A SHIP FOR THE KING

A thrilling maritime adventure, the first in a new series set against the backdrop of the English Civil War

Bristol, England, 1618. Kit Faulkner is a young vagrant orphan, but his life changes forever when two gentlemen spot his potential and he is taken aboard their merchant ship, the *Swallow*, to be trained for a life at sea. As he rises through the ranks, he risks all in encounters with pirates and French corsairs. Meanwhile, England edges ever closer to civil war, and very soon Kit must choose which side he will fight for...

A SHIP FOR THE KING

Richard Woodman

Severn House Large Print
London & New York

This first large print edition published 2012
in Great Britain and the USA by
SEVERN HOUSE PUBLISHERS LTD of
9-15 High Street, Sutton, Surrey, SM1 1DF.
First world regular print edition published 2011 by
Severn House Publishers Ltd., London and New York.

British Library Cataloguing in Publication Data

Woodman, Richard, 1944-
  A ship for the king.
  1. Seafaring life--History--17th century--Fiction.
  2. Sailors--Great Britain--History--17th century--
  Fiction. 3. Great Britain--History--Civil War,
  1642-1649--Fiction. 4. Historical fiction. 5. Large type
  books.
  I. Title
  823.9'14-dc23

ISBN-13: 978-0-7278-9832-6

Severn House Publishers support The Forest Stewardship Council
[FSC], the leading international forest certification organisation. All
our titles that are printed on Greenpeace-approved FSC-certified paper
carry the FSC logo.

MIX
Paper from
responsible sources
FSC
www.fsc.org
FSC® C018575

Printed and bound in Great Britain by the
MPG Books Group, Bodmin, Cornwall.

For Arlo

Prologue

Mr Rat

Bristol, January, 1618

The youth was cold and hungry.

Gaunt and filthy, clothed in the ragged remains of a shirt and breeches, his calloused feet black with the slurry on the wet quayside. The rain had stopped and with it the strong wind that had blown relentlessly for several days, but the January air remained damp and cold, so that he shivered uncontrollably, his teeth chattering. Crouching, he waited, partly concealed by two giant hogsheads of sugar, all that was left of the discharged cargo of the ship alongside the quay. In a few moments they would be rolled away into the warehouse close by, and then he would have nowhere to hide and yet keep the two gentlemen under observation. Why were they dawdling? He knew, with the ship now emptied of her lading, one or other of them would return to board her and finish the business of her discharge – always a matter for well-heeled gentlemen – now that the dock-labourers had finished their toil. The ship's crew had long since been paid off and the vessel left in the hands of a ship-keeper, a wily old bird who had, besides a raddled wife, a son who looked out for him and took his duties seriously. The hungry lad, who had no liking for a kicking, sensed his physical inferiority to the ship-keeper's son, who was of roughly his own age, and kept out of sight on that account. There was no sign of the youngster at that moment, only the tantalizingly slow approach of the two gentlemen who had paused alongside the bow of the ship and were regarding some appointment in her rigging. The lad could not hear what they said but their discussion was sufficiently serious to suspend the eating of the apples each held. Those apples were the lad's objective and his heart was pounding lest the labourers come and roll away the hogsheads before he had secured the core of at least one of them. Suppose one of the gentlemen, on coming no nearer, tossed his into the dock? Suppose...

But no, they had resumed their leisurely stroll slowly towards the ship's short gangway whose landward end was not ten yards from where he crouched in anticipation. He heard a noise behind him and without looking, knew the labourers were coming for the final hogsheads. Everything now happened quickly. The first gentleman had almost reached the gangway and, regarding the remains of his apple, dropped it with a fastidious gesture. Even as he rushed forward, the youth knew that much remained of the apple's flesh and it had not rolled on the quay more than once before his hand shot out and grabbed it.

Just as it did so the brown shoe of the second gentleman pressed his wrist to the ground and, as the lad looked up with a yelp of pain, the shoe's owner called to his fellow, 'Had you a mind to let this urchin gowk thee, Gideon?'

The other, a step on the gangway, turned and looked at his colleague and then down at the squirming boy. 'What have you there, Harry? A rat?'

'Indeed, so it would seem, though an uncommon large rat.'

'Please, sir, you're hurting...' the lad pleaded.

'A talking rat, by God!'

'I only want the core, sir ... I wasn't about to...' The lad faltered, sensing danger in what he was about to say.

'Weren't about to what, Mr Rat?' The two exchanged looks. 'Weren't about to rob me? Filch my handkerchief, or were you after my watch, eh?'

'No, I was not, sir!' the lad protested. 'Had I wished to I should have got aboard your ship and stolen from her deck; there's no one about, sir, no one. I could have done that, sir, if I'd wished to, but I have been here awaiting your return for half an hour.'

This little speech had caused the man named Gideon to cast an eye over the ship's deserted deck, but the other seemed more interested in the youth. 'What do you mean you have waited for me? Eh?' He leaned forward and added a

9

little weight to his foot.

'I knew you'd come back when the cargo was ashore, sir, and then I thought...'

'Thought what? Go on.'

'To beg of you, sir, to plead of your charity.'

'But you tried to steal an apple?'

'Only the core, sir, and it wasn't your'n...'

'Was it not? No, it was my friend's – but it was not yours, was it? You did not pay for it?'

'No sir, but it was dropped ... your friend had dropped it...'

'But suppose that were an accident, eh? Suppose my friend had not finished with his apple. See, I note there is some flesh remaining upon it.' The boy's tormentor looked at the other man who had ascended a further step up the gangway and seemed torn between locating his ship-keeper and watching the little drama being staged by the man he had called Harry. 'Had you finished with your apple, Gideon?'

'Of course,' the other replied a touch testily.

'See, sir,' said the trapped lad.

'Now you have spoiled the argument, Gideon,' the lad's torturer said in mock exasperation, looking down at his victim. 'And just when my young friend and I were debating an exquisite point of moral philosophy.'

'Come, Henry,' said the now impatient Gideon more formally, at which point the ship-keeper emerged on deck and effusively greeted his employers. For a second the lad thought his ordeal was over, that he would be free of the booted foot of the man called Henry and he could break

10

his overlong fast. Somewhere behind him the second of the two hogsheads was being rolled away and on board, hidden now by the ship's rail, the man called Gideon and the ship-keeper were in conversation.

'When did you last eat, Mr Rat?'

'I found some slops yesterday, sir.'

'Slops?'

'Cast out of a pie-shop...'

'And before that?'

'You dropped an apple core in New Street, sir.'

'I did?'

'Aye, sir. You bought them off the girl on the corner of Union Street and...'

'Oh yes. So I did, so I did...' Henry paused a moment, recalling the girl with a brief flash of pleasure. Then his weathered face hardened. 'It was full of maggots, which these,' and here he held out his own partly consumed apple which he had not yet finished, 'these are delicious, as was the girl from whom we purchased them.'

The youth felt the pressure on his wrist ease; he closed his fist on the dropped apple core. Above him the man Henry sighed and lifted his foot. Gathering himself to escape, the boy said in a rush, 'If you find a length of leather hose is missing from your vessel, sir, I know who took it.'

'Wait!' A gloved hand restrained the boy's retreat. 'Don't run away ... What did you say about leather hose?'

'Aye, sir, and with copper rivets. That devil that belongs to the ship-keeper, he made off with it this morning.'

'Stap me, that's a new hosepipe! Are you telling lies in the hope of reward, Mr Rat?'

'No, sir. I am telling the truth for the love of it.'

'Are you by God!' The man smiled, his broad, open countenance revealing a kindly aspect. 'Well, well, where did you learn such high-mindedness, Mr Rat? Not in these gutters, I think.'

'No, sir.'

'Where then?'

'From my mother, before the fever took her.'

'And your father, Mr Rat? What about him? D'you know his name?'

'I'm no bastard, sir. He went to sea and never came back. The ship was lost, sir, some say to the Sallee Rovers, some say she was wrecked on the far Bermudas, sir.'

'Indeed.' The man raised an eyebrow at this intelligence. 'And what do you say, Mr Rat, for the love of truth, eh?'

'I don't know, sir, but please, sir, may I go and eat this apple?' The lad lifted the morsel to his mouth but Henry's hand shot out and prevented him putting it anywhere near his mouth.

'No! It is covered in filth. You cannot eat it, Mr Rat. Come aboard, we shall find you some-thing better to your ratty liking.' He raised his voice. 'Hey, Gideon, we are coming aboard and I bring you a guest: Mr Rat!'

They mounted the gangway and descended to the deck. The youth looked about him and knew the chaos of a discharged ship. He had spent the last three years eking a living along the city's waterfront and the nickname of Mr Rat was not so far from the truth. Like the rats that filled the warehouses, he had scavenged the surpluses every cargo deposited. What he could not eat, he garnered and sold or bartered, but he alone among the other waifs never took what was not lying about. He was peculiar in that, most peculiar; though why, he could not tell.

Gideon and the ship-keeper had concluded their business and, as the old man shuffled forward towards the galley, Gideon turned to his friend. 'Have we to feed this, Henry? Is this another of your acts of charity by which means you intend to prove the Good Book wrong?'

'Unlike you, my dear Gideon, I am not a rich man, so may yet squeeze through the eye of the needle, though why the Good Lord in his infinite wisdom should contrive to make the gates of Heaven so confounded narrow, I am at a loss to know. Let us give our young acquaintance some burgoo, or something of that nature. Hey, sirra!'

The old ship-keeper turned from the threshold of the companionway.

'Bring me something sustaining and hot,' Henry called. 'And be quick about it!'

The lad could see the old man's mouth working abusively. Beside him Gideon chuckled. 'Wait there, Mr Rat,' he said and followed his colleague under the poop and into the great cabin. The lad crouched on the step of a gun-carriage, drew up his knees and put his arms about him. He was growing cold as the fading day grew chilly. There would be more cold rain by nightfall and he was *so* hungry. He thought of the food that might be coming his way and began to salivate. Was this a dream? For the first time for three years he felt tears start to his eyes. Then he wiped them away as the old ship-keeper emerged from the forecastle. He held a small tin pan from which a wisp of steam rose. He drew closer and passed the lad, glaring. Just as he raised his hand to knock on the door, it opened and the man named Henry emerged. He had removed his hat and cloak, revealing a dark tunic with slashed sleeves, black hose and thick worsted stockings. The lad recalled he had said he was not rich, but he looked so to the eager starveling, who could smell the cooked food. Taking the bowl the man stared into it and then looked up at the ship-keeper.

'Is this a portion that you would give to your son, Mr Jones?'

The old man sensed a trap but could not quite fathom it. 'Why, Captain, I, er ... er my wife...'

'Tell your wife to produce another such pannikin at once. Be off! And bring the boy a spoon, he is not a dog.'

He handed the lad the pan of thin stew. 'Eat it before it cools.'

The youth took it and wolfed it down, slurping at the rim of the pan, scooping up the small lumps of salt meat and sucking on them greedily. When he had finished Henry bent and said,

'Open your mouth wide.' He obeyed and the man remarked, 'Good teeth, by heaven. How the devil did you manage that?' The lad shrugged. 'The query was rhetorical, Mr Rat. But, heavens, I cannot call you that. Forgive me. I asked if you knew your father's name; do you know your own?'

'My mother called me Kit, sir.'

'And your father's name?'

'Robert Faulkner, and he was married to my mother.'

'So you are Kit ... no, no, that is not what you were baptised, assuming you were baptised; you are therefore Christopher Faulkner.' He paused, scrutinizing the thin pale face with its over-large eyes. 'D'you recognize the cognomen?'

'You mean the name, sir? Christopher Faulkner?'

'Just so.'

'Aye, sir. I do.' It was the lad's turn to pause, and then he asked, 'Is that what cognomen means, sir; my name?'

'Indeed. And where are you from?'

The lad shrugged. 'Hereabouts, sir. I live on the waterfront as best I may, sir...'

'And what would you do with yourself?' the man named Henry asked, his tone dallying as he awaited the slow and resentful approach of the ship-keeper with a second pan of stew.

'Why, find somewhere dry and warm, sir, for the night.'

'Eat this and go and curl up in the galley near the stove...'

'Cap'n, have I to look after vagabonds?' the ship-keeper protested.

'Indeed, Jones, you do not. You shall attend this young fellow on your son's account, payment for which was a length of leather hose fastened by rivets of excellent Welsh copper, which belonged to this ship and which has since passed into the hands of others without the prior knowledge of Captain Gideon Strange, or myself. And if I find one hair of this child's head has been touched by you or your son tomorrow, I shall see you answer for the crime of theft, even though you instruct your son to recover the hose this night.'

The ship-keeper visibly cringed at the mention of the word 'theft' and indicated to the lad, who had now finished the stew, that he should follow him forward into the warm shelter of the galley.

'Thank you, sir,' said the lad, half-fearful of following the old man.

'One moment, young Kit. Tell me, had you a wish upon which your life depended, what would it be?'

'Why, sir, to go to sea and make my way like you, sir.'

A broad grin spread across the gentleman's face. 'Like me? Oh, I think not. Not like me at all, but to go to sea is an easy road to which one has only to trim your sails. It is the coming back that proves the greater problem.'

'Would you take me on your ship, sir?'

'Do I have a ship?'

'Is this ship not yours, sir?'

'I am part-owner of her, yes, but I have in mind something better. Have you the stomach for a fight, Mr Kit Faulkner; and perhaps a gamble on life's hazard?'

The lad frowned, conscious that he was being dallied with, while the old ship-keeper stood by sucking what remained of his caried teeth, and awaited his release, whereupon, the lad feared, he would receive a beating in exchange for his night's lodging. 'I do not understand what you mean, sir...'

'Henry, for God's sake has that boy not had sufficient of your charity that you must make an evening's entertainment of him?'

The gentleman turned back to his companion who had emerged from the cabin and, wrapped in his cloak and carrying a satchel under his arm, seemed destined for the shore again. 'A moment, Gideon,' the gentleman said fishing in his pocket and withdrawing some silver which he passed to the ship-keeper. 'Tend this boy, Jones, and tomorrow see him clothed decently and brought to my lodgings by noon. Discharge this and recover our hose and I shall drop the matter of reporting the theft. D'you hear me?'

'Aye, sir. Shall be done as you say, sir.'

The man named Jones led the youth forward to where a small deckhouse stood; it housed the ship's galley. Inside it was dark, but the glow of the galley stove threw out a seductive warmth. With much grunting and tongue-clicking Jones drew the galley fire, then indicated that the lad could sleep nearby. Carrying the bucket of hot

17

coals on deck to dump over the ship's side for fear of fire, and which the port regulations required, he left the lad to himself.

Kit Faulkner lay down and curled up as close to the warm cast-iron stove as he could. The sudden transformation in his circumstances reminded him of happier times and he was all but overcome with tears for a second time that day. For many months the sheer necessity of staying alive had denied him the indulgence of self-pity and he might have sobbed himself to sleep had not a distraction caused him to rub a hand across his grimy face. The cat's miaow might have been interpreted in many ways; outrage, perhaps, at finding the hearth occupied, or a welcome to another whose existence was as perilous as its own. Whatever feline logic drove the animal, it nudged up to the adolescent boy and he found himself stroking its inquisitive head. A moment later it curled up beside him and both were soon asleep.

The two men, Captain Gideon Strange and Captain Henry Mainwaring, were less eager to retire and spent the evening dining on mutton and some rotgut Portuguese wine that their landlord had the effrontery to attempt to pass off as claret. Both men declared they had drunk better but had matters more pressing, conducting their conversation in Strange's private lodging rooms, where Mainwaring was his guest. Both were part-owners of the *Swallow*, the ship in which Kit Faulkner had found temporary refuge and which had but lately arrived from the Mediterranean. Although not the sole owners, the two partners held the largest number of shares in the vessel, between them commanding forty-eight sixty-fourths, with Mainwaring holding a moiety more than Strange. The latter, however, was the master and the two regarded each other as equals in their business. Having pored over the accounts to their mutual satisfaction, filled themselves with the landlord's mutton and filthy wine, Mainwaring called for pipes and tobacco before turning the conversation to other matters. When both had wreathed their heads in an aromatic blue haze, he ventured his news.

'Gideon, I have news for you that will upset the tranquillity of our arrangements, I fear.'

'Oh? Pray, what is amiss? Is it that wretched boy?' Strange waved his hand to dissipate the cloud of smoke in order to see his companion better. Mainwaring removed his own pipe and stared into the distance. He was a handsome man, clean-shaven and in his early thirties. He had a strong face, a straight nose and a well-formed mouth. A hint of coming fat hung on his cheeks but he was not ill-made, with a strong, lean body that spoke of physical power, even when seated after a hearty meal. Not for the first time Gideon Strange thought it was his friend who should have borne his own surname, for there was something indefinable about Mainwaring: the man was an enigma. In truth, Strange knew that the suspicion arose from his ambivalent past, and the reflection was given added weight by the consideration that had Mainwaring not had a chequered career he, Gideon Strange, would not be sitting in lodgings in the city of Bristol, comfortable in the knowledge that he had just completed a prosperous voyage to Smyrna. Indeed, he was only too conscious – and the thought made him cold with sweaty apprehension – he would still be toiling under the hot sun of Barbary, a slave to the Moors. Thank God, however, Providence delivered him through the timely agency of one Captain Henry Mainwaring.

As if sensing Strange's reflections, Mainwaring turned to his friend and smiled, an open, charming smile that could turn a woman's head and never failed to elicit a similar response from Strange himself. 'No, Gideon, not the boy, though I shall come to him later. No, what I have to impart to you concerns you directly since I am summoned to London and will, perforce, hand over my part in the management of the *Swallow* to your goodself, assuming, of course, that you are willing to undertake it.' Here Mainwaring held up his hand to prevent Strange from interjecting. 'I would not impose on our friendship and would yield eight sixty-fourths in the *Swallow* to make you both master and majority shareholder if you agree.'

'That is a most generous offer...'

'And take Mr Rat as apprentice – not with the object of making of him cheap labour, but advancing him quickly in seamanship and navigation...'

Strange frowned. 'What on earth for?'

'Gideon, the country has need of competent seamen, men to command, not simply to hand, reef and steer. A youth who knows nothing else, who is bred to the sea, and one, moreover, who thinks that all his ambition lies thither, is the perfect clay with which to mould so necessary an object. Take him and make him ... that is all I ask.'

Strange shrugged. 'Very well. I shall if you wish it, but think you he has the mind for it?'

'By my reckoning the lad is sharp and shrewd and I may well have need of him. To such natural talents he has nothing to add beyond a hunger and with it, I suspect, a hunger for knowledge would surely follow his appetite for apple cores.'

Strange rubbed his chin in contemplation. If he was less eager to espouse Mr Rat's cause, he was even less eager to challenge Mainwaring's judgement. His partner was not infallible by any means, but he was not often wrong in judging men. Had he been prone to such a fault he would not have so transformed himself. 'So,' he said, 'may I ask why you intend to relinquish your business here and go to London?'

'I have been granted audience of the King,' Mainwaring said casually, blowing a cloud of smoke into the thick air and staring at it as it roiled upwards towards the low, stained and dingy ceiling.

'By heaven, you have not!'

'Indeed, Gideon, I have.' Mainwaring turned and looked at his friend. 'You are surprised?'

Strange shrugged. 'Were it any other shipmaster in Bristol, I should be astounded, but you – no, I am not surprised, though I am continually amazed. However, think you that our gracious King might not have a motive in so commanding you?'

'Undoubtedly His Majesty has a motive...'

'I mean one more devious than mere curiosity at setting his royal eyes upon a lately pardoned pirate.'

Mainwaring laughed. 'Lately pardoned? Come, come, Gideon, you are unjust, I have been pardoned two years. Besides, what mean you by devious? They say His Majesty is a mighty devious shrewd prince, which surely is a necessary quality for one whose business is with ambassadors, bishops, courtiers—'

'And catamites,' Strange interrupted.

'Catamites? Mean you to impute some unnaturalness to Jacobus Rex, Gideon? Have a care or you will end your days in two pieces upon Tower Hill – if you are lucky.'

'Come Hal, 'tis well known that the King has his favourites. This boy George Villiers, lately made Marquess of Buckingham, is said to be pretty and with a delicacy about his features better fitting a lady than aught else.'

'I suppose it is said so in every tavern from here to Wapping, and it may well be true, but what has this to do with me?'

'Why, that the King, our master, may have

many favourites and you have already attracted his attention thanks to your pardon. How you managed it is a mystery to me, but I would warn you that there must be a price to pay.'

'Come, Gideon, I was granted that on account of taking a Moorish ship in the Thames, besides other captures of the King's enemies, one of which yielded you your freedom.'

'True, and for that I am grateful, and it is in gratitude that I warn you to be careful when you attend the King.'

'You are in serious vein,' Mainwaring said staring hard at Strange and smiling at the concerned expression of his face.

'Well then, why else would His Majesty trouble himself further on your account?'

'Because, my dear Gideon, I have written a work upon the suppression of piracy and His Majesty has graciously consented to accept a copy from my hand. His Majesty, being himself an author, has a great love of books. On that account I am to wait upon His Majesty.'

'His Majesty would do better to commission some vessels of his own to cruise upon the coast as a guard to frighten and deter these villainous Moors from our shores...'

'Ah! You have the rudiments of a verse there, Gideon, damned if you haven't...'

'Hal, 'tis a serious matter. These descents upon our people and the carrying of them off into slavery in Barbary are now a matter of regular occurrence. Why, whole parishes have been abducted!'

'I know very well what has been happening and do not need to be told, though I comprehend your bitterness...'

'I lost five years of my life to them...'

'And *I* risked all by placing my existence on account, Gideon...'

'But I was forced into slavery, Hal. You chose to go *on account*, as you put it, and I have never understood why. Were you not in a fair way to becoming a man of parts without so desperate a measure?'

Strange paused, sensing he had been importunate, trespassing on Mainwaring's feelings, though the conundrum had long fascinated him. Mainwaring he knew to have been of good family and, at the age of thirteen, or thereabouts, attended Brasenose College before being admitted to the Inner Temple. Some years later, conceiving himself a military rather than a legal man, he had been granted the Captaincy of St Andrew's Castle in Hampshire. Mainwaring had bought an armed ship, the *Resistance*, from the King's own master shipwright, Phineas Pett. He had also solicited and then been granted a commission from the Lord Admiral to cruise against pirates. Here was the great irony: having been entrusted with this task by the Lord Admiral, the Earl of Nottingham, Mainwaring had gone to sea and, in company with another ship, the *Nightingale*, had turned his coat. Instead of attacking pirates, of which there were numerous groups – both native-born and Moorish – off the coasts, many of which used remote bays in

Ireland for their recruitment, Mainwaring had revived the sentiments of *El Draco*, Sir Francis Drake. Declaring his hatred of the Spanish and of Popery he thereby suborned his entire crew, announcing he intended to attack Spanish trade for the purpose of enrichment. Thus turning pirate himself he embarked on an indiscriminate and private war of which dark tales were told of his consorting with the King of Morocco and selling into slavery those of his captives who would not join him. It was in one such foray that he had discovered Strange, chained to the oar of a Moorish galley, and, trading Catholics for Protestants, obtained his release. In three years Mainwaring had acquired a squadron of five armed ships with which, in 1615, he appeared among the cod-fishing fleets on the Grand Bank of Newfoundland. His name had been linked with that of Peter Easton, the self-declared Admiral of a loose confederation of seamen, who, dispossessed of their living by King James's indifference to his Navy Royal, had found themselves driven to this extremity.

Easton had subsequently made himself useful to the Duke of Savoy; had been ennobled and, taking a wealthy Catholic lady to his wife, retired a Savoyard Marquess, luxuriating in wealth and status. After Easton's departure Henry Mainwaring succeeded him as the pirates' 'admiral'.

By this time, however, other forces were stirring. Exasperated by English weakness at sea and King James's reluctance to clear his own waters of the plague, the Dutch, whose trade had suffered from the captures of Easton and his cronies, took matters into their own hands. In 1614, a powerful Dutch squadron had descended upon Crookhaven, one piratical lair in the south-west extremity of Ireland. It was clear that matters were coming to a head and Mainwaring considered his future, a fact well known to Strange who had, by this time, become one of Mainwaring's lieutenants.

Mainwaring's skills in negotiating the release of Protestant slaves from the Moroccan Sultan conveyed an odour of morality to his conduct and allowed him to seek a reconciliation with the English King. James's conciliating policies towards the European powers had earned him no friends at home and he was in need of men of action beholden to him. Gone were the glorious days of Elizabeth; the country had sunk into despondency, her navy rotting, her trade stagnant, except for some wildly gambled enterprises to the East Indies, the outcome of which remained uncertain. James's unpopularity was made manifest when, calling a Parliament to raise funds, his efforts were rebuffed and the so-called 'Addled Parliament' was dissolved for failing to finance him. Amid this stalemate came news of a victory at sea; one Henry Mainwaring had taken five Spanish ships and he was even now cruising off Ireland with two vessels, seeking an accommodation and pardon from King James. James was mooting a change of policy and released Sir Walter Raleigh from the Tower on the supposition that the old adventurer could capitalize on a treasure-seeking voyage to *El Dorado*. Raleigh had failed and lost his head, but Mainwaring, hearing of the King's intention of pardoning him, sailed up-Channel and captured a Moorish pirate in the estuary of the Thames itself. He could hardly have accomplished a more appropriate feat: it cleared his name and legitimized his pardon. He became a gentleman and thereafter he acquired shares in several ships, to which he acted as ship's husband, entering a legitimate trade with the West Indies and the Mediterranean, which he knew well.

This much Strange knew, but while Strange took the *Swallow* to Smyrna, Mainwaring had been composing his *Discourse of Pirates and the Suppression Thereof*, admission of which had caused Strange his importunate curiosity.

Mainwaring's silence was on the verge of becoming awkward when he removed the pipe from his mouth, blew smoke and turned to his friend. 'My dear Gideon, you and I have made money from our partnership. You came from a mercantile background and while I rescued you from slavery, you came back to your family's shareholdings in the *Swallow*, the *Lark* and the *Bristol Rover*. It does not suit me to languish here in this city. I have a mind for more and have friends at court, as you know through my connections with old Walsingham's family. But their stars are in the wane, as is Nottingham's, and I look to new. Buckingham may be pretty as a girl, and the King may nurse an unseemly passion for his prettiness, but Buckingham has a need for competent sea-officers, for the King's policies will draw our enemies upon us and I have the stomach for a fight—'

'You seek a commission!' Strange almost shouted as he divined Mainwaring's intentions, but his friend merely raised an eyebrow in mock astonishment.

'Is that what you think?'

'You shall be an admiral again, only this time your flag will be atop the mainmast of a King's ship, by God. Harry, I drink to your success.' Strange raised his glass and swallowed its contents with a wince. 'God's truth, but that is vile wine!'

Mainwaring made a self-deprecatory gesture, allowing Strange to add, 'And you intend to make Mr Rat one of your lieutenants after I have trained him.'

Mainwaring lowered an empty glass to the table and regarded Strange through the haze of blue tobacco smoke. 'You have divined my mind, Gideon, and tomorrow we shall see what young Mr Rat makes of my proposal ... at least the first part of it. We have no need to reveal it all until we see whether he possesses the qualities I believe he does. Now,' he went on purposefully, 'I want to consider some other worthy seafaring men of our acquaintance...'

'God, you would strip my ships of the most able, damn you, Harry. You are already thinking like a naval officer!'

'Why not, Gideon. 'Tis not so very different from being a pirate.'

Kit Faulkner woke to the new day uncertain of his surroundings. The cat had gone, though the warmth of its companionship lingered. Inured to sleeping on a hard surface in any odd corner, it was the slight movement of the *Swallow* that reminded him of the previous day's events and his quickening heartbeat woke him fully. All previous attempts to board ships in the dock had run the risk of a thrashing from the elderly ship-keepers who tended them, and while a nimble chap could usually elude the grunting and rheumaticky pursuit of these guardians, they had their nasty accomplices, like the boy Kit had witnessed stealing hosepipe from his bene-factors. As if the thought conjured a spectre, the galley door was flung open and a figure stood silhouetted against the grey autumnal daylight. A shadow fell across the stirring Kit as he drew up his legs and scrambled to his feet.

'You little bastard,' the ship-keeper's son said. 'The old boy took it into his head that I had lifted some pipe and I have you to thank for the lie...'

''Twas not a lie, and you know it.' Kit was standing now and backed himself against the bulkhead. His right hand was behind him, fumbling briefly until it closed round a handle hanging from a hook.

'It was a filthy lie,' the other said, advancing into the galley as Kit, his heart thundering in his chest, carefully twisted his hand and freed the implement from its hook. Just as the youth lunged for him he brought his hand round and caught his attacker a sharp blow across his outstretched wrist. Fortunately it was a sharpening steel that Kit had alighted on, and not a knife; nevertheless, the youth squealed and withdrew his hand. Although he made a move as though to renew his assault he thought better of it. A moment later he had hopped backwards, slammed the door and shot the bolt. Kit could hear him running off and settled to wait, scouring the galley for food. Curiously there was nothing beyond a small bag of oats from which he broke his fast. He was vaguely aware of raised voices somewhere in the vessel.

An hour later he heard footsteps approach. He took up the steel again, but the door opened to reveal the old ship-keeper. 'Come with me,' he grumbled, making no mention of the encounter between the two youngsters. Kit followed as Jones led him ashore, muttering testily, by which means he indicated to his charge that he thoroughly disapproved of his present task. It took some time for Jones to execute his master's commission, for it required a series of commercial transactions for which the old man was unfitted. During the course of these Kit realized this and he was able to cajole a number of decent garments out of the vendors, calling upon the skills that his vagrant life had equipped him with. Thus he emerged from the pawnbrokers' shops and the cobblers, in and out of which

Jones led him, with two sets of under-drawers, three pairs of stockings, two pairs of breeches, three blouses and a rough coat of the kind that sailors wore. He also argued for a decent pair of shoes that were too big for him and a hat that was likewise oversized but marked him for a fledgling dandy. Jones, who grumbled incessantly at the diminishing stock of coin he held, nevertheless managed to accomplish his task with the minimum of outlay, as Mrs Jones had insisted: all-in-all, it would get this infested boy out of his hair and his own son off the hook of his own stupidity.

It was not far short of noon when Jones and his charge, weighed down by his bundle, hung about with his shoes and sporting a stubby clay-pipe that the cobbler had thrown in for good measure, reached Captain Strange's lodgings. If Kit thought, by acquisition of the pipe, that he had been elevated to the estate of manhood, he was swiftly disabused for Captain Mainwaring, barely looking up from some papers he was studying with Captain Strange, dismissed Jones and summoned a chambermaid.

'Take this boy, Miss, and scrub him under the pump. Then have a barber shave him ... No, Mr Rat, leave those clothes here. You may take a pair of breeches and throw those rags you are wearing away before you come back.'

Kit Faulkner endured twenty minutes of humiliation under the yard-pump, with several servants, men as well as women, looking on as his skinny frame was soused and scrubbed. The chambermaid had no liking for her task, and took her own displeasure out on the boy, though she warmed to her part with the encouraging shouts and advice from her fellows. Kit's backside was red from rubbing and he clutched his private parts lest her enthusiasm should entirely dispossess him of them. However, when finally released and clad in rough breeches, he privately acknowledged an invigoration as he fled for the stairs leading to Strange's rooms.

Mainwaring was still working on his papers, but Strange was enjoying a pipe by the window that overlooked the street below. Turning as the boy knocked and entered the room, Strange gestured to the screen behind which the pisspot stood on a stool and said quietly, 'You had better dress yourself properly, Mr Rat.'

Awkward in his new clothes, the hat clasped in his hand and the overlarge boots making of him a figure of fun, he emerged and stood before the two men. Mainwaring looked up, laid down his quill, and sat back in his chair, suppressing a smile. 'Well, Gideon, where has Mr Rat gone? I think we are looking at the makings of a gentleman.'

At which, in some imitated reflex, Kit Faulkner shyly advanced one foot, flicked his broadbrimmed hat and made a not inelegant bow.

'Indeed, Harry, I think maybe you are right. Well, sir, you are welcome,' Strange said kindly. 'Please take a seat and –' Strange came forward and, searching among the papers before Mainwaring, drew one and laid it before Faulkner as

32

he sat awkwardly at the table – 'can you read?'

'A little, sir.'

'Do read that, and when you have digested its contents you may make your mark here ... It is an indenture, boy, binding you to serve me as your master for four years, during which I undertake at my own expense to teach you the business of a seaman...'

'And if you prove resolute and efficient, if you learn your duty quickly, Captain Strange will impart to you the business of navigation, conning and lodemanage,' Mainwaring added, 'after which you shall, if you wish, seek advancement.'

Faulkner stared at the two men and then at the bewildering document before him. It was covered with words, only a few of which he could decipher, though his mouth tried to form those he could not. 'Read it to him, Gideon, while I finish these accounts.'

And so Kit Faulkner, a semi-illiterate vagrant orphan aged somewhere between twelve and fourteen years old went to sea, bound apprentice to Captain Gideon Strange, Master under God of the ship *Swallow*, of two hundred tons burthen and ten guns. In March 1618 the vessel slipped down the Avon and took a strong ebb tide to the westward, passed between the islands of Flatholm and Steepholm and for three days anchored under the lee of Lundy Island, where marauding Barbary pirates had raised ramparts in defiance of the King's Majesty, before catching a slant of wind from the north-west, whereupon

Captain Strange set course for the Mediterranean.

The same day Henry Mainwaring, having previously waited upon His Majesty King James and presented his sovereign with his *Discourse upon Pirates and their Suppression Thereof*, was summoned to attend the King at Woking. Here he was knighted and appointed a Gentleman of the Bedchamber, whereupon the first person to offer his congratulations was George Villiers, the Marquess of Buckingham. The court favourite was eagerly seeking new allies among seafaring men, for his intrigues had recently secured the ousting of the Howards from the King's favour. The Earl of Nottingham, once the victorious admiral who had turned aside the Spanish Armada, wrecked by age and corruption had given way to a younger man of subtle skills – considerable administrative ability but infinitely greater venality. Buckingham's star was rising, for soon he would be a Duke and not merely the Lord Admiral as Nottingham had been, but Lord High Admiral of England.

Far to the westward of these grand proceedings the *Swallow* lay over to the wind, her yards braced sharply, her sails full and the sea a-roiling along her lee tumblehome. Here, the boy Kit Faulkner, damp and unhappy, threw up the contents of his stomach and wished he was scavenging apples on the waterfront of Bristol.

Part One

The King's Whelp

Whelp

1 The young of the dog. Now little used, superseded by *puppy*.

2 An ill-conditioned or low fellow; later, in milder use, and especially of a boy or young man. A saucy or impertinent young fellow; an 'unlicked cub', a 'puppy'.

3 (*Nautical?*) One of the longitudinal projections on the barrel of a capstan or windlass [by which the nipper or anchor cable was more readily drawn round].

4 (*Nautical?*) One of a fleet of auxiliary war vessels established in Charles I's reign, so-called because designed to attend on HMS *Lion*.

Oxford English Dictionary

One

Awaiting *El Dorado*

Summer 1620 – Spring 1623

It was to be many, many months before Kit Faulkner next encountered Sir Henry Mainwaring, four years during which he served Captain Strange, who in turn taught him the business of seamanship in accordance with the indenture Kit had marked with a curiously assured monogram. Although Strange had discovered this was almost the limit of the boy's literacy, it was quickly apparent that Mainwaring's instinct had proved correct: Faulkner was exceedingly quick on the uptake, a bright, intelligent adolescent who swiftly turned into a tough, sinewy youth for whom the crude victuals of the *Swallow* seemed like manna from heaven.

The equinoctial outward passage of the *Swallow* had been rough and for three days the wretched Faulkner had repeatedly spewed-up his guts. Strange left him to his misery and the cuffings he received from the boatswain on the occasions when he failed to make the rail before voiding himself. Happily the decks were sluiced incessantly by green seas so that Faulkner was relieved of the humiliation of cleaning up his own vomit, but much of the time Strange observed his charge lying shivering in the lee scuppers, indifferent to the cold seawater that swirled about him, a bight of rope cast about him by the same boatswain who admonished him for fouling the decks. From time-to-time a pannikin of hot burgoo was offered to him by another of the able seamen and for most of the three days this act of solicitude was rejected by the lad. But on the fourth day out, after a veering of the wind produced a ray or two of sunshine which, with the southing they were making, combined to throw a patch of comparative warmth upon the *Swallow* sufficient to dry her damp decks, Strange observed Faulkner take the pannikin and spoon its contents into his mouth. Almost as he watched, Faulkner seemed to lose his greenish pallor and assume something of the countenance of normality, and by the time they raised Cape Ortegal Kit Faulkner had not only turned-to to wash decks with the morning watch, but had made his first ascent of the rigging at sea. That evening he assisted at the whip-staff and began to learn to box the compass in quarter-points. From that moment he forsook boyhood and aspired to do everything that was undertaken by the able seamen, and it was Faulkner who first spotted the approaching pirate as they closed the Straits. The action was brief and spirited; the *Swallow*, aided by a fresh and fair wind which allowed her to play her guns to advantage, deterred the sea-rovers from Sallee from making a close approach. Discouraged, they made off after easier prey.

Having once fallen into the hands of the Barbary corsairs, Captain Strange made more than adequate provision for such an encounter, employing, besides competent seamen, a gunner of skill. Moreover, he had laid in a quantity of powder and shot, especially bar-shot, which would give his ship the edge against all but a most determined attack. It was not in the interest of the mixture of Moors, Arabs, and renegade Christians who made up the crews of the corsairs, whether they emerged from Sallee, Algiers, Tunis or Tripoli, to press their attack if there was much danger of losing their lives. They were usually after easy pickings, but the experience made its mark on young Faulkner and he gradually learned the story of his commander from the seamen who increasingly regarded him as a useful addition to their complement.

Nor was Gideon Strange unique in his history, for every year hundreds of seamen were captured and enslaved by the so-called Moors. Many turned apostate, renouncing their Christianity, submitting to circumcision, and finding liberty of a kind in the service of the pirates. They were generally treated well, unless, like Strange, they refused to recant and tried to escape. Captain Strange had spent several years chained to the oar of a galley until ransomed by Mainwaring during one of his periodic spells in Algiers. Mainwaring had got wind of Strange's predicament on account of his being a commander in the service of the Levant Company. A condition of release was that Strange served under Mainwaring until the latter obtained his pardon from King James, whereupon Mainwaring retained Strange's services, setting him up in a Bristol ship as a partner, an offer Strange could not refuse. A single man whose father had died in his youth and whose mother had succumbed to grief at the capture of her son and expired at the onset of an epidemic of the plague, Strange rapidly recovered lost ground and was, within a short time, a comparatively wealthy man. Apart from serving as master and part-owner of the *Swallow*, he was also a partner with Mainwaring in the ownership of several other vessels, assisting his liberator and colleague in turning his ill-gotten gains into legitimate assets, stock and money.

The two men's affairs were thus intimately linked and they had consequently become firm friends. Such was the confidence between the two that shortly before the *Swallow* had sailed, Strange had received a letter from Mainwaring outlining the state of his affairs at court. *My Friend*, Mainwaring had written,

I find matters here of so complicated a nature as to offer me a considerable future. The King in his wisdom has appointed me

one of a Commission to enquire into the state of the Navy Royal and to make such commendations as best serve the State in these difficult times. I had some notion of this when leaving the boy F. in your charge but I do urge you to bring him on with all haste if, as I suspect and hope, he proves able. At least he knows nothing else and is thus devoid of distractions. Should there be other young men come among the crew who show ability, treat them in like wise but do not deprive yourself of able seamen on this account. Two or three is all that I seek for the King's service which is woefully in want of proper men bred to the sea and able to give him good return. As for myself, I am in a fair way to receiving a greater commission but upon this it is premature to speculate. I wish thee God-speed to Smyrna and a good voyage withal.

Your affectionate Friend,
Hy. Mainwaring

The *Swallow* had indeed had a good voyage, making first for Leghorn and then the island of Zante, before loading her final homeward cargo of silk, oil and raisins at Smyrna. This had been followed by several more equally successful voyages in which several subsequent encounters with pirates had met with similar receptions to that initial brief exchange of fire. Only one of these had turned out to be serious and it occurred when the *Swallow* lay becalmed off the

41

north coast of Malta. One morning, pulling down the glittering path of the rising sun, an Algerine galley had come upon them, surprising the morning watch.

Had the captain of the galley held his fire for a moment longer, his surprise would have been complete, but his first shot, fired from the heavy cannon mounted over the galley's long beak-head, not only startled the *Swallow*'s mate with its detonation as he directed the trimming of the sails to a cat's paw of wind, but it ricocheted over the ship's waist, tearing through a foremast backstay before falling into the sea.

'On deck! On deck! All hands to arms!' the terrified mate roared as the seamen on watch ran to the guns, casting off the lashings. Thanks to Strange's precautions these were kept loaded when there was any danger of attack, the charges being drawn and changed every morning. As the galley drew close, its crew assembling on its forecastle in anticipation of boarding, two guns loaded with langridge barked from the *Swallow*'s waist and cut a swathe through the men, robbing them of their ardour.

Both Strange and Faulkner had been below but they, like the others off watch, were soon on deck and bearing arms. Nevertheless, the galley came on and ran alongside, her starboard oars trailing, as stink-pots of Greek fire were hurled aboard the *Swallow*. These inextinguishable devices meant the enemy were intent on the capture of men, rather than cargo, though they would take both if they overcame resistance rapidly. Seeing the missiles, Strange shouted for them to be thrown overboard before their contents had a chance to spread.

One had hit the bunt of the mainsail but failed to ignite it and fell to the deck, where several others lay, their burning contents running out over the wooden deck. Fortunately this was still wet from the swabbing the watch had been giving it, but the persistent nature of the Greek fire meant that they had only a second or two to deal with the threat.

Darting out from among the seamen, Kit Faulkner picked up a burning stink-pot, hurled it back whence it came, over the heads of the men straining to get another round off from the guns.

'Good lad!' hollered the mate, as he drove a boarding pike at one of the pirates trying to clamber aboard. Behind Faulkner, others similarly disposed of the other stink-pots. What followed was a confused violent struggle about which Kit afterwards recalled very little except that his hand was burned – though from the heat of the stink-pot not its infernal contents. The last he saw of the galley was it drifting astern, several of its huge starboard oars broken. A miraculous breeze, of which the earlier cat's paw had been a precursor, sprang up with the rising sun and the two vessels drew apart. The enemy made one attempt to chase them but the breeze strengthened, and although it seemed for a while that the Algerine would persist, a few cannon shot were fired from the stern-chase guns, one of which – judging from the cries that came faintly downwind – fell among the slaves on their benches, causing havoc and dissuading further aggression.

Thus by the summer of 1620, when the *Swallow* lay in Bristol, the tall youth with his brown hair clubbed and wearing breeches, a long waistcoat under a cutaway coat and sporting a broad-brimmed hat, carried himself with the air of an experienced mariner who had learned sufficient of his business to be released from his indenture prematurely, and to be carried upon the ship's books as second mate. It was in this capacity that, having cleared the *Swallow* inwards at the Customs House, Captain Strange summoned both his mates to his cabin. Pouring each a glass of wine and pledging them a toast on the conclusion of a successful voyage, he invited them to be seated.

'Well, gentlemen,' Strange began, taking a letter from his satchel, 'I have here a letter of some import for us and I thought it best to take you into my confidence before we sign off the crew. I must first ask for your word as to remaining silent upon the detail of the matter contained herein.' Strange looked up. 'Mr Quinn?'

'Of course, Cap'n Strange.'

Strange looked at Faulkner. 'Aye, sir, my word upon it.' The lad's formal response in a voice long broken was in such contrast to Quinn's rough assertion that it amused Strange. Faulkner had acquired – from God alone knew where – a certain rough polish.

'Very well,' he said, holding up the letter to the

light coming in through the stern glazings. 'It is from Sir Henry Mainwaring.'

Reuben Quinn, the mate, threw a quizzical look at Faulkner as Strange began to read that portion of the missive that contained the content that he wished to share.

'In accordance with directions from the Lord High Admiral I am charged to muster a number of armed merchantmen to act in support of a squadron of His Majesty's ships-of-war, the whole of which is to be placed under the command of Sir Robert Mansell as admiral, having Sir Thomas Button as his vice admiral and Sir Richard Hawkins as his rear admiral. To which purpose and our mutual advantage, I have commended the services of yourself and the *Swallow*, as both knowing the seas unto which the squadron will presently be dispatched and for that you have acquitted yourselves notably in several sea-fights against the pirates of Barbary. To this end you are commanded to recruit a crew suitable for an enterprise to the Mediterranean, to augment your armament by some swivels and murderers besides shipping any extra great-guns as you think desirable and the ship may bear; lay in powder and stores for six months, and such water as will hold sweet for as long as half that time...' Strange paused, passed over the rest of the letter which he set down before him. 'Well, you see the way the wind blows gentlemen; we are to become a King's ship.'

'And under favourable charter, I wouldn't wonder, sir,' remarked Quinn, rolling his eyes with amusement.

'No doubt,' responded Strange with a smile. 'Sir Henry was scarcely to be expected to let such an opportunity escape us. The question is – our crew. They will want paying-off but I have to have the ship ready to sail in...' he consulted the letter, 'ten days'.

'I am content to stand by, sir, having no other place to go,' offered Faulkner. Strange nodded. Until released from his indentures the young man had usually been lodged ashore at Strange's own expense whenever the *Swallow* lay in her home port. 'Mr Quinn?'

'Well, Cap'n, it does not seem unreasonable for a man to want to lie in his marriage bed for a night or two, and I imagine the men will feel the same, if only with a whore, but my guess is that if thou puts it to them, they will oblige.'

'We must of necessity conceal our destination, so I purpose that we put it about that we are to embark upon a Guinea voyage...'

'That will not be popular, Cap'n,' said Quinn, 'what with the stinking fever rife and word of the *Gloucester* losing half her men before ever she left the Sherbro.'

'True,' said Strange, 'but we need an explanation for the additional ordnance...'

'Might we not need that if we were intending a short voyage to Spain, sir?' said Faulkner.

'Good idea,' said Quinn quickly, 'and the promise of a short voyage is inducement enough.'

'We'll have to break it, though,' ruminated

46

Strange, 'and I do not like to mislead men.'

'They will understand if the enterprise goes well, Cap'n.'

'Maybe,' said Strange, 'and if it goes ill, they will not forgive me my deception'.

Quinn laughed. ''Twill not miscarry, Cap'n Strange. Why, we have seen off the Moors ourselves and didn't Cap'n Mainwaring do some such thing with his crew when he first went on account? I have certainly heard something of the affair.'

'One does not enquire too deeply in such directions, Mr Quinn,' Strange said quickly.

'Maybe not, Captain, but if we go in goodly company with the King's ships, how can we fail?'

But they did fail and a year later Kit Faulkner stood once again before his benefactor, having been summoned to attend Sir Henry Mainwaring when the *Swallow* arrived home. Mainwaring was fuller in the face than Kit remembered, but retained his kindly, encouraging smile and it was difficult to cast him as a former pirate. For his part, Mainwaring noticed the greater change evident in the younger man who, for all his youth, had matured both physically and intellectually.

'Well, Mr Rat, you have grown mightily. Pray be seated ... A glass of wine...' Mainwaring proffered a glass brimful of a rich *Oporto*.

They sat for a moment and then Mainwaring asked his protégé, 'I have spoken to Sir Robert

Mansell as to the Mediterranean enterprise but, tell me, why in your opinion did the expedition miscarry?'

'In my opinion, sir?'

'Aye, in your opinion, Kit. You are not without wits, I think.'

'Well, sir, the place – Algiers, I mean – is formidable. The harbour is protected by a vast mole, well embrasured and filled with artillery enfilading any approach. We were, it has to be admitted, tardy in pressing our suit. Our embassy had failed despite the Dey promising much, but in truth giving us nothing, so we withdrew and then two or three times came again before the place, making sundry demonstrations without effect...' Faulkner appeared to falter and Mainwaring prompted.

'And then?'

'May I speak frankly, sir?'

'Indeed, I would have you so, even if you impute some blame to those of us here at home.'

'That is part of the seat of our dilemma, sir. As time passed and we expected stores and reinforcement, nothing came and the admiral grew exceeding vexed, as did Sir Thomas Button, while Sir Richard Hawkins so fulminated against the inactivity that he seemed sometimes fair set to split himself asunder as I believe he since has...'

'Alas, yes,' Mainwaring said, reflecting on the death of Mansell's vice admiral. 'He was beset by a fit in the presence of the Privy Council when informed that his expenses would not be

48

met ... a sad end for a man who saw action against the Armada...'

'I am sorry for it, sir, for he was much esteemed in the fleet.'

'But perhaps past the age for active service?'

'It was said so, sir, among those who pretended to know.'

'So, but you made several attempts to carry the harbour, did you not?'

'Indeed, sir, we spent much time in preparation and practice with fireships, but every time we essayed the venture, the wind turned contrary and when, in desperation, we pressed the attack by boat, we were caught in crossfire and driven off. We set alight but two of the piratical vessels, but those fires were, I believe, put out.'

Mainwaring nodded, rubbing his chin ruminatively before looking up at the young man. 'And what part did you take in these proceedings, Kit?'

'I was pretty forward, sir, taking part in the final boat attack.'

'Yes, Captain Strange has written that you earned the approval of Sir Richard on several occasions. That is good, for I want you to leave the *Swallow* and come into my private service if you are not unwilling.'

'To leave the *Swallow*...?' The young man was suddenly uncertain and Mainwaring realized that the little merchantman had provided him with the security of a home, while the prospect of advancement yawned before him as a chasm, full of the unknown. 'I owe Captain Strange a great deal, Sir Henry,' Faulkner said awkwardly.

'He knows that,' Mainwaring responded, 'but since you have acquitted yourself well, I have other plans for you. It depends upon your inclination, but the country is greatly in want of good sea-officers in the King's ships and I have it in mind that you should be one of them. I am a Commissioner of the Navy and am empowered to recruit new officers, and would have a proportion of experienced seamen to offset the courtiers that plague the service.' He paused a moment to allow the import of his proposition to strike home. 'Come now, what do you say?' Seeing the lad was confused and hesitant, Mainwaring added, a hint of exasperation in his tone: 'For heaven's sake, Mr Rat, you have nothing to fear! I am offering you a future as a gentleman ... *El Dorado* awaits you.'

Faulkner looked at the older man. 'I understand, Sir Henry, but my lack of means ... my penury...'

Mainwaring held up a hand and shook his head, smiling. 'My dear fellow, I perfectly understand your misgivings, but a year in my service will equip you for preferment, that I promise you. Come, what do you say?'

'If you are certain Captain Strange will not think me ungrateful—' he began, but Mainwaring cut him short.

'Of that I can assure you. He and I are of one mind and while I have no doubt but that he will miss your society and your ability, he can fill the deficiency in the latter well enough in Bristol; as for the former, well that shall be my advantage and recompense for the gamble I took upon your good character and abilities.'

Looking relieved, Faulkner nodded with a sudden and, for Mainwaring, pleasing decisiveness. 'Very well, Sir Henry. I am at your service.'

Mainwaring's face cracked in a warm smile and he rose to put out his hand. 'Welcome, Kit, we shall do famously.'

Thus, for nigh two years Faulkner attended his new master, initially in the capacity of clerk, rapidly improving his ability to write, acquiring a polish in his manners, and learning something of the various projects in which his new master was then engaged. These involved negotiations with the Venetian ambassador (which fell through), and a prolonged engagement with Dover, whither Sir Henry repaired regularly, having been appointed Lieutenant of Dover Castle, Deputy Warden of the Cinque Ports and Member of Parliament for the town. During this period Faulkner was chiefly employed assisting Mainwaring in the writing of his book on seamanship, a dictionary entitled *Nomenclator Navalis*. By this time Faulkner had become Mainwaring's private secretary, and while he found the work of interest and grew into the part Mainwaring had cast him, assuming the character of a gentleman who moved in the shadows of important men and acquired a passing acquaintance with the outer circles of the Court of King

James, he sometimes pined to go to sea again. There the chores and daily round allowed him to stand upon his own two feet, a watch-keeping officer directing others. Now he was continually subservient, ever on his guard, not against Mainwaring, but wary of some of those among whom his master moved. Mainwaring's duties were many and varied. He attended and conferred regularly with Lord Zouch, the Governor of Dover Castle with whom he maintained a fractious relationship. Faulkner was involved with arrangements for ordnance, powder and ammunition to be supplied from London, then followed his master to the Assize Court to try French fishermen caught fishing illegally in English waters. But, once having had ambition awakened, Faulkner chafed increasingly at the constraints necessary to his life. If he had been turned into a quasi-gentleman, was apparelled accordingly and spoke with a certain witty and ready tongue, he was yet a whelp to Mainwaring, the old hound and a man of indefatigable energy.

Sir Henry rarely seemed to take pleasure in anything other than work, having made himself almost indispensable to the King's service and, paradoxically, it was this that suddenly ended the stasis in which the irked Faulkner found himself.

The variety of Mainwaring's involvement in public affairs led him to make enemies within the castle and he was accused by Lord Zouch of neglect of duty. Hints that he slept outside the castle in order to lie with a woman brought about a heavier suggestion that his resignation would be pleasing to His Lordship. Much amazed, and declaring the charge trumped-up, Mainwaring asserted he indeed sought the company of a woman, but not on the occasion in question. He had, he responded, been assaulted by a troublemaker and afterwards spent the night with an old friend, one Captain Wilsford. It was also true that he was then also raising men for a squadron fitting out for foreign service and therefore his absence from Dover was legitimate. Taking Faulkner with him, he had also waited upon the King at Windsor to discuss with His Majesty the issue of impressments, but Lord Zouch dismissed him, nonetheless, remarking that a man, even a man of Mainwaring's acknowledged talents, could not properly serve two masters.

Aware of this furore, Faulkner was apprehensive for Mainwaring's future as much as for his own. Despite his misgivings, his youthful sights had been raised considerably and he had slowly but inevitably become a victim of his own self-conceit. In due course, his head turned, he had abandoned any idea of returning to his old life sailing out of Bristol, increasingly enamoured of the notion of serving in a King's ship-of-war.

In the event Mainwaring had lost nothing in the King's eyes during his altercations with Lord Zouch. Having made representations to the Earl of Rutland, Mainwaring found himself in receipt of a letter in the King's own hand. He and Faulkner were lodging in London when it was delivered and, aware of its origin and fearful of its content, the latter watched his master anxiously as Mainwaring cracked open the royal seal. Without looking up and before he had finished reading, he ordered Faulkner to pour two cups of wine. As Faulkner set them on the table, Mainwaring laid the letter down and picked up the wine.

'You are aware that the Prince of Wales and the Duke of Buckingham are in Spain, seeking a Spanish *Infanta* as a bride for Prince Charles, are you not?'

'Indeed, Sir Henry. There has been much talk of it and the fear of Their Highnesses being held hostage by His Most Catholic Majesty.'

Mainwaring smiled. 'I should have known better than to have asked,' he laughed, pleased at his protégé's grasp of affairs of state. 'Though the whole affair is a mad-cap adventure wherein the impetuous Buckingham has imperilled the Prince, undone much diplomacy and made something of a fool of the King's Majesty. But you will know that some of our present business has related to the fitting-out of a squadron intended to proceed to Spain to bring home Their Highnesses.'

'Yes, of course.'

'But you will not know,' Mainwaring went on, the fingers of his left hand tapping the King's letter with a slight and portentous rustle, 'that I am appointed to command the *Prince Royal* in which the Earl of Rutland will shortly hoist his flag and take command of the fleet destined for

54

Spain. Moreover, you will not know that I shall appoint you among my lieutenants.' Mainwaring paused to let the import of his words sink in. Then, looking at Faulkner, he added: 'By God, this is a long way from foraging for apple cores, Mr Rat!'

And he was pleased when the lad smiled.

Two

The *Prince Royal*

Summer 1623

Mainwaring had joined the *Prince Royal* at Chatham, leaving Faulkner in London to attend to some domestic affairs relating to their departure. The ship had sailed to Spithead from where, early in July 1623, Faulkner was summoned 'before the middle of the month'.

With that attention to detail that marked all his dealings, Mainwaring had given Faulkner a list of instructions enabling him to prepare himself for his new role. These had arrived along with his orders to join Sir Henry in the ship and included an inventory of personal effects with which Faulkner should equip himself. Studying the list made the young man aware of the daunting nature of his new life, and while he had learned to conduct himself with an assumed confidence, he was astute enough to know that in the close company of courtiers he would be found wanting. In his solicitude Mainwaring had addressed this, writing,

Get thyself a new doublet, some decent boots and some goodish lace. Nothing ostentatious, but of sober and undoubted quality. Match this with some small clothes, for you shall have a servant and none tittle-tattles more. Do not acquire a new sword, that will mark you too obviously, but take mine which I left purposefully for you. Buy also a red sash that will mark you as a new lieutenant – your commission I have with me over the King's Sign Manual – for there is no dishonour in promotion. Purchase also a decent cuirass; half-armour will be beyond the means I left in your charge, but there will be sufficient funds for a b'plate...

Faulkner hefted the purse Mainwaring had left with him 'for contingent and other expenses such as I shall advise you of soon', and smiled grimly to himself.

'Well,' he muttered, 'there is nothing for it, then,' and picking up his hat he made to leave upon an expedition to acquire the necessary additions to the stock of his belongings. Pausing on the threshold of his lodgings he regarded his hat and its bedraggled feather. 'And perhaps a new hat and,' he added sensibly to himself, 'a portmanteau of sufficient capacity.'

Halfway down the stairs he paused again. 'God's blood – a servant!' and with that he strolled out on to the street, whistling softly to himself and mightily pleased.

Faulkner had only ever seen a King's ship at a distance and she had been half the size of the *Prince Royal*. Now, as the hired boat pulled him from the Sally Port towards the anchorage at Spithead, reality bore down heavily upon him as he sat in the boat's stern sheets, his feet tucked to one side of his portmanteau and his left hand about the satchel containing Mainwaring's correspondence. The euphoria of the four days begun with the making of his purchases and preparations in London, and ending with his journey in some style (an inside seat in the coach), were whipped away in the breeze that even on a day of brilliant sunshine in high summer, had something of the chill of the distant waters whence it blew. To his disgust, Faulkner's stomach reminded him it was some time since he had trodden a deck; knowing that his claim to advancement relied upon his professionalism rather than his breeding, he feared a humiliation and in an attempt to overcome his nausea, addressed the nearer of the two straining boatmen.

'Tell me, which is the *Prince Royal*?' It was a question he instantly regretted, for he had made it without consideration. The man spat to leeward and raised an eyebrow which, as he leaned forward to ply his oar, gave him the appearance of leering at Faulkner.

'Why, the flagship, o'course...' the man observed with unhelpful contempt.

Faulkner peered over the undulating shoulders of the two boatmen; the anchorage was crowded with shipping. Coasting vessels and tenders slipped between the larger shapes of men-of-war which were in silhouette against the bright sunlight dancing in reflections off the short, choppy seas cut up by a wind blowing over the tide. This contrary quality of nature caused the squadron to lie athwart both wind and tide and lie almost end-on to anyone approaching from Portsmouth. Seeing his passenger's eyes darting about from one man-of-war to another, the boatman spat to leeward again.

'From London are ye, sir?'

'Aye...' Faulkner answered warily.

'An' the first time you've joined a ship, eh?'

'In Portsmouth, yes, but I've seen a deal of service...'

'Have ye now...' The boatman seemed to consider this and reassess his passenger. He was anxious to get a good tip beyond the shilling he had already extorted from him. 'You see the three largest vessels, over against the island, sir...'

'Yes, I do...'

'The westernmost one is the *Swiftsure*, of forty-two guns wearing the flag of Lord Windsor; the easternmost is the *St Andrew*, also of forty-two guns and flying the flag of Vice

Admiral Lord Morley. The *Prince Royal* lies between the two, sir, a full fifty-five guns and Sir Henry Mainwaring in command with the Earl of Rutland expected tomorrow, but you'll know that coming from Court, sir,' the man added ingratiatingly.

Faulkner was no longer listening; he was peering at the ship the boatman had identified. She presented her huge stern to the mainland and, as they drew nearer, the vast size of the ship began to impress itself upon him. Why, the *Swallow* might nestle in her waist! She was huge! And he could see as she swung slightly that she sported *four* masts! Something entirely new opened up in the pit of Faulkner's stomach; all fear of seasickness vanished in the face of a naked apprehension: could he cope with handling this monster? Why she must have a crew of ... of perhaps four hundred men?

Something of this may have betrayed him, for the boatman added, 'Some twelve hundred tons she measures, sir, and with a crew of five hundred men.'

'*Five* hundred!' Faulkner was unable to conceal his astonishment: five hundred men! Why, the *Swallow*, even with her crew augmented by gunners to ward off the Sallee Rovers mustered no more than twenty-eight!

'And her guns on three decks, sir,' added the boatman, aware that he was impressing his young passenger and doling out the information as if he himself were the author of all this naval puissance. Faulkner stared at the looming bulk of the great man-of-war as he was pulled past the lesser vessels in the squadron, though even these, except perhaps the pinnaces *Charles* and *Seven Stars*, would dwarf the *Swallow*. He counted the gun-ports in the larboard side of the *Antelope* and, doubling them, guessed her to mount about three dozen pieces, the *Bonaventure* perhaps the same and the *Rainbow* more. Two heavier ships were too distant for him to make any such estimate, nor would he learn their names until later as the *St George* and *Defiance*. They were now closing the *Prince Royal* and Faulkner had only a moment or two to register the enormous height of her poop, richly encrusted with ornate and gilded carvings, of fabled beasts, armorial bearings and acanthus leaves. These surrounded the royal coat of arms and embraced the monogram H.P. – *Henricus Princeps* – the royal prince after whom the great ship had been named before Henry, Prince of Wales, predeceased his father.

This grandiloquence soared above the wherry as the boatmen worked her closer, against the tide sloshing alongside the huge man-of-war. Faulkner felt the chill as they came in under the looming shadow of the monstrous vessel and then all introspection was driven from his mind as a hail from the entry port had the bow oarsman stow his oars and reach for a boat-hook, making the signal for an officer for the ship. Then they were tossing alongside in the chop and Faulkner, having pressed a shilling and two pence into the warm and horny hand of the boatman and slung the satchel on his back, stumbled clumsily before catching his balance. Stepping lightly upon a thwart he grabbed both baize-covered man-ropes, stepped on to the treads proud of the ship's side and ascended her sloping tumblehome. A moment later he had passed through the entry-port and stood in the gloom of the middle gun-deck where a young man wearing his sash of office awaited him. Faulkner seemed to be expected.

'Mr Faulkner, I'll warrant.'

'Indeed, sir, yes.'

The young man, his face half hidden in the prevailing gloom by long dark hair, appeared cordial enough and extended his hand.

'You were expected. I'm Harry Brenton, fifth lieutenant, and we are messmates. I'll have your gear hauled aboard instanter and then I shall conduct you to Sir Henry. My Lord of Rutland, though he joined us in the Downs, has gone ashore.' Brenton turned away and summoned a hand to assist. Turning back with a broad grin, he said: 'He seeks his sea-legs thither for by God he has none here!' The young man laughed carelessly and a smiling sailor, girded by his frock and an apron, with a red woollen cap upon his head, knuckled his brow and said he would attend to Faulkner's portmanteau.

Between decks the great ship seemed even larger, the darkness teeming with people of both sexes, many of whom seemed intent upon selling either themselves or their wares to the rest, who were dressed in similar fashion to the sailor

61

now supervising the dragging up the ship's side of Faulkner's luggage.

'Come, sir, follow me. Adams will see your dunnage safely in your cabin.' Brenton led Faulkner along the deck, shoving aside the whores, the vendors and the usurers with bloody oaths and condemnations, followed by a bewildered Faulkner. He would never have allowed such chaos aboard the *Swallow*, he thought, his eye caught by a score of impressions in as many seconds, but how could one keep order among such a throng? A drunken face here, a bawd's leer there, the neat well-dressed appearance of a hirsute Jewish money lender, dim relief in the darkness beyond which there loomed the dull gleam of heavy artillery and the pots and kids of the men's messes. He felt a pang of misgiving: would he ever be able to master all this? If Brenton was fifth lieutenant he devoutly hoped he himself was the sixth or seventh. How many lieutenants did such a vessel own? He had no idea. Suddenly all his knowledge and experience, all his cunning and skill, seemed worthless in the face of this behemoth. And then they stood beside a door and, a moment later, entered the comparative haven of the captain's cabin. Certainly there were cannon ranged either side, but the space was carpeted and lit by glazed windows through which streamed daylight, casting the familiar figure of Sir Henry Mainwaring in dark outline against the brilliance as he sat at a long table that ran the beam of the ship. The table was surrounded by chairs at another of which sat an older man who had thrust his wig aside and pored over several charts, wielding dividers and writing in a notebook.

Brenton coughed and in a lower voice than he had just been using said, 'Excuse me, Sir Henry...'

Mainwaring looked up and then, with evident pleasure, rose smiling and holding out his hand. 'Faulkner, my dear fellow, have you brought my papers?'

'Aye, Sir Henry.' Faulkner fished the satchel round and took it off, handing it to Mainwaring.

'Brenton, pour us all a glass of wine,' Mainwaring commanded. 'And were you able to fit yourself out as I instructed?'

'Indeed I was, thanks to your assistance...'

Mainwaring cut him short, waving away his thanks. 'We'll hear no more of that. Thank you, Brenton,' he added as Brenton did duty with a tray and filled glasses. 'Now, sir, Mr Brenton will show you the ship. He has the advantage of you having served in her before, but he will be junior to you...' Faulkner shot a swift glance at Brenton, alarmed at this news but seeking any sign of resentment on the part of his new colleague. Brenton caught his eye and smiled with a nonchalant shrug. Mainwaring, meanwhile, reached behind him among the litter of papers on the desk and drew out a stiff parchment leaf. 'Here is your commission as fourth lieutenant.'

Faulkner hid his surprise and apprehension. 'Thank you, Sir Henry...'

'Now, let me introduce Mr Whiting, the Master. Whiting, this is the young fellow of whom I spoke, Kit Faulkner. You will find him as good as the best of your mates at the traverse, the helm and with a quadrant...'

Whiting rose and turned his weathered face towards the young man, making a half-bow. 'Mr Faulkner,' he acknowledged. 'A tarpaulin then,' he said to Mainwaring, adding pointedly with a barely perceptible and probably involuntary movement towards Brenton, 'rather than another gentleman.'

'Both tarpaulin and gentleman, Mr Whiting,' Mainwaring said with a hint of asperity, 'as I would hope all my officers are.'

Whiting laughed. 'No fear of *my* being mistaken for a gentleman, Sir Henry.'

'Ah, Whiting, but you are a *natural* gentleman, which maketh all the difference.'

Having raised his glass perfunctorily to Mainwaring, Whiting went back to his charts and Mainwaring gestured to Faulkner and Brenton to occupy two chairs.

'Since I have you both here I shall tell you what I have told Mr Whiting. The first lieutenant informs me that we shall complete our stores tomorrow forenoon after which I want the ship cleared of the landlubbers and only the permitted women to remain. They are to be mustered and entered upon the watch and quarter-bills. We will also stand the men to their stations for action. After the noon gun I expect some signal that Lord Rutland is rejoining us, following

64

which I anticipate that we shall put to sea. For that purpose I shall require you, Mr Faulkner, to attend me upon the poop, thereafter keeping your watch as directed by the first lieutenant. You are familiar with your station, Mr Brenton, are you not?'

'I am, Sir Henry.'

'Good. Well, stow your gear, Mr Faulkner, and make yourself known to the first lieutenant. Then we shall await the arrival of the admiral and our orders to weigh.'

The two young men lowered their glasses, rose, made their bows and withdrew. As they returned to the chaos of the gun-deck Brenton remarked that the hour of their departure could not come soon enough. Within hours Kit Faulkner was devoutly praying for the same outcome.

In the following weeks Faulkner learned something of the complexities of organizing a naval squadron. The means by which time was wasted seemed infinite: first Rutland sent word that he was unwell and obliged to stay in his house on the Strand in London; then Mainwaring caught an infection that seemed rife in the ship and which affected Faulkner to the extent of a slight quinsy and a shivering fit or two; then a man stole some kit from a messmate and must needs be ducked from the foreyard, then towed behind a ship's boat, landed and dismissed. The following day there came aboard an odd man who claimed to be rowing a boat down Channel from the Thames with the purpose of visiting the West

Country, an occupation that struck Faulkner as being absurd, though Mainwaring warmly welcomed him and introduced him to such of his officers then on board.

'This gentleman is John Taylor,' he told them, 'the well-known Water-Poet of London's River, to whom we owe much in the matter of advertising the importance of watermen and mariners to the common people and the court.'

The hearty and bluff soul who wore a gentleman's ruff over a plain doublet bowed, struck a pose and declaimed in a strong voice:

'From London Town to Bristol City, I pull my scull the Channel to disarm,
And prove a point that Wiltshire's Avon and the sea could lie as one,
And thus to Spithead and this mighty ship I come
To find Sir Henry Man'ring and his mighty charm,
Fulfils all expectations of my gratitude, in such a southern latitude.'

There was a silence, as if the gentlemen in range of the poet's declamation awaited more, and then Mainwaring led a polite clapping.

'Great Jupiter, is that poesy, or am I a Double-Dutchman?' asked Brenton in Faulkner's ear as the assembled officers went their separate ways. 'What the devil does he mean about the Wiltshire Avon?'

'Oh, there was some talk in Bristol about

digging a canal through from Salisbury to the sea,' said Faulkner, amused by the ridiculous scene, despite himself. 'D'you know the fellow?'

'I know *of* him,' replied Brenton, 'but so does half London. He has a natural wit and much of his verse is tolerable. That execrable piece was no doubt improvised upon the spot, though why he came aboard, Heaven only knows ... unless he expected the King to be here, it is not beyond his importunity to thrust himself into the royal regard.'

'The King, here...?' Faulkner said, surprised.

'Why not? We are for Spain to recover his son and his...' Brenton shrugged enigmatically. 'He is presently lodging at Beaulieu.'

This curious interlude was the only event of note that broke the monotony of their waiting time. The Earl of Rutland had still not joined his flagship when Mainwaring ordered her moved to Stokes Bay, a new anchorage closer to the mainland. Here, on the 20th August, King James, attended by numerous Lords and a large retinue, did indeed board the *Prince Royal*. The occasion was of such dazzling splendour, with a full royal salute fired by the assembled fleet and answered by the guns of the flagship, that Faulkner thought they might have destroyed the entire Barbary fleet by the expenditure of powder. There was, besides, such a hoisting and lowering of flags and standards, that he caught only fleeting impressions. This reaction, it seemed to him as he rolled into his berth that night, characterized naval service as a life of rich idleness interspersed with incomprehensible interludes of almost theatrical portentousness, whether to the point of silliness in the visit of John Taylor, or extravagant grandeur as in the condescension of King James.

Not that Faulkner – assembled among the officers, his sword upon his hip and his new hat upon his head to uncover when presented to His Majesty – even recalled much of the encounter itself. That he was honoured, he was aware, but the need to avoid the King's eyes and to make his bow at once elegant and deep, almost exhausted his concentration. Even a sly glance as King James spoke with Mainwaring, told Faulkner little beyond the fact that His Majesty had a long, pallid, lugubrious and bearded face, and wore a hat that seemed too tall for him. Somehow the huge royal standard that spent the day at the truck of the *Prince Royal*'s main-mast seemed more splendid than the King himself – a consequential impression that stuck in Faulkner's imagination for many a long year.

There was, however, one moment which made a deeper and indelible mark upon him, though he was not yet to realize it. Among the several ladies accompanying the King, and whose embarkation had caused anxiety to the *Prince Royal*'s people, was the slim, richly dressed figure of a girl. His eye had first been caught by her dainty feet in embroidered shoes as the yard-arm whip had lowered her to the deck. Later Faulkner caught sight of her at dinner in the

68

great cabin, sitting near the King. He was astonished chiefly at her youth and her proximity to King James, but it was the round luminosity of her fine eyes, the colour of which he could not see, that struck him like a blow. She had, he thought, cast him a single glance, before attending to the gentleman on her right, who Faulkner thought was perhaps Lord Pembroke, the Lord Chamberlain. It seemed to him as he later considered of the events of the day, that a vast gulf existed between such as she and the likes of himself. He felt a vague resentment at the inequities of life and wondered whether he would have been so troubled if she had neither had such fine eyes, nor looked his way.

Then he chid himself for a fool; the look she had given him was of no significance, marking – if anything at all – only a general curiosity. Besides, he must remember that he might still be seeking food and employment along Bristol's waterfront and in the city's gutter. He reflected that, having come so far, perhaps the inequities of life were not entirely insurmountable. And with that comforting thought, he drifted off to sleep, aware of a faint ringing in his ears that had been caused hours earlier by the combined gunfire of the entire fleet as it saluted the departing royal barge.

The Earl of Rutland did, eventually, hoist his flag and on the day he did so – a few days after King James had dined on board – Faulkner's life took another strange turn. The long period of enforced idleness at Spithead had at least given him time to take stock; to familiarize himself with the huge ship and her working; to realize that fundamentally she was little different in principle than the little *Swallow*; to recognize significant members of her crew, particularly among the petty and warrant officers; to grow used to Adams's solicitations on his and Brenton's behalf, since they shared Adams's services between them. He also better understood his own many and varied duties which emerged from the confusion of naval protocols and privileges, discoveries which gradually reduced the apparent chaos of the great ship, slowly and subtly reducing it to something approaching order.

The delay also gave him time to impress his own character upon others. As his own confidence and comprehension grew, he swiftly lost his uncertainty and brought to bear his skills and native good sense to the daily round. Identifying those aspects of his job that tallied with those he had acquired in the service of Strange aboard the *Swallow* he was able to make his mark, so that when a seaman fouled a line as they hoisted the mizzen lateen yard, Faulkner swiftly cleared the lead before trouble followed, an initiative which drew a grudging appreciation from the boatswain who would otherwise have taken action against the wretched perpetrator of the error. It might not be what a gentleman officer did, but it clearly demonstrated that Lieutenant Faulkner not only appreciated the technicalities of the task, but also the dangers of hesitation; in short, it was clear to all who witnessed the momentary hitch, that he was a thorough-going sailor.

Word reached them one morning that the Earl of Rutland would come off to the ship that day and orders were passed for his barge to be prepared. Brenton was to go in it and embark the admiral whom Faulkner by now knew was a court appointee and no seaman. Under such a titular head, all depended upon Mainwaring and his officers, of whom several others were courtiers or soldiers, rather than men bred to the sea.

At last word was passed to the ship's company to stand by to receive the admiral and men ran to their preordained posts and an unnatural stillness descended upon the ship. Those on the upper decks could see the approaching barge, its oars rising and falling, the blades flashing in the sunshine, astern of which came a procession of wherries piled with baggage, and another boat with an ornate canopy over the stern.

'We shall need a chair and a whip at the mainyard, Mr Slessor,' Mainwaring called to the first lieutenant, indicating the presence of ladies in the Earl of Rutland's entourage.

'It won't be just the Earl and his suite who join us today,' Brenton had remarked earlier that morning as they were advised of the admiral's coming while they were shaving and Adams was dressing their hair. 'There will be a number of courtiers come to provide a fitting welcome for the Prince of Wales and the Duke of Buckingham and that, my dear Kit, is why you and I

71

have to live like rabbits in this hutch.'

The two officers were obliged to share a cabin intended for one for, although the *Prince Royal* had been built as a flagship and thus carried accommodation for an admiral and his staff, the numerous suites of those considered indispensable to the reception of the Prince of Wales and the Duke of Buckingham almost beggared belief. 'We have to remember,' Brenton had remarked as they sat over a glass of wine the previous evening, 'that besides being the King's favourite, My Lord of Muckingham is the Lord High Admiral and therefore his flag will take precedence over Rutland's.'

'Muckingham...?' queried Faulkner.

''Tis my name for him,' Brenton said, lowering his voice, 'though I shall be hanged yet for saying so...'

'Then why say it?'

'Because, my dear innocent Kit, I abhor what he is and what he stands for. He is not merely venal to the point of stinking corruption, but is also the King's catamite.' Faulkner stared, puzzled. 'You do not know what a catamite is?' Faulkner shook his head and Brenton reduced his voice to a whisper. 'Why, the King's creature; he who lies with the King for the purposes of carnal lust ... sodomy ... buggery...'

'I know what sodomy is,' Faulkner hissed, 'and I know that such indiscretions aboard a ship such as this may indeed lead you to the gallows, or a slow disembowelling...'

Brenton grinned with an insouciance that

72

Faulkner found profoundly unnerving. Although there was a difference in rank between them, they were of the same age and the previous fortnight had cast them as friends. Nevertheless, Faulkner was compelled to acknowledge the other's more sophisticated worldliness. 'Why, 'tis spoken of everywhere,' Brenton said.

'But perhaps not so loudly here when the ship is full of courtiers,' Faulkner remarked.

'Indeed not, but tonight it is full of honest Jacks and I take thee for an honest Jack, Kit Faulkner.'

'Indeed, I hope you do, and now, before you preach more sedition I think we ought to get some rest...' And so they had turned in, though Faulkner had lain awake long after the snores of the foolhardy young Brenton filled the stale air and the great ship creaked and groaned about him as she swum, straining to her anchor and cable in the tide.

The following forenoon the sight of the approaching boats had reminded Faulkner of the conversation and the influence of great men. When he had first entered Mainwaring's service he had half expected great men to reflect something of the goodness that Sir Henry had manifested towards himself, and although he had long since lost that naivety, there remained some sense of disappointment that they did not. On the one hand it reduced their high social standing in respect of himself, but on the other it seemed to increase their unworthiness to enjoy any such superiority. Indeed, if he were truthful, he found the very notion of a king engaged in fondling another man, let alone enjoying any form of congress, profoundly disturbing. Was not a king God's anointed? And was not sodomy forbidden by biblical proscription? Faulkner was no expert on such theological matters, but the notion made him distinctly uncomfortable and in a moment of rare self-doubt, he wished himself clear of all such muddles, spiritual, intellectual or physical. Indeed, he wished himself back on the deck of the little *Swallow*, with the Scilly Isles astern and the broad bosom of the Atlantic ahead, the horizon sharp under the spritsail yard and the world full only of the potent evil of Sallee Rovers.

But now the tweeting of the boatswain's call and the shouted orders as the *Prince Royal*'s people prepared to receive the approaching boats took over his attention and for half an hour Faulkner's mind was attentive to the formalities of seeing the crowd of courtiers aboard and conducted to their allotted accommodation. And that is how he came face-to-face with the young girl with the dark and luminous eyes and felt such a violent twist in his bowels the like of which he had never previously experienced.

He had returned to the deck from seeing three gentlemen into a cabin under the poop, the smallness of which sent them into paroxysms of confusion and complaint from which he extricated himself only with some difficulty. 'I assure you gentlemen,' he had explained, 'this is accommodation superior to anything enjoyed by the ship's officers and I am sure that you will find us as attentive to your needs as our duties will allow...'

'I do hope so,' one mincing wag said, rolling his eyes in Faulkner's direction as he withdrew. 'I don't know which I prefer,' he heard another say, 'those hearty tars or their petty officers...'

The clean air of the deck washed over him as he watched one of the canvas chairs descend on deck on its yard-arm whip. A seaman reached up a hand and steadied it as it was lowered to the deck. Catching Faulkner's eye, the first lieutenant, Edward Slessor, beckoned him and then turned to its occupant.

'Milady,' he said, 'Mr Faulkner will show you to your apartment...'

Faulkner stepped forward, made a perfunctory bow and looked up into the luminous eyes that had momentarily transfixed him earlier when the King had dined on board.

'Milady,' he said, holding out his hand and steadying her as she took it and stepped out of the chair. He was aware that his heart had begun pounding and that he was uncertain whether he was blushing like a loon or had gone as white as a corpse. He felt her fingers through her glove, tiny, delicate, and he was unsure whether to withdraw his hand now his assistance was no longer required, or to remain leading her towards the door under the poop and the great cabin, which had been partitioned and hung with velvet drapes to accommodate the ladies. In the end he led her, only half looking at her as he said in as steady a voice as he could muster – and with a second, awkward crabwise bow made between one step and another – 'Lieutenant Faulkner at your service, ma'am...'

It was the first time he had referred to himself by rank and he drew strength from his new status. He felt a slight pressure from her hand as she stepped across the deck and the great ship moved slightly as she trimmed herself to the wind and tide.

'I shall hope so, sir,' he heard her say as she looked about her apprehensively, 'for I find this shipboard world a most confusing universe.'

The turn of phrase struck him as apt and the intimacy somewhat disarmed him. 'Indeed, ma'am, so it seems at first, so it seemed to me but a month ago...'

'Then you are no seaman?' she asked, her tone astonished, and stopped, compelling him to stop and face her. He felt foolish, confused, and then he mastered himself. It was pointless to act otherwise than truthfully. Besides, he felt compelled to tell this girl who he was and he knew it was unlikely he would have another chance like this moment.

'You misunderstand, ma'am; I am but newly commissioned into the *Prince Royal* but have been bred to the sea since boyhood. As a flagship this is said to be the largest man-of-war in the world and she awes us all...'

'Awes us all ... why there is a nautical pun there, sir, if I am not mistaken.' She smiled and walked on, and Faulkner felt stupidly irradiated by her regard.

'I did not intend it so...'

They were under the poop, now, entering the subdivided space and encountering servants and others fluttering around the influx of grandees. A ladies' maid bobbed a curtsey at his charge and she withdrew her hand. 'I am Katherine Villiers, Lieutenant Faulkner,' she said, meeting his eyes and smiting him with her deep, level gaze, 'and I hope to see more of you during the voyage.'

Stunned into silence, his heart leaping foolishly in his breast, Faulkner footed the most elegant bow he could muster and returned, reluctantly, to the drab duties about the deck.

And yet they were not so drab for it now seemed his every movement might be scrutinized by those beguiling eyes, his every order heard by her. It did not matter that in revealing her name he learned that she was associated with the King's catamite, or that her social standing was lunar to his earthly ambition. He carried himself with new authority, gave orders with a crisp clarity and found himself eager to be on deck, attentive, conspicuous.

Brenton caught him an hour later as they drew breath with the hoisting in of the last of the interminable portmanteaux. 'You had the best of the advantages there, Kit, I think. What a pretty girl and related to the Lord High Muckingham. You are playing with fire, don't you know, for she will break your heart or pox thee – perhaps both, I shouldn't wonder.'

'Hold your damned tongue, Harry,' he responded sharply, at which Brenton merely went off laughing. 'Come, we must dine before we labour further,' he called, over his shoulder.

Not during the several days that followed her boarding did Faulkner set eyes upon Katherine Villiers and yet he constantly fancied that hers never left him.

The fleet weighed on 25th August and headed west with a favourable tide, but the easterly wind proved fickle and the following day the ships rode again at their anchors off Weymouth. Two days later, however, the wind came away from the east and the fleet headed down Channel. Faulkner, high upon the *Prince Royal*'s quarterdeck, stood amazed at the ponderous progress of the great ship which contrasted with the swift, weatherly wallow of the little *Swallow*. She lolled at the end of every roll and she hung before coming back, so that her topgallant yards were not hoisted if the wind was anywhere forward of her quarters. Nor, it was clear to him as they had worked to sea to gain an offing from the Isle of Wight, was she handy; sufficient time and sea-room had to be allowed for any manoeuvre, a liability complicated by the proximity of the other ships in the squadron. On the 28th the wind hauled ahead, veering to the south and then the south-west, compelling Rutland – at Mainwaring's instigation – to hang out the signal to come to an anchor in Plymouth Sound. Here they all lay at the end of the month, when Faulkner, along with Slessor, Brenton, Whiting and the other officers, found themselves called to council in Rutland's cabin. Here they were joined by the inferior flag officers, Lords Morely and Windsor, and their flag captains and the commanders of the other men-of-war in the squadron, Trevor of the *Defiance*, Steward of the *St George*, St Leger of the *Bonaventure*, Palmer of the *Rainbow* – all of whom were knights – and Love of the *Charles* with the lesser captains of the two pinnaces, *Charles* and *Seven Stars*. The admiral stood resplendent in red and black slashed silk, the pale-blue sash of the Garter across his breast, his hand on the basket-hilt of a long and highly chased rapier. Behind him were two courtiers, Sir John Finett and Sir Thomas Somerset, both men part of the suite whose duty was to conduct any diplomacy contingent upon receiving Prince Charles or Buckingham and of extricating them from any impasse into which their dubious conduct had embroiled them during the course of their importunate Spanish adventure. They watched the assembled sea-officers with a mixture of hauteur and rank curiosity, though several were known to them. However, it was Mainwaring who, after a brief welcome by Rutland, addressed the assembled officers.

'My Lords and gentlemen, as you all know, our progress has been hampered thus far by contrary winds and the season is already well advanced. We must therefore hold ourselves ready to move with all despatch the instant the wind lies fair. To this end all ships are required to make good their deficiencies in stores and water...'

'What about men?' asked Sir Sackville Trevor. 'I am two score short of my establishment.'

'What rating, Sir Sackville?' asked Rutland wearily.

'Why, able seamen, my Lord, we are always in want of them...'

'I suggest a press in Plymouth might solve your problem, Sir Sackville, though the sight of our fleet has likely driven able men inland faster than their kine,' remarked Lord Morley, 'though we all want seamen.'

'Aye, and provender too...' added St Leger, a remark accompanied by a grumbling of assent from the other captains. Faulkner heard one or two of them mention Finett's name, as though blaming the courtiers for these deficiencies. There was, he knew from Whiting and Slessor, some justification at the slight, for Faulkner had learned of the desperate want of good provisions, both fresh and casked, that the fleet stood in need of and without which they would not only be on short commons but soon find sickness rampant among them. The observant Faulkner also noticed Mainwaring mutter something from the corner of his mouth as Rutland drew himself up and faced his officers.

'Gentlemen, I must ask you to do what you can in the short time we have available. May I remind you that we are bound on a diplomatic service of the utmost importance to the country and our Royal Master. To this end Sir Henry has other matters to impart to you, matters which My Lords Morley and Windsor are already privy to and have given their assent.'

The grumbling subsided and attention again focussed upon Mainwaring, who made a motion to Whiting. The master spread a rolled chart across the cabin table and Mainwaring spoke again.

'My Lords and gentlemen,' he began, 'in consideration of the lateness of the season, the prevalence of the likely winds as being from the south-west, and in anticipation of the Equinoctial gales that will shortly belabour us, I propose that our progress is made not to Corunna, as has been planned, but to here,' and at this point Mainwaring stabbed the chart somewhat to the westwards of the sharp, right-angled turn of the coastline from east-west to north-south, just where the Pyrenees fell into the Atlantic between France and Spain. 'Here,' he repeated, 'at Santander.'

There was a moment's silence and then St Leger said, 'But my Lord, while I can see that the winds will better serve such a course, is not the entrance to Santander both narrow and fortified?'

'Aye, and we will be either enfiladed coming in or going out...' said Trevor.

'Or mewed-in by a boom or other devilish device of the Spanish...' A chorus of agreement met this final closing of the trap behind them.

Rutland laughed and commanded them all to

silence. 'I think not. Our embassy may not have met with the success hoped for but we are not at war with His Most Catholic Majesty and there is no possible reason to consider the Spanish are hostile towards us...'

'Not until they have the flower of our Navy Royal within their rocky fastnesses,' St Leger said, pressing his point. 'As far as I am aware the diplomacy of our Royal Master has been compromised by the reckless passions of what Your Lordship is pleased to call our embassy, but which others I have heard refer to in less respectful terms. And besides this, are there not rumours of great Armadas being again at sea? I have heard tell of such as are armed and intended against us. My Lord, I do not mean to question your orders, or the good and seaman-like arguments of Sir Henry, but I like it not. God knows the Dons have little cause to love us. Did not the Prince's suit fail on his refusal to turn Catholic? Might not such a refusal ignite passions inimical to the English crown? The Spanish have no love of us in our heresy...'

'Aye,' added the bluff Captain Love, 'and from what I have heard of the delicacy of Spanish sensibilities, the young men have caused some offence in the manner of their conduct in the Escorial...'

'That is not a matter for us,' snapped Rutland, clearly bored and irritated by the prevaricating tone of his officers. 'You have your orders, gentlemen. Kindly see that they are obeyed. Now Sir Henry will issue the order of sailing and such signals as seem requisite at this time. The minute the wind is favourable, you can expect the signal to weigh.'

Fifteen minutes later the dismissed flag officers and captains, escorted by the *Prince Royal*'s lieutenants, spilled out on to the quarterdeck where, in the calm of the anchorage, the ladies were taking the air. It was a calm and balmy afternoon, with the sun westering over the Cornish shore and the heights of the hoe black with townsfolk out to see the fleet assembled in the Sound. In order of seniority the senior officers descended into their boats, accompanied by a twittering of the bosun's pipe. As he stood watching them go, Faulkner was suddenly aware of the sweet scent of perfume and turned to find Katherine Villiers at his side.

He removed his hat and bowed. 'My Lady, 'tis a pleasure to see you. I hope the voyage thus far has not...' He paused, not quite knowing what to say, '...er, o'er taxed you.'

'O'er taxed me, sir?' she replied, her voice light with amusement. 'If you are concerned about my suffering from seasickness, I am happy to say that I appear immune, though that is not true of others of my sex; if, on the other hand, you ask whether I have been bored, then I have to confess that I have been bored to excess.'

'I am sorry to hear it,' he said, wanting to add that the handling of the great ship was of such consuming fascination that, while he understood it would lie outside a woman's interest, he would have liked to have explained it all to her. As he stood tongue-tied and irritated that he could find no way of expressing this, she added, 'I suppose you find it absorbing, all these ropes and sails and the men to command, but my want of instruction renders it incomprehensible, while my sex confines me to attempt genteel point-work in light one can scarcely see to dress in, let alone thread a needle.'

Almost without realizing what he was saying he looked directly at her and said, 'My Lady, if you can find a way to slip the leash of confinement I would be only too happy to explain the workings of the ship.'

'And you would not find it too tedious?' she asked, and he was not certain if she was mocking him. But he saw that her eyes were so curious a blue that they might almost be described as violet, and that her red lips parted to reveal teeth as white as the bleached bones of the fish he used to scavenge along the Bristol waterfront. Despite himself, despite the constraints and inhibitions he felt in her presence, despite the melting in his bowels as he looked at her, his open face split into a wide grin. 'Tedious, ma'am, oh yes, I should find it tedious in the extreme, but anything less and I should be wanting in my duty.'

She caught the joke. 'Then I shall be compelled to so impose upon you, Lieutenant Faulkner, for I understand from my cousin that it is important that officers in the King's service are frequently brought to their duty and so kept there that they are like chained dogs.'

'That, Mistress Villiers,' he said, still grinning and footing an exaggerated bow, 'is advice that I do not deserve. Please send me word when I may be of service, though if the King's duties supervene I must, alas, give them precedence.'

'Tush, sir,' she said turning on her heel with a lightness that almost took his breath away, 'I should expect nothing less: we are all subject to the King.'

He went to bed that night with the exchange buzzing in his head, simultaneously exhilarated and terrified by what they had said; thrilled by her flirtatious interest, yet scared that that was all it was; at once reminded by her allusion to her cousin that in her relationship with the Duke of Buckingham she stood high in court society, and reminded that they were all bound by their obligations to the King. Suddenly the jest between himself and Brenton as to the latter's risk of disembowelling caught at his imagination with an image of pure horror. And as if that were not enough there were other thoughts that rushed into his overheated head – a broken heart or the pox? He was, as Brenton had said, playing with fire.

Three

The Spanish Voyage

Autumn 1623

The wind came fair on 2nd September and, weighing their anchor and setting sail, the *Prince Royal* headed south, doubling the Rame Head and thereafter laying a course for the Bay of Biscay. For the best part of the passage the wind was fresh but not too strong, and the squadron laboured south under courses and top-sails, making good a progress that drove them steadily towards the north coast of Spain. Occasional rain marred the days, and clouds denied them any truly clement weather, while the sea ran uncomfortably enough to confine the ladies for the most part to their beds. A few ventured on deck but most, if not overcome themselves by seasickness, found the stench of the vomit of others too much, persuading them that they too were ill, as indeed, they soon were.

After his moments of elation, Faulkner considered that he would be lucky if Katherine Villiers escaped her prison, but he was proved wrong for she sent word by her maid, a girl named Sarah, that she 'would be attentive to his instruction as to the conduct of the ship and the time of a meeting'. He replied that that afternoon he was relieved of duty and would be honoured to wait upon her, and so, in due course, he stood with her in full view of the watch on deck and showed her the ropes.

'The masts are supported by stays, both fore and aft and athwartships, the latter are crossed by ratlines up which the seamen ascend to tend the sails when it is necessary. These lower sails we call the courses, the sails above are named the topsails and above them come the topgallants, which are only set in the best of weather and the most favourable of winds. The sails are stretched along yards as you see. The yards are swung by braces and the lower corners of the courses – their clews – by sheets and tacks.'

'Why two ropes to control the corners, the...'

'Clews. Well, the sheets lead aft to pull the clew in that direction, the latter forward so that the sail may always be controlled and on one side may be led aft, while on the other forward when we are steering on a wind...'

'Does not that twist the sail?' she asked quickly. He watched her as she took in the information, admiring her quick-wittedness as much as her ability to maintain her footing on the gently sloping but lively deck.

'Indeed, which is precisely what we want, and by so doing thereby harness the energy in the wind to drive the ship.'

She stared about her for a moment, seemingly

tracing the thin ropes against the grey sky, before observing, 'So that is what we are presently doing.'

'Aye, ma'am. You see we are heading south,' he explained, waving his hand forward, 'with the wind near west.' He swung his arm until it pointed a little forward of the starboard beam. 'That is to say that we are near to being close-hauled on the wind and so our larboard, and therefore leeward, sheets are hauled aft and the larboard tacks are slack, whereas to starboard, it being the weather side, the tacks are hauled forward and the sheets are slack.'

The ship pitched and then struck a sea with a shudder. Her hand went out and he felt the pressure of her on his arm as she braced herself against him, and then, as the ship settled again and the shower of spray spattered on to the deck, she withdrew her hand. She took the slight contretemps in her stride and made no foolish allusion to it.

'I see,' she said nodding slowly as she took in the information, and then, craning round and pointing at the two after masts, remarked: 'These sails are a different shape, triangular...'

'Indeed, Mistress Villiers, and you will be surprised to learn that we stole the idea from the Arabs. We call them lateen courses and their yards lie diagonally...'

'Why did we steal them from the Arabs?'

'Because they are a good idea, allowing us to lie in comfort in heavy weather, keeping our head up into the sea, and yet they add to the power of the ship and improve her ability to turn swiftly in action without burying her, as a large square sail would if carried this far aft.'

'And we sail all night. Tell me, why do we not anchor?'

He laughed. 'Our cables are too short and the sea so far from shore too boisterous. We are in deep, deep water here, my Lady, far deeper than our lead-line can reach...'

'A depth without telling,' she said, a tone of awe in her voice, adding, 'How thrilling.' She again touched him lightly on the arm and this time it was a gesture of shared intimacy.

'I am glad you find it so.'

'I do, but you are failing in your attentiveness. You have named but half a dozen ropes and yet I see many, many more. See how many are tied here at the foot of this mast! Why, there must be a score or so. Tell me their names...'

'Haul-yards, buntlines, clewlines, clew-gar-nets, bowlines – more than one to every sail and each one carefully denominated so that a sea-man knows every one, where it is and where to find it in the dark.'

'And do you know all this?'

'Aye, ma'am, I do. It is my business.'

'It is the business of an officer to know all this detail?'

'A good sea-officer must know all such mat-ters. How can he not if he is to handle the ship efficiently.'

'I'll wager there are some who do not,' she said slyly, and he caught her smile and laughingly shrugged.

'It is not my place to know the faults of other men, ma'am...'

'Oh, come Lieutenant Faulkner, you need not play the courtier with me. I'll warrant you do and your knowing will doubtless make their not knowing the worse for them.' And she pulled his arm playfully, smiling at him so that he saw her teeth and the wide curve of her mouth and knew what he wanted to do but dared not.

'There is much else to tell you. Matters concerning anchors and navigation, and stowing the hold and manning the guns...'

'Have you ever manned the guns, Lieutenant Faulkner?'

'I have seen action, Mistress Villiers, in a merchantman against the Barbary pirates.'

'Truly?' Her dark eyes widened.

'Truly – but it was nothing. We drove them off...'

'Otherwise you would have been enslaved and made to turn Mussulman. Is that not so?'

'It is what they intend.'

'Shall we see Barbary pirates?' she asked, suddenly serious.

He laughed. 'I doubt it, but if we do they will not approach so large a fleet as this.' He gestured round the horizon where the other men-of-war wallowed, their hulls dashing aside the seas as they rose and fell under the press of their canvas.

'I have heard talk among the ladies that there is a Spanish fleet at sea on the lookout for us. Is this true?'

'I have heard the selfsame thing, but if it is I cannot think that we shall suffer, being so powerful a squadron. Besides,' Faulkner indicated the farthest distance beyond the bowsprit where two purple nicks spoilt the hard line of the horizon, 'the two pinnaces lie ahead of us. If any should approach they will warn us.'

'And then what?'

'We will send the people to their stations for action at their guns, take post ourselves and the squadron will form line of battle.'

'And what will happen to me – to us – those of the fairer sex?'

'Why, ma'am, we shall require you to go below and seek shelter in the orlop out of harm's way.'

'Why cannot I stand here and share the danger with you?'

'Why, Mistress Villiers, you have no commission from the King obliging you to hold yourself in a post of danger and exposure.'

She frowned. 'No, but I should like to share the danger and not like to be cooped up in the ... where did you say?'

'The orlop, below the waterline where no cannon shot can reach you.'

'Great heavens, sir, I have been cooped up for days now. I should not wish to spend any further time sent into the bowels of the ship – danger or no danger!'

Faulkner chuckled. 'I would hope that matters do not come to that pass, Mistress Villiers, most sincerely.'

'I shall hold you responsible if they do, sir,' she said with mock severity.

'Mr Faulkner!' Faulkner turned. Some paces behind them the Earl of Rutland and Sir Henry Mainwaring had come on deck, unnoticed by either himself or the girl. Faulkner whipped his hat off and bowed awkwardly as the ship gave a leeward lurch. He felt Katherine's hand swiftly withdrawn.

'My Lord?' he said, straightening up, then, aware that he was compromising the young woman beside him, he bowed low and said in as loud a voice as he dared, 'Mistress Villiers, if I can be of further service to you...' He let the sentence hang as she nodded.

'I am much obliged to you, sir, you have been most kind and helpful.' And with a wide smile and a conspiratorial wink she withdrew, curtseying to Rutland as she passed and leaving Faulkner to approach the admiral.

'I am not aware, Mr Faulkner, that any privilege has been granted you to undertake the nautical education of Mistress Villiers. In its absence I am surprised at you.' Rutland's voice rose and for the first time Faulkner sensed the extent of his impropriety. 'It is not your place to address the young women of the court, let alone Mistress Villiers...' Faulkner bowed his head in submission, his face colouring at the public humiliation. Only now did he consider the others about the deck who had seen the animated conversation between the two of them and of

92

which they themselves had been sublimely oblivious. Rutland seemed to have run out of words. 'Have you nothing to say, sir?'

Faulkner avoided Mainwaring's eyes. 'Only that if I have caused any offence, my Lord, I am abject. I merely responded to Mistress Villiers's request to be informed about the working of the ship.'

'Did you indeed.'

'My Lord...' He inclined his head again. This was awful; it ripped the delight out of the day and was like to the morning he had been kicked bodily out of the warehouse in Bristol for spending the night in its comparative warmth.

'I'll have no tomcats on my ship, sir, d'you hear me? Eh? And you are a damned tomcat! By God, if you were a seaman I would have you flogged for your insolence!'

'But he is not a seaman, my Lord,' said Mainwaring, his voice cool and self-possessed. 'He is a gentleman and a King's sea-officer.'

Rutland was having none of it and turned archly upon his flag-captain. 'He may be a sea-officer, *Sir* Henry, but what maketh that manner of man a gentleman, eh?' The earl lowered his voice. 'Why, I am told that a man may be a sea-officer that hath been a pirate!'

Faulkner, who had kept his head low, could not resist looking up. Expecting fury from Mainwaring, he saw Sir Henry confront Rutland with a broad smile. 'You are right, my Lord, but we shine best where we have learned our manners.' Then, as Rutland seemed uncertain as to

93

whether to explode again, Mainwaring looked at Faulkner and with an abrupt movement of his head said, 'Be off, Lieutenant, you are now a tomcat and no longer a rat. That is promotion and who knows where it will end.'

As Rutland asked Mainwaring what the devil he meant, Faulkner went below, entering his cabin and flinging himself into his wooden bunk. A few moments later Brenton came in, having seen what had happened, but eager to know precisely what had been said.

'Damn it, Kit, the ship fair buzzes! You steal a march on every other lusty lad aboard and then get blown out of the water. I told you, you are playing a dangerous game, but hell's teeth, what on earth did old Mainwaring say that so discommoded Rutland?'

'What?' Faulkner frowned. Brenton repeated the question while he, completely unaware that the admiral had been discommoded, was only grateful that Mainwaring had softened the admiral's blow – though that was little enough comfort.

'Come on, tell Harry before Harry explodes with curiosity!'

Faulkner frowned. The remark about the rat becoming a tomcat would mean nothing to Brenton, nor was he eager to share it with a man who knew nothing of his humiliatingly humble origins. He could only repeat what he could recall of Mainwaring's remark about shining 'where best we learned our manners'.

'He said *what*?' Brenton gawped with aston-

94

ishment. Still uncomprehending, Faulkner repeated himself. 'Why, the old devil,' said Brenton, smacking his thigh in appreciation. 'Sir Henry has a carelessness for his skin that I greatly admire!'

'What the hell are you talking about, Harry? For the love of Christ I have been held up to ridicule and feel as though I am for the block, while you sit there burbling about Sir Henry's skin! He got me off the hook, that is all...'

'The devil, it is, Kit,' Brenton said rubbing his hands with a kind of manic glee. 'The devil it is...' He paused, realizing that Faulkner really had no idea what had transpired. 'He did more than get you off the hook, he poked the hook in Rutland's eye!' But all Faulkner could do was stare at him. 'A pun, Kit! A bloody pun. Not the greatest or wittiest pun ever made, I'll allow, but one which, improvised in pressing circumstances, will have given His Lordship more to think of than your little indiscretion with Mistress Villiers.'

'What pun?' Faulkner asked, exasperated.

'Why, manners, Kit, manners. Manners is Rutland's family name. You are a tomcat, Mainwaring is a pirate and by implication of his pun, Sir Henry attributed an ungentlemanly lack of manners on Francis Manners, Sixth Earl of Rutland and our beloved admiral!'

For a long moment this intelligence meant nothing to Faulkner. He was still shocked and humiliated by what had so publicly taken place on deck. Then it began to dawn upon him that

95

something vaguely amusing had been said, a mere play upon words but sufficiently witty to make an impression, to defuse – or perhaps to ignite? – a powder train. He shook his head.

'Such things are beyond me, Harry. By God I wish I were back aboard the *Swallow*. I'd rather be reefing her mainsail in a squall than stand another hour upon the deck of this, this...'

Brenton was laughing at him and holding out a glass of wine. 'Rise above the petty anxieties of the day, Kit. Had you not picked up the gauntlet laid for you by pretty Mistress Villiers you would have shown a want of spirit which, lacking in a King's officer, would have condemned you. Why, Kit, if the whole Spanish Armada heaves in sight tomorrow, I'll lay my life that every man jack in this ship will follow you rather than that thin-blooded Rutland. Down that glass and have another, and let's drink to dark eyes and a beguiling smile! Here's to Mistress Villiers!'

A week later they came in sight of the Spanish coast some leagues to the westward of where they intended. The wind had begun to rise and it was under reduced sail that they coasted east, to enter the narrows at Santander on the 11th where the squadron came again to anchor.

Faulkner heard nothing more of the incident, but then he did not speak to Mainwaring, apart from making one report about the stowing of the mainsail. Happily he did not set eyes on Rutland until they were anchored. But then he saw

96

nothing of Katherine either, and sensed that an atmosphere surrounded him. Ned Slessor was curt, though not unfriendly, Whiting ignored him and only Harry Brenton winked, cajoled and consoled him.

'You are in love, Kit. Drown your sorrows, catch a Spanish whore in Santander and save the trouble of poxing yourself in a more complicated manner...' and at the use of that word, Brenton laughed again at his own wit. Faulkner himself rode out the storm; he had no alternative. The dalliance with Katherine was just that, and he was foolish to think any more of it. Besides, he was not certain that the ways of the court held any appeal for him. Mainwaring might have been a pirate, but he had been to Oxford University, had held the King's Commission as Lieutenant Governor of Dover and understood these things. He, on the other hand, was nothing more than a King's sea-officer by Mainwaring's grace and perhaps would not have to be that for very much longer.

As for now, well the *Prince Royal* had hardly anchored before great events were under way and the affair of Lieutenant Faulkner and the Earl of Rutland was forgotten. As Harry Brenton remarked a day or so later, it would have mattered if Faulkner had been nicknamed 'Tom Cat', but he had not. Mainwaring's barb in the other direction seemed to have gone home and was better remembered.

Within an hour of the ship coming to her anchor, Sir John Finnet and Sir Thomas Somerset were landed by boat and went in quest of Prince Charles and the Duke of Buckingham who, it was said, were coming over the mountains hotfoot, having greatly embarrassed both themselves and the entire Spanish court. Their sundry improprieties had, it was said, included the invasion of the Infanta Maria's privacy by climbing a wall into a garden wherein walked the Princess and her ladies, thereby putting in danger the life of the ancient marquess charged with her protection.

The following days were, for Faulkner, a period of miserable and relentless duty. The misery arose out of his humiliation by Rutland in front of Katherine Villiers, and was compounded by solitary reflections – for he and Brenton had little liberty to discuss anything – that he was a damned fool, a fool for thinking anything could come of his encounter with the young woman, and a fool for behaving as he had. To this was added the constant irritant that once Prince Charles and Buckingham had been embarked, the ship took on a different air. Suddenly the courtiers, prostrated for the greater part on the outward voyage by seasickness, suddenly seemed to take over the *Prince Royal*. It was as though the presence of the Prince not only galvanized them, which was understandable, but enabled them to assume rights that extended to the very running of the ship. Now, everything was subservient to their demands and these came day and night – an unending stream of stupid requests, of demands for wine and food, the services of an officer to carry some message or to pay some act of respect, ceremonial or otherwise, to either Prince Charles or Buckingham. Indeed, Faulkner formed the indelible impression that the latter was the greater man for he made the most noise, took the lead in everything and seemed to arrange matters entirely to his own convenience.

This too added to Faulkner's unhappiness, or it further marked the wide social distinction between Katherine Villiers and himself, adding to his impression that she had been only toying with him, engaged in a frivolous flirtation.

The days that followed were full of comings and goings. An exciting few hours were spent by the *Prince Royal*'s bargemen who, in rowing Prince Charles ashore in a strong wind and tide one night, were nearly swept out to sea. Had not Sir Sackville Trevor of the *Defiance* not appreciated what was happening and thrown out ropes attached to lantern-lit buoys, the barge would have been lost.

Held by the weather from the beginning of the homeward passage, the Prince entertained the Spanish envoys and Cardinal Zapata, in some hope of mollifying the Spanish in their wounded pride. Finally, on Thursday 18th September, the wind came fair from the south and with much ceremony, including the blaring of fanfares and thunder of drums and guns, the fleet weighed and headed out of the ria of Santander for the open sea. The wind held steadily from the south for several hours before it veered, first to the south-west and then further into the north-west. So distracted was Faulkner by the constant demands of his duty, and so convinced did he become that he meant nothing to Katherine, that he buried himself in it all, worked constantly and made himself – at least to the satisfaction of his self-conceit – indispensable to the efficient working of the ship. Thus it was that one morning, about five days after they had departed from Santander, that he carried the news down to Mainwaring that the deterioration in the weather had compelled him to reef the topsails and the *Prince Royal* was going full-and-bye on the larboard tack at five knots in a stiff north-westerly breeze. It was the end of the morning watch and he had handed the deck over to the third lieutenant and Brenton for the forenoon. He nodded at the sentry leaning on his spontoon outside Mainwaring's cabin and knocked, entering at Sir Henry's behest. A sudden patch of brilliant sunlight reflected off the sea threw dancing lights on the white-painted deck-head and showed Sir Henry's silhouette against the roiling wake that rose up, and then subsided under the transom, accompanied by the creaking of the rudder stock. Another figure sat at table with the captain and Faulkner assumed it to be Rutland, breaking his fast with Mainwaring since the two were obliged to mess together, the admiral's cabin having been taken over as a royal suite. Faulkner had no wish to appear before Rutland as anything other than an efficient officer and he delivered his message with a studied if laconic authority, which Mainwaring acknowledged with his usual courtesy. Faulkner was about to turn and leave the two men to their breakfast when Mainwaring said, 'Stay, sir. Will you break your fast with us, Mr Faulkner?'

Faulkner flushed. He did not wish to make small talk with Rutland, though he knew that Mainwaring's invitation was an act of kindness, an opportunity for him to make a good impression on the admiral after their unfortunate encounter some weeks earlier.

'Sit, Faulkner! I command it.'

Surprised at the unfamiliar voice, Faulkner squinted against the sunlight and found himself staring at the Duke of Buckingham. He bowed deeply as Mainwaring said, with a touch of irony, 'His Grace commands as Lord High Admiral, Faulkner.'

'Indeed I do,' said Buckingham, rising and moving towards Faulkner, one hand braced upon the corner of the table until he reached a chair and drew it out. 'Come, Mr Faulkner, I pray you sit.'

The act was of such condescension that it seemed obscene to allow the chair to remain un-occupied a moment more than was absolutely needful to allow Buckingham to return to his own seat. A moment later a servant was at Faulkner's elbow with a plate of smoked fish and a pot of hot coffee. 'I am obliged, Your Grace, Sir Henry.'

'You will be hungry after your watch,

Faulkner,' remarked Buckingham with a solicitude that seemed unfeigned, and Faulkner looked up at a face that reminded him of another: the same eyes and almost the same lips – odd on a man, but the curling moustache and the short, pointed beard declared the effeminately beautiful face to be male.

'Aye, Your Grace, and it is a raw morning, though a bright one and the wind—'

'Remains foul. Yes, I heard you report it so to Sir Henry.'

'Just so, Your Grace.' Faulkner felt crushed.

'Come, eat up your fish else it will spoil.'

Faulkner picked up knife and fork and suppressed the shaking of his hands. Then, just as he had filled his mouth, Buckingham spoke again. 'Sir Henry speaks well of you; in fact he tells me you are a coming man and the King has need of good men at sea.'

Faulkner swallowed and almost coughed. He wondered where on earth Rutland was hiding. 'That is kind of Sir Henry,' he managed, his face red and reddening further as he saw Buckingham smile at his discomfiture.

'I am torturing the poor fellow, Sir Henry,' Buckingham said laughingly.

'I fear you are, Your Grace. I fear too that the Earl of Rutland has worn away Mr Faulkner's natural armour. He will be himself when he has mastered the herring.'

Filled with confusion as both older men laughed at him, Faulkner could only mumble his apologies.

'Oh, fie, sir,' said Buckingham, his tone friendly, 'you must not mind us. What is the Lord High Admiral to do if not to tweak the noses of junior officers. Besides, I gather you gave the Earl a lesson in manners...'

'Good Lord! Not I, Your Grace,' Faulkner said hurriedly. 'I should not have dared such an impropriety!'

'He left that to me, Your Grace,' Mainwaring remarked casually.

Buckingham chuckled. 'Well, well, subordination is a necessary thing aboard a man-of-war, as no doubt you would agree, Faulkner.'

'Indeed, sir, I would.' He paused a moment, shot a glance at Mainwaring who was watching him, it seemed, with an expression denoting encouragement. 'I trust I have given no offence or committed any impropriety as my Lord of Rutland imputed, Your Grace.'

Buckingham threw back his head and laughed. The sunlight shimmered off his gorgeous doublet of sky-blue slashed with silver silk, and caught his long locks as he shook his head like an elegant hound. 'I trust not too, Faulkner, though I am scarce the one to judge. It seems that I upset half the *duennas* in Madrid and was near banned the entire Escorial, so minor infractions of etiquette...' He let the sentence trail off. 'No, Mr Faulkner,' Buckingham resumed after a moment's consideration, 'I value a man who sticks to his last. If you are half the sea-officer of which Sir Henry sings, then stand firm, sir, and do your duty.'

Faulkner sensed dismissal and pushed his chair back. 'Your Grace; Sir Henry ... with Your Grace's permission I have other duties to attend to.'

'Of course.' Buckingham flicked his left hand dismissively and Faulkner rose. Outside the cabin he paused a moment. Whatever impression he had made on Buckingham seemed less important than the impression Buckingham had made on him – was this the corrupt Duke of Muckingham of whom Brenton was so disparaging? Certainly his manner contained a high-bred hauteur, but there was withal a certain warmth, even an inspiration. Pondering on the complexities of human nature – Brenton's as much as Buckingham's – he went in search of his bunk.

Afterwards, however, the encounter troubled Faulkner. The incident with Rutland had so thoroughly unsettled him that he could not fling it off. He was aware that Mainwaring had gone to some lengths to divert Rutland's ire, even to the extent of damaging his own relationship with the admiral. Of course, it was common knowledge that Rutland was no seaman, but he possessed enormous influence and it was inconceivable that Mainwaring would not have suffered some damage – now, or later – from his pun on Rutland's name. That being so, it might have been of some comfort that he had received so encouraging a meeting with Buckingham who, whatever his deficiencies in other directions, remained the Lord High Admiral and therefore Rutland's senior in the naval hierarchy. On the other hand, it was equally probable that Rutland, with his older lineage, would consider Buckingham a parvenu and any man raised by him, such as it was clear Mainwaring intended for his protégé, risked acquiring a similar name, to which might be added the obloquy of Rutland and his faction at court. These considerations discommoded Faulkner, increasing his misery and blighting his spirit on the homeward passage which otherwise – despite the onset of the season of strong winds – was marked by a good passage.

Though the wind necessitated the fleet tacking, the weather failed to discourage the royal party from frequently appearing on deck. The Prince and Buckingham promenaded ostentatiously, a little gaggle of courtiers in close and sycophantic attendance, Katherine Villiers among them. On these occasions it became obligatory for all the commissioned officers, irrespective of their routine duties, to appear on deck and gather on the opposite side of the half deck where they were expected to maintain a respectful interest, though what in, Faulkner could not quite comprehend. Despite his discomfiture he was nevertheless anxious that Brenon's irreverent asides were not heard by anyone other than himself. Unfortunately, Slessor caught Brenton's aside on one such afternoon, and shot Brenton and Faulkner – into whose left ear the former was so obviously 'whispering' – a glare of such fury that would have stopped the heart of a more timorous man. Faulkner, oversensitive, flushed scarlet just as Buckingham, looking up from his discourse with the shorter Prince Charles, saw the knot of be-sashed officers and drew the Prince's attention to them.

The two men, braced against the lurch of the ship as she shouldered aside a sea heavier than its predecessors, crossed the deck. The officers uncovered and footed their bows with a sweep of their feathered headgear. Was Brenton sniggering as they executed their dutiful obeisance? Faulkner certainly thought so as they straightened up and he found himself looking directly into the face of the Prince of Wales. He hurriedly lowered his gaze but was left with an indelible impression of sensitive weakness, of a thin, pallid countenance, of deep-set, dark eyes of indeterminate colour set either side of a large nose. A thin, adolescent and drooping moustache bracketed a feminine mouth below which the vertical wisps of a boyish beard bisected a pointed chin. The Prince's dark-blue doublet was in marked contrast with the Duke's silver and sky-blue, though the lace collar at his throat was of exquisite workmanship, even to Faulkner's ignorant eye.

'Allow me to introduce these *gallants*, Highness,' purred Buckingham as he guided his charge in a manner that bespoke deferential, but absolute, control. 'Mr Slessor, the First Lieutenant to Sir Henry...' Slessor bowed again.

'M–M–Mr S–S–Slessor and I have met

be–f–f–f–fore,' stuttered the Prince, smiling wanly and holding out a gloved hand which Slessor took briefly. When it came to Faulkner's turn, Buckingham said, 'Christopher Faulkner, Highness, of whom Sir Henry speaks highly, having employed him in trade.'

Faulkner wished the deck could have opened up and consumed him. Such particularity would stand him in ill stead among his fellow officers, especially Slessor.

'F–F–Faulkner,' stammered Prince Charles, 'trade, eh? Have you been much in action?'

Faulkner attempted to speak but found he had lost his voice for a moment. Then he managed, 'Only against the Barbary pirates, Your Highness.'

'*Only?*' The royal tone was ironic. 'W–W–Why, sir, they tell me a man must fight for his life against the Moors...'

'At the risk of his foreskin at the least, Highness,' Buckingham put in, raising a polite titter among the officers.

'I t–trust yours is intact, Faulkner?'

The harmless ridicule stirred something in Faulkner, paring him to some previous sharpness he appeared to have abandoned since his attempts to become a gentleman. And yet, in losing his paralysing diffidence it suddenly seemed to the others, particularly Slessor, that he was indeed a man to watch. 'I thank Your Highness for your solicitude and, yes, I am intact, sir.'

'We are glad to hear of it,' said Buckingham

intrusively ending the brief preoccupation of his charge with Faulkner, and moving on to Brenton in whose mouth butter could not have been melted even on the hottest summer's day.

On the following Friday, at two bells in the afternoon watch, they came in sight of the Scilly Isles and the outlying reefs stretching south-westwards towards the Bishop Rock. Faulkner had the deck and Whiting was fussing about the bearing of the rocks, which lay, hard-edged and spiky, against the sharp line of the horizon. 'The tide, Mr Faulkner, has a strong set hereabouts on to the reef.'

'Very well, Mr Whiting, I shall call the watch to tack the ship,' Faulkner responded and the pipes twittered, calling the hands on deck to their stations as Whiting carefully took a compass bearing of the rocks, which were coming appreciably nearer as the strong flood-tide swept them closer. Faulkner swept his gaze around the horizon, noting the respective positions of the squadron. Calling the duty yeoman to hoist the signal to follow the admiral's motions, and the duty gunner to prepare a chase-gun in order to draw the attention of the other men-of-war to the impending manoeuvre of the flagship lying in the van, Faulkner sent word below to warn the royal party of the imminent concussion and alteration of course.

The news brought Prince Charles on deck alone. He approached Faulkner directly and, for a moment, lost his hesitant stammer. 'You are about to discharge your falconet, sir?' he queried, standing behind Faulkner, who was pre-occupied by the imminent manoeuvre.

'Aye, sir,' Faulkner replied and then, turning, saw to whom he was speaking. He stepped back, uncovered and bowed. 'Your Highness,' he murmured.

'P–pray tell me the name of those rocks,' said the Prince, pointing.

'They are the outer Scillies, your Highness, and you can just see the island of St Agnes,' he pointed, 'in the distance beyond.' From forward came the crack of the gun and the yeoman and his mates ran aloft two brightly coloured flags.

'D–d–d–do lend me your glass, if you please, Mr...'

'Faulkner, Your Highness,' he responded helpfully, forgetful of the Prince's impediment and thinking his name had slipped the Prince's memory.

'Yes, yes, I know, Mr Faulkner. Your glass, pray.' The gloved hand extended with a peremptoriness that signalled the Prince's irritation and Faulkner coloured at the double embarrassment.

'I regret, Your Highness, I do not possess my own glass. Mr Whiting, the Master, has one though. With your permission...?' The Prince made a second gesture and Faulkner hurriedly crossed the deck to where an anxious Whiting stood awaiting Faulkner's order to put the helm down. Faulkner held his hand out. 'May I borrow your glass a moment? His Highness wishes to survey the Scillies.'

'His Highness will be wiping his nose on the Scillies if we do not tack instanter, Mr Faulkner,' hissed Whiting, fishing his small telescope from his pocket and handing it to him.

'Do give the order immediately then,' snapped Faulkner, as discomfited as Whiting. He spun on his heel and returned to where the Prince stood gazing at the closing prospect of the jagged reef, surrounded by the breaking swells of the Atlantic. Faulkner held out the glass. 'With Mr Whiting's compliments, Your Highness.'

The Prince took the telescope and, bracing himself against a stay, focussed it upon the reef. 'Pray thank him for me,' he said abstractedly as Whiting began shouting orders to the quarter-masters at the whip-staff. The *Prince Royal* dipped her bow and rose, her beakhead slewing to starboard as the helm was put over. Faulkner turned again to the Prince as he slowly brought the glass round with the alteration of the ship's heading. Meanwhile the men at the braces swung the main yards and, as the *Prince Royal* paid off on the opposite tack, those on the fore-mast came round with a rattle of parrel beads and the clicking of the blocks. After a few moments, Prince Charles lowered the telescope and handed it to Faulkner.

'A sublime s–s–sight, Mr Faulkner. Most sublime.' He paused a moment and then added, 'Is it not a great inconvenience not having a glass? I m–m–mean an officer without a glass is somewhat like a falconer without his t–tiercel, is he not?'

'Indeed he is, Your Highness,' said Faulkner, thinking quickly and unwilling to admit that he could not afford one, that Mainwaring had neither advised him to acquire one nor given him the means to do so. 'I had the misfortune to lose mine overboard on the outward passage,' he lied smoothly.

'An expensive item to replace, no doubt,' the Prince remarked conversationally.

'Tolerably so, sir,' Faulkner said, with only the vaguest notion of what a telescope cost. He had never thought to acquire one previously, having relied upon Strange providing a battered French glass for general use aboard the *Swallow*. Thankfully the Prince's attention was distracted as one of his gentlemen came on deck, made a low bow and remarked that His Grace the Duke wondered if His Highness would care to take a hand at a game of chance. After a final bow as the small, almost delicate figure made his way below, Faulkner had a chance to look about him to find the squadron had conformed and followed the *Prince Royal*'s change of direction. The entire incident had taken no more than a quarter of an hour, but it was to have a profound effect upon Faulkner's subsequent life.

Shortly afterwards, however, the squadron came in sight of a number of ships which, as they drew near, were seen to be four Dunkirkers being chased by seven Dutch men-of-war. They came close to the *Rainbow* and were directed to heave to under the lee of the *Prince Royal*, which herself hove to for the purpose of receiving their commanders. In a vain attempt to end hostilities in the English Channel, Prince Charles bade them to desist from their actions, which the Dutch admiral refused, so that the Prince was obliged to detain him until the Dunkirkers had got away. The wind now veered again into the north-east and the fleet remained hove-to off the Scillies, the Prince conceiving the notion of landing on the principal island of St Mary's, since several local pilots, perceiving the royal standard flying from the largest man-of-war, scented pecuniary gain and had come aboard from their boats. A council was held aboard the *Prince Royal* and it was decided that the Prince and Buckingham would land at St Mary's. The longboat was launched, the royal party, Captain Mainwaring and Mr Whiting descended into it and it was streamed astern. Here one of the pinnaces came alongside it and, with every man shifting for himself without ceremony, they all embarked, along with a pilot, and made for the islands.

There was now a further gathering of the *Prince Royal*'s remaining officers, and Slessor, having consulted with two pilots, decided to follow the pinnace before it grew dark. Accordingly, the other ships in the squadron took their stations and followed the *Prince Royal* through the rock-strewn sound into St Mary's Road, all hands touched by the sight of Prince Charles and Buckingham standing on the shore cheering them and waving their hats. A curious interlude ensued, lasting four days, but on 5th October the

112

Prince Royal led her squadron into Spithead and within hours had once again been transformed. Emptied of the Prince and his entourage with a thundering of artillery and much fluttering of standards and other flags, she and the other ships pressed on to the eastwards and anchored in the Downs. Here they were ordered to the Medway for paying off. Void of the presence of the Earl of Rutland and with none but her ship's company to fill her, she made the short passage. No longer crowded, it seemed all hands heaved a collective sigh of relief; their duty was done and before them was the prospect of laying up for the winter, receiving their pay and discharge, followed by a return to their families. For those, like Faulkner, who had no family the future was less rosy, though it was difficult to resist the sense of accomplishment that accompanied the return of the ship's boats after Rutland's guests had left and they had only the passage round the North Foreland into the Thames Estuary ahead of them. The following few days were spent tearing down temporary bulkheads and preparing for the short voyage to the Medway and the ship's winter berth. This kept them busy and gave Mainwaring time to dine his officers in compliment to their diligence. The invitation was brought by the captain's manservant as both Faulkner and Brenton returned to the cabins intended for them under the half-deck, vacated now by the courtiers who had left them dirty and untidy.

'It is astonishing, is it not, Kit, that two ladies-in-waiting whom, one would have thought, possessed refined tastes, can so be-powder a few square feet of wretched cabin-space that it looks as though a market has been held herein?'

'Well, I suppose...'

'Oh, you suppose the luscious Mistress Villiers inhabited one such hutch and made it a bower of unrequited love, do you?'

'Oh, hold your tongue!' His reaction surprised Faulkner himself.

'Come, Kit, she was a flirt – a damned pretty flirt, I'll grant you, but a flirt nonetheless – and a cousin distant to his High-and-Mightyness the Duke of Muckingham.'

'Oh, come now,' Faulkner responded, 'Buckingham was not so bad. He seemed civil enough to me.'

'Of course he did. He beguiles the susceptible. Now see how you are defending him. The man bends for the King – what good will come from that unnatural conjunction?'

Faulkner fell silent. The truth was he remained ill-at-ease over the entire voyage. Of course, he had no hope of seeing Katherine Villiers again, had no expectations of further advancement, despite Buckingham's encouragement – which he took for mere condescending civility on the Duke's part – and remained concerned about the animus he must have aroused in Rutland. Indeed, as he smartened himself up for Mainwaring's dinner, his most profound hope was to escape and return to Bristol and the life of mate aboard the *Swallow* or another merchantman.

All hopes of advancement in the King's service had evaporated, not least because his encounters with Rutland, Buckingham, even the lovely Katherine, had disarmed his ambition and made him realize his inadequacies and the impediment of his low birth. That was something he could only disguise in the short-term – exposure was, in the end, inevitable. He should henceforth count himself lucky to have come thus far, and return to trade and the merchants' service.

The dinner was a convivial enough affair; Mainwaring's generosity lubricated the occasion, encouraging Brenton's irreverent sparking and drawing from Edward Slessor a short but pointed diatribe on the unwisdom of courtly influence on the sea-service. Mainwaring presided genially, his easy manner demonstrating his skill at handling others. Only Faulkner failed to enjoy the evening, his reticence seemingly overwhelming him so that he was tempted to get drunk at Mainwaring's expense and would have done so had not Slessor's words given him pause for thought, for it was clear that Slessor's inspiration arose in part from Rutland's attitude towards Faulkner. Slessor did not mention either the admiral or his junior colleague, nor was it clear what he thought of Faulkner, which had at least the effect of diverting Faulkner's thoughts from himself. Instead he toyed with the unlikely idea of continuing in the naval service before rejecting it, and in doing so realized that the officers were rising – somewhat unsteadily – from their seats. He followed suit, only to be restrained by Mainwaring who motioned for him to remain behind.

'A word with you, Kit,' he said with the quiet intimacy of former times, as he bid the rest of his guests goodnight. Fortunately, Slessor was amused at some remark of Brenton's while Whiting and the others had already withdrawn. When they had gone, Mainwaring indicated to Faulkner that he should be seated. 'A word with you, if you please,' he repeated, and Faulkner again felt the cold hand of apprehension seize his stomach.

'I am well pleased with you, Kit, notwith-standing your, er, contretemps with my Lord of Rutland.' Mainwaring smiled and Faulkner bowed his head.

'I apologise, Sir Henry, for forcing you to the extremity of intervening on my behalf. It was perhaps foolish of me to have engaged Mistress Villiers in such intimacy as I did...'

Mainwaring waved his explanation aside. 'Between ourselves, it did not do the admiral any harm to mind his manners for, in all justice, his appointment to flag rank was exactly what I am opposed to, as are those of us intent, by com-mand of the King and the Commissioners he set so recently above us, to man His Majesty's ships with only competent officers – though I daresay we shall have to accommodate and make allow-ances for the high-born from time to time.' Mainwaring paused a moment, gathering his thoughts. 'What I have to say to you bears directly upon you and your prospects. Whether or not Mistress Villiers plays any part in them,' he added with a wry smile, 'is a matter for yourself, but I must caution you to be wary where the Duke is concerned. He showed an interest in you, and this may have been on my recommendation as a tarpaulin officer of merit and prospect, but might be from some personal desire of His Grace towards your person in a less flattering manner, if you take my meaning.'

'If I take your meaning, Sir Henry, I must, perforce, be most careful.'

'Indeed. In such circumstances a healthy interest in Mistress Villiers may be out of place, but would not be inappropriate.'

'I thank you for your advice.' Faulkner made to rise from his seat, but Mainwaring put up his hand to restrain him.

'There is more, Kit. I am charged by His Grace whom, for all his sodomitical faults, does not lack energy or determination to do good by the King's service. You and Brenton have promise and I would see you continue in it. My Lord Duke and the Commissioners of the Naval Board had the task of reforming the Service and have put their hands to the building of new ships, ten in five years, of which the last two have most recently been put in commission. Four of these – the *St George*, *St Andrew*, *Swiftsure* and *Bonaventure* – were most recently in our company. Much is therefore afoot and, hearing some word that you were minded to return to Strange's employ, I thought it better to offer you some more permanent part in what is under way.'

Faulkner was surprised and coloured at the reference to his intended return to the merchants' service. 'I had intended to speak with you, Sir Henry. I am in want of sufficient funds to continue in the King's Service without some assurance of payment. As you well know I am without means and I do not wish to be a burden upon yourself.'

'You need not labour the point and you are not a burden. Believe me, if you accept my offer, I shall make certain that you are not idle. To this end I am going to make over to you thirty-two shares in the vessels in which I have an interest, and by which means you will enter into partnership with myself and Gideon Strange. Spread among five or six ships, they will yield you a small competence to which additional benefits will undoubtedly accrue. Gideon will attend to the matter of business insofar as it is necessary, leaving you to more effectively assist me in the implementation of those reforms, surveys and reorganisations that the Naval Board deem requisite. I will do all in my power to advance you, though it will be necessary for you to venture from my protection and make a name for yourself when opportunity arises.' Mainwaring paused, looking at his young protégé for a moment, before asking, 'Come now, what do you say?'

Faulkner shook his head. 'Sir Henry,' he said, a catch in his voice, 'what can I say but express my gratitude for all the interest you have taken in me. You have been most kind. It is true that, not knowing what the future held for me in your own service, I was contemplating returning to Bristol. But now that you have so graciously—'

'My dear Kit,' Mainwaring broke in impatiently, 'will you cease this prattle. You are beginning to sound too like a damned courtier for my liking. My motives are entirely devoted to the King's Service, for which I think you are an ideal officer and I would simply have it so. Since you still wear the King's sash I could order you, but I prefer to carry you within the stream of my intention. So, yea or nay?'

Faulkner rose to his feet and held out his hand. 'A most assured yea, Sir Henry.'

'Excellent.' Mainwaring took his outstretched hand and wrung it warmly, then Faulkner turned and left the great cabin. For a moment Mainwaring stared after the younger man. 'Excellent,' he breathed, sitting down and reaching for his pipe. What an odd encounter that had been all those years ago, when he and Gideon had walked back to the *Swallow* and found Mr Rat scavenging for food. Suppose they had not had an eye for the apple-seller and bought of her wares? Would he otherwise have extended a charitable hand to the starveling? He doubted it, yet there were certain acts of expiation a man had to carry out if he sought redemption from charges of piracy. Besides, he had sworn to work in the interests of the King in exchange for his pardon. He had made enemies, though. Rutland would probably not forgive him his impudence! And as for Lord Zouch at Dover, well there was no love lost between them. In the end he could only launch Mr Rat upon the wide waters of the world. For his personal voyage, the young man would have to find his own fair winds. As for Mistress Villiers...

'Well, well,' Mainwaring chuckled, 'Mr Rat will not cut that pretty flirt out from under the guns of her great protector. Not in a hundred lifetimes!'

Four

Bristol, 1623–1627

In the four years that followed the Spanish voyage, Faulkner busied himself at Mainwaring's side. Although he continued to act as Mainwaring's secretary, thereby improving his literary style and expanding his view of the world in which Mainwaring moved, he also undertook independent commissions which were of increasing significance and were concluded as his own, rather than his principal's work. Most involved surveying and taking inventories in the dockyards, and on three occasions he acted as pilot, moving men-of-war from the Thames and Medway to the westwards, but they also included several commercial transactions. It was true that he assisted, in a collaborative sense, in drawing up the tables of dimensions for the spars and sails appropriate to men-of-war, which with other data was included in the draft of Mainwaring's *Nomenclator Navalis*, the Seaman's Dictionary, which made but slow progress. Faulkner also worked alongside and grew to know others, such as the Master Shipwright Phineas Pett whom he had first met – but had little to do with – aboard the *Prince Royal* on the passage to Santander. Among the most significant of the several charges given to Faulkner in this period was that of preparing a report on the reviving of Portsmouth as a Royal Dockyard, the place having fallen out of favour since Tudor times. The final document laid before the King's Council bore Mainwaring's imprint, but many of the arguments adduced therein had originated with Faulkner, not least a remark that by comparison with Chatham, a fleet based on Portsmouth was 'as for one to have his sword in his hand, whilst the other is rusty in its scabbard'. Though approved of by many influential persons, the decision was not then implemented, falling as it did at the time of the death of King James and the accession of his son as King Charles I. Other circumstances were said to have militated against the project; several rumours being circulated affirmed that the nomination of Mainwaring as the controller of the new dockyard stank of self-interest. Such blackening of Mainwaring's name coincided with other events of note, none of which enhanced Sir

Henry's reputation or advanced the career of Faulkner. To some extent Mainwaring himself had a hand in the latter, preventing Faulkner being appointed to any ship commissioned under the command of Sir Edward Cecil when war was declared on Spain in the aftermath of the disastrous 'Spanish Adventure' of the Prince of Wales and Buckingham.

'Cecil is entirely devoid of experience at sea,' Mainwaring explained when the two discussed the matter. 'The Victualling Commissioners are corrupt and you yourself have personally seen the stores intended for the squadron and reported on the rotten state of the ropes and cables. That they should send to the *St George*, a vessel built only in 'twenty-two, the sails from the *Triumph* that were put ashore in 'eighty-eight, is evidence enough!'

The expedition was a fiasco, as was a second sent under another soldier's flag. The Lord Willoughby's fleet was in open mutiny, his ships – even some of the new tonnage – leaked abominably, the lack of good food increased the incidence of disease, there was no money to pay the seamen, and many of the officers were obliged to petition the Lord High Admiral for relief, stating that neither the food supplied nor the money paid them was adequate to sustain life. Three hundred angry sailors marched on London and mobbed the house of the Treasurer of the Navy who escaped with his life only on promises of redress. Nevertheless, both Cecil and Willoughby were honoured, Cecil with a viscountcy and Willoughby with an earldom, honours which rang hollow and began a prejudice in Faulkner's own mind against such trumpery things. Nevertheless both grandees were appointed to a 'Council of the Sea' to enquire into the two disasters, joining Phineas Pett and Sir Henry Mainwaring, who sat among several grizzled veterans who had fought the Spanish Armada thirty-five years earlier.

In this work Faulkner continued at Mainwaring's side and was therefore regularly in the company of the Commissioners, coming again under the eye of Buckingham who headed the Commission, though he was not always present, particularly during the inspection of the ships lying in the Medway. Thus in the cold January of 1627 Faulkner was at Chatham when instructions were received from Buckingham which required the completion of the Commission's surveys, after which twenty men-of-war were to be made ready for service by the end of February. It fell to Faulkner to carry a written request for the shipwrights to attend the Commissioners in order to receive this news and in consequence was present when they did so.

The men, led by the masters of their craft, came into the Commissioners' lodgings in sober state, presenting a petition and refusing to lift a finger to prepare the ships. 'We have had not a penny of pay these last twelve months,' their spokesman explained, 'no allowance for food nor drink. We have pawned all we can and many among our company have been turned out-of-doors for failure to pay their rents; our wives and children starve and we must forage for whatever necessaries we may find, which is precious little. In such circumstances, My Lords and gentlemen we have neither energy nor means to carry your orders forward.'

After the delegation had departed the members of the Commission ruefully shook their heads and mumbled among themselves, expressions of impotent frustration clear on every face.

'Is this treasonable?' someone asked.

'Would that His Grace could see the indigence to which these men have been reduced,' one of the older Commissioners remarked sourly.

'Aye,' said another, 'it is damnably shameful,' to which the Earl of Denbigh responded, 'I find it difficult to comprehend the depths of corruption which, having regard to the sums expended upon the King's ships, has reduced us to this woeful state of affairs.'

'Is that not the purpose to which we have been appointed?' Pett asked with his customary pointed testiness. 'I have spoken often enough about the difficulties of building these ships and there are those that hold their private purses wide-open when they are fitting them out, such that nothing but rotten stores, putrid or rancid victuals are supplied. We shall have no better luck with those of the ships' companies presently mustered,' Pett asserted.

'I hope thy purse is not thus filled, Mr Pett,' Denbigh said.

'Indeed not!' snapped Pett.

'Or yours, Sir Henry?'

'Your Lordship is welcome to scrutinize my accounts,' said Mainwaring warmly, adding, 'as I hope is the case with all presently assembled.' Several pairs of eyes swivelled towards Denbigh, whereupon Mainwaring snapped, 'This is to no purpose. These men speak the truth and Mr Pett says likewise of the seamen. I have seen men compelled to lie on the bare decks of the *Vanguard*, gentlemen, devoid of food, clothing, fire, and this in a time of freezing weather...'

'It is beyond our power to redress any of these grievances,' said Denbigh loftily, 'but we must inform His Grace...'

'I think, My Lord,' offered Faulkner from the window, 'that we must hasten, for the men are assembling below. I imagine they intend to take their petitions to the Lord High Admiral themselves.'

'Very well, sit and write, Mr Faulkner. Gentlemen, your corrections to my dictation, if you please.'

By the end of the month Mainwaring and Faulkner were, with the other Commissioners, on their way back to London. 'It passes belief,' Mainwaring remarked to his young companion, 'that ships scarcely three and a half years old can be found so wanting that we cannot recommend them for service. That damned scoundrel Burrell had the building of them and three hundred per annum for the doing of it. Such a state of affairs would not be tolerated in the merchants' fleets.'

'Then surely something must be done,' remarked Faulkner.

Mainwaring turned to him and said with utter conviction, 'No. Nothing will be done. Nothing at all. Pett informs me – and he ought to know being himself a shipwright – besides Burrell and his complicit, villainous shipwrights, Edisbury the Paymaster, Norreys the Surveyor and Wells the Storekeeper, not to mention the whole confounded pack of the Victualling Commission, have their noses so firmly entrenched in the arses of others lying closer to the Court, that decent seamen will be left to starve.' Mainwaring paused, before going on. 'And talking of arses, I would wager a guinea or two on His Grace of Buckingham being a recipient of such filthy profit; his absence from Chatham was most marked and that disappoints me.' Mainwaring dropped his voice and muttered so that Faulkner only half heard him, 'And they have the effrontery to call me a quondam pirate!'

The Commission reported to King Charles at an assembly in the Star Chamber where its spokesman was Buckingham himself. Mainwaring returned to his lodging at the conclusion of this session, fulminating at the outcome and doubtful of Parliamentary sanction for the raising of sufficient funds to accomplish the task of reconstruction.

'Devil take it, Kit!' he had said, tearing off his wig and taking from Faulkner the glass of wine extended to him. 'I think I have asked you to hitch yourself to the wrong cause. There is no sense in this, no sense at all! We have a thousand private ships a-trading to earn our keep, and no confounded fleet capable of seeing the coast is clear! God damn, damn, damn! I'll warrant that by summer we'll have not only Barbary and Sallee rovers in the Channel, but the fleet of the French and Spanish off Dover ere long...' He drew deeply on his wine. 'Gideon tells me the French corsairs are active and Mitchell nearly lost the *Garvey* to a Malouin last month! Haven't you shares in her?'

'Aye, four...'

'You'd have lost a pretty penny then, had Mitchell not kept his head.' Mainwaring lapsed into silence for a moment and then looked up at Faulkner. 'I think we are in peril, Kit; real peril. I have heard that Richelieu has asked the Assembly for a fleet of fifty men-of-war for the Atlantic, many to be armed by some new-fangled gun, and is boasting therewith to hammer the very gates of London.'

'Is the King not alarmed, Sir Henry?'

'The King,' Mainwaring spluttered, 'the King is concerned, but leaves all to Buckingham and is content with the Noble Duke's considerable blandishments. God rot me, Kit, he does not lack nerve in that direction. Listening to his honeyed words one would think that all was well in the world, while it is obvious as pox on a whore's breath that this damned Cardinal will steal a march on us, and instead of our commanding the Narrow Seas, will see that France, with her ally Spain, does what it is our duty to do!'

'Then we shall—'

'We shall have to fight, Kit. We shall have to fight! And what with, in the name of God?' Mainwaring tossed off his glass and suddenly tore at the pocket in his coat tails. 'Heavens, Kit, I quite forgot amid all this damnable turmoil, I have a commission which, despite everything, it gives me great pleasure to execute – and by-the-by, I must ask you to regard my treasonable criticism of His Majesty as the meanderings of an overanxious man, as it seems you may be marked for rapid promotion,' he laughed, 'though what in, I hesitate to guess!' And with-drawing his hand he held a silk package out to Faulkner. 'I am commanded by His Grace the Duke to present this to you. He spoke of you personally, Kit – a mark of singular condescension – and, furthermore, His Majesty added his own compliments.'

Faulkner was astonished. 'What have I done to merit –' he broke off as he unrolled the silk to reveal a small, silver-mounted telescope round which was a scrap of paper bearing Buckingham's signature – '...to merit this favour?' He finished the query in a whisper.

'Perhaps,' said Mainwaring with a wide smile, rising to refill his glass, 'a certain lady may have spoken in your favour. But if not, you will take my advice and watch your step. The condescension of princes is apt to cut another way – usually when one least expects it.'

'But why, Sir Henry? I ... I recall mentioning that I had no glass when asked to lend it to His Majesty ... when His Majesty was Prince of Wales, I mean, but I had no expectation...'

'I recall it being mentioned at the time, that Prince Charles had remarked it was a deficiency in a naval officer. Would that he remedied all such faults in the naval service with such personal assiduity, as I am sure that it comes on His Majesty's prompting.'

Later, lying in bed musing over the extraordinary and unexpected gift for which he was at a loss to know how to respond, Faulkner wondered whether he might use the circumstance to get in touch with Katherine Villiers. The possibility tantalized him for some time until he recalled that remark of Mainwaring's, that the favour of princes can 'cut another way'. Certainly the gift had swept out of his head any sense of the outrage he had felt earlier over the treatment of the men in the fleet at Chatham, or the starving shipwrights, or the elevation of Lords Cecil and Willoughby. Faulkner knew what it was like to starve better than most, and far better than his social superiors. But to what end did Buckingham or King Charles wish to purchase so deep an obligation in him by such a disarming gift? For a moment he enjoyed a flight of fancy that this was a mark of approbation and he was looked kindly upon sufficient to encourage his pursuit of Mistress Villiers. But almost immediately he realized the stupidity of such a hare-brained conclusion, and then his pleasure began to wither and he sensed also a foretaste of gall, that the gift in some way compromised him, took from him some of the independence that he was slowly establishing for himself, and seducing him away from his obligations to Mainwaring.

This had nothing to do with Katherine; she had no interest in him and he felt a sudden bilious anger rise within, so that he was raised from his torpid, half-fantasizing drowsiness. For months now he had succeeded in expelling all thoughts of Katherine Villiers from his mind. And now he was entertaining ridiculous notions of wild promise again. What a loon he was; he had not spoken to her since that moment Rutland's interjection had separated them. Even then the admiral had done little, for they had scarcely made each other's acquaintance. God, he was a purblind fool!

Perhaps he should suffocate himself in the arms of a doxy just as Harry Brenton had advised. Better still he should resign his commission and return to sea in a merchantman. As a shareholder in several ships, he could make himself master of one of them and thereby abandon all these foolish ideas. It was an idea he mused and matured for several weeks and, in coming to a determination to carry it out, he awaited a favourable opportunity in which the move would seem sensible to his benefactor and not cast himself in the light of ingratitude. Such opportunity was not long in coming. In the wake of the Council of the Sea's findings and a subsequent inquiry in which the several dockyard officers were examined, without serious consequences, Parliament was asked for money to rebuild the fleet. Partial payment was made to those owed wages from a new and fixed pay-scale. Mainwaring was not therefore proved quite correct in his claim that nothing would be done. On the subject of new men-of-war, however, Parliament was intransigent and little was indeed forthcoming. Only ten small vessels were added to the Royal Navy, individually denominated by number and intended to support one of the only large men-of-war fit for service, the *Red Lion*, they were collectively known as the *Lion's Whelps*. However, significantly, they were to be built at the Duke of Buckingham's expense, his Lordship thereby securing his position against the various charges of corruption levelled against him and appearing as a great public benefactor. It was a typically shrewd and clever move for the *Whelps* were actually intended as privateers and as such would pay back their owner.

Faulkner was with Mainwaring when he received the news of their ordering. That same day they received other, private news which, for Faulkner, proved timely. The letter was addressed to Mainwaring but its content was of equal importance to Faulkner, for Gideon Strange wrote to say he was ill with a wasting disease and the physician he had consulted was not hopeful.

By this time Buckingham's malign influence upon the King had provoked war with France for, in spite of his marriage to a French Princess, Henrietta Maria, the Duke had persuaded Charles to come to the aid of the French Huguenots then under siege at La Rochelle by Cardinal Richelieu and the forces of King Louis XIII. Buckingham had hoisted his flag aboard the *Triumph*, and with a considerable fleet and thousands of soldiers had sailed to establish a base on the Île de Rhé from where operations would commence to relieve the beleaguered Protestant forces in La Rochelle. None of this augured well for the two men and, since Faulkner was privately determined to go to Bristol and avoid returning to the King's service, he seized upon an opportunity in the shape of a second letter from Bristol. It was written by one Gooding, the counting-house clerk employed by Strange, and warned that his master was gravely ill. As Mainwaring's Naval Board sought to cope with the logistical problems arising from the appalling mess that Buckingham was, by all accounts, embroiling the King's forces in before La Rochelle, Faulkner suggested that both their business interests demanded that he at least proceeded to Bristol with all despatch to learn what ailed Gideon Strange.

Then worse news came from the Île de Rhé and, hard on its heels, Mainwaring received a letter from the King. A lack of proper preparation, of stores, men and victuals, combined with the vigorous actions of Richelieu, had quickly bogged Buckingham down and disaster loomed. The Duke sent for urgent reinforcements and the

King summoned Mainwaring. Ordered to Plymouth to expedite the sailing of a relieving force, Sir Henry left Faulkner on the road to Bristol.

'I leave matters entirely to your discretion, Kit. As far as I know from what Gideon hath told me, Gooding lives up to his name and may be relied upon.'

Faulkner took leave of his patron with mixed feelings. The sense of independence, of freedom and a coming-of-age was only tempered by a concern for Captain Strange. He had seen enough of disease and death at sea to know of their horrors but, for the young man riding west that day, such evils beset others. And there was something else lurking in his subconscious, an unacknowledged sense that by returning to Bristol a made man he was finally turning his back not only on the King's navy, but the shadowy obligation he had placed himself under by accepting the telescope and the whole miserable experience of the Spanish voyage. Mistress Villiers, being nothing but a chit of a spoiled child, was exorcised from his unrequited affections. With a lifting heart he reflected that she was not the world's only beauty.

Such frivolous thoughts were, however, soon displaced, for in Bristol Faulkner found Strange abed, a shockingly pallid and thin figure whose face was scarcely recognisable. His woman attended him and she let Faulkner into a room scattered with ledgers and papers. 'See that my Molly is provided for, Kit,' Strange said, his voice strained by the pain of his ravaged body. 'She has been good to me.'

'Of course, sir, but you will recover...'

'No,' Strange said through clenched teeth. 'But listen, Kit. The books are up to date and the ships are all employed. My confidential clerk, Nathan Gooding, is entirely trustworthy and I have secured his interest by virtue of a bequest in my will...' Strange broke off as a wave of pain wracked him. 'I know that neither you not Henry can give our affairs...' He stopped and turned his attention to the hovering woman whose loving concern disfigured her otherwise handsome face. 'Molly, send for Nathan...' Repressing a sniffling, the woman did as she was bid and Strange lapsed into silence, rousing himself every few minutes to issue an instruction to Faulkner regarding one or other of their ships. It was a slow, gasping process; he was painfully telling Faulkner that Captain Mitchell would be due in with the *Garvey* the following month when Molly returned with Nathan Gooding, a tall youngish man dressed soberly in black, his reddish hair cut short to his shoulders, but with an open countenance that Faulkner immediately took to.

'Explain to Mr Faulkner the present state of affairs in our business, Nathan...'

'Certainly, Captain Strange.' The young man turned to Faulkner with a deferential air, though he was probably some three or four years Faulkner's senior, and began a lengthy disquisition Faulkner found difficult to follow with Strange so pathetic a figure lying beneath his coverlet and breathing hard. From time-to-time Gooding drew his attention to an entry in a ledger, each of which related to the affairs of one of their ships. At the termination of this Gooding closed the last of the books, that referring to the *Bristol Rover*, and looked at Strange who, without opening his eyes, said, 'That was well done, Nathan. Now pray tell Mr Faulkner what provisions are consequent, but contingent on my death.'

'I believe, sir,' Gooding began, turning to Faulkner, 'that Captain Strange, knowing your own preoccupations, and having no issue of his own, has settled the greater part of his own shares – with some exceptions in yours and Sir Henry's favour – upon myself. I also understand that this is to ensure the continuation of the business and that I shall thereby be bound to act in—'

'I understand, Mr Gooding,' Faulkner interrupted, 'and this is all as it should be, I have no doubt, but,' he turned to Strange, addressing the dying man, 'I am come to Bristol to take up my former trade and to take command of one of our vessels...'

'No, no, that is not our purpose, Kit,' Strange said, struggling to lift himself. 'Sir Henry...'

'I pray you do not upset yourself, Captain Strange. Sir Henry is aware...' Faulkner was almost immediately ashamed of the lie. It was meant to soothe Strange, but Mainwaring was not yet fully aware of his intention to throw up

135

his naval commission.

'But great matters are afoot in France. Your future lies there, not kicking your heels on the waterfront. Besides,' he said with an effort, 'you would not dispossess Mitchell, or Simpson, or Willoughby of their livings, would you?'

Faulkner had not considered such a thing. 'Well, I, er...'

Strange paused, frowning as he focussed his tired eyes upon Faulkner. 'You are not yet married, are you?'

'No, no...'

'Perhaps we can discuss this matter elsewhere, sir,' Gooding remarked, indicating the distressed state Strange now appeared to be in. The woman Molly seemed to concur, coming forward and wiping Strange's sweating forehead with a none-too-clean cloth. Faulkner felt the disapproval, as though he had brought unwanted problems into the sickroom.

'Come sir,' said Gooding, rising and nodding to Strange and Molly. 'I shall apprise Mr Faulkner of all our circumstances, Captain Strange. Please do not distress yourself.'

The two men withdrew to Strange's counting-house, which occupied the ground floor, where Gooding sent his junior for a jug of cider. 'Sir, it is none of my affair and I should greatly welcome some help here in Bristol, but I am conversant with the Captain's business and have kept his books for nigh on ten years without, insofar as I am able to affirm, having given him cause for concern.' Gooding looked awkward, but struggled on. 'The Captain has proved a friend to me and I must provide for a sick mother and a sister, and am scarce likely to compromise my position...'

'Are you asking me not to poke my nose in where it is not wanted?' Faulkner asked, with only the faintest hint of sarcasm. He felt bad about his conduct in the sickroom but had no idea how he could have made matters easier for the dying man. Despite his connections he was not able to dissemble – thanks perhaps to Mainwaring's curiously twisted moral sense – but one white lie was enough. Now Gooding looked as though Faulkner had struck him.

'Good heavens, no, sir! It is not my place to even hint at such a thing. All I am saying is that I hope that you will find me as reliable as Captain Strange has done.'

'You are making a protestation of honesty then?'

'I cannot do that, sir! I am merely anxious that in coming to Bristol you do not assume that I cannot be of service to you.'

The desperation in Gooding's voice shamed Faulkner. It suddenly struck him that the good fortune that had lifted him from the gutter had all but prevented him from recognizing Gooding's desire to please, that a man placed as Gooding was, was insecure. Indeed, the man was terrified that he, Faulkner, was going to sweep with the zeal of a new broom. Whether Strange had confided the story of Faulkner's origins or not, Gooding was plainly consumed with fear for his future.

'Oh, dear Mr Gooding,' Faulkner began. 'This is going fearfully wrong. Please forgive me. I had no idea exactly what to expect on my arrival and I have been unconscionably forward with my own affairs and for that I apologize. Come now, we are shortly to be partners it seems and therefore it is meet that we consider ourselves equals.' He held out his hand which Gooding seized eagerly. 'I am known to my friends as Kit.'

'And I as Nat.'

'I am sorry that we find ourselves drawn together in such circumstances,' Faulkner remarked, 'but let us establish a comity of purpose between ourselves, if only in our benefactor's interest.'

'Yes, Captain Strange has been good to me.'

'And I.'

The two sat for a moment in silence, then Gooding asked, 'Will you dine with us? I can have Julia – my sister – make up a bed, if you are content to stay with us. You must be tired after your journey.'

'That is kind of you. I have not thought of sleeping, the appearance of poor Captain Strange having driven all such thoughts away from my mind.'

'I will send word. Shall you come immediately? I can close the house now, for we have little business to transact until the *Garvey* comes in and I already have a full lading awaiting her – or at least promised – for Jamaica...'

Faulkner nodded. 'That is kind. Give me an hour; I think I should sit awhile with him and make him sensible that he can compose his mind. I have troubled him overmuch. Has he asked for a priest?'

Gooding shook his head. 'No. He is not so inclined, though he may change his mind as his end draws nigh.'

'You do not approve?'

Strange shrugged. 'It is for Captain Strange to settle his soul's shriving.'

'Very well.' Faulkner rose from the bench and made his way back to the sickroom.

As he left Gooding asked, 'Where is your horse, Kit?'

'I left it at the King's Arms, with my portmanteau.'

'I'll have the horse tended there, and send for the latter and have it taken home, if you wish.'

'That would be a kindness. Thank you.'

An hour later he had joined Gooding as they walked a few hundred yards to his dwelling. His father had been a haberdasher and although his father's business was now in the hands of others, its sale necessary to pay his father's considerable and unsuspected debts, his mother, sister and himself continued to live above their old premises.

'We have four rooms,' Gooding explained as they made their way through streets scoured by a raw westerly wind that carried more than a hint of rain to come. 'We manage to hold on to a single maid to tend my mother. Julia cooks and otherwise runs the house, and I do not know what I shall do when she marries, though my anxiety is eased by Captain Strange's consideration – though I would not have you think I wish him dead...' Gooding said with evident and awkward embarrassment.

Faulkner gained the impression that Gooding was preparing him for meeting a pair of dragons and asked, conversationally, 'Is your sister intending to marry?'

'Ha! I wish I knew. She has rejected two men of her own age, though none of them could offer her much, but there is an eager suitor, quite unsuitable in my opinion, in the person of a city alderman of ample girth and considerable wealth.'

Faulkner was tempted to ask his name but thought better of it. He did not wish to involve himself, nor to show interest in affairs that were not his business, though he wondered idly why Mistress Gooding should have turned down so many offers of marriage. Nat must have divined his mind, for he volunteered the information that: 'My sister has strong opinions, political opinions quite unsuitable for a woman...' The explanation tailed off. 'Here we are.'

They entered a door in an old building and immediately ascended a staircase, Gooding's shoes and Faulkner's boots making a thunder of their approach. His host threw open a door and Faulkner hesitated while he announced the arrival of their guest. Then, doffing his hat – which seemed overlarge for the low-ceilinged room – he followed.

'Mother, Lieutenant Kit Faulkner, a partner of Captain Strange.'

'Kit, my mother...' The old lady was of formidable appearance. Shrunk in a winged armchair, her features were half-lit by the light coming in through a grimy window of paned glass and showed a face of indelible character. Her rheumy eyes were sunk in her skull, her wispy hair was drawn severely back and hidden under a lace mob-cap, and her head was sunk upon a plain collar of white linen. The rest of her shrivelled figure lay under a dark woollen blanket, only two tiny black shoes peeping out upon a low footstool.

Faulkner flourished his feathered hat and footed his most elegant bow. 'Mistress Gooding, your servant.'

The eyes regarded him with a shrewd light and a claw-like hand emerged from under its covers. Bowing over it he put it to his lips. It was cold, bony and dry. 'You are welcome, sir...' she wheezed. She seemed to scrutinize him, her eyes travelling up and down his travel-stained figure. Wrapped in his cloak in the dark room it was difficult for her to see what manner of man he was, though she had noted the plumed, wide-brimmed hat and the heavy, spurred boots. The claw gestured and she said, 'Megan, take the gentleman's cloak ... So, sir, you are a partner of Captain Strange ... pray give the girl your cloak and sit here beside me.' She indicated a second, higher stool upon which lay an upturned but open book. 'Nathan, remove the book to the table so that our guest may sit.' Her command was instantly obeyed.

His cloak removed, Faulkner perched awkwardly on the stool. A quick glance about the room revealed no indication of the whereabouts of the sister. Perhaps, he thought, she had lately been sitting where he now was, reading to her mother.

'Nathan,' she said in a peremptory manner, 'on receipt of your note which arrived with this gentleman's effects, Julia has gone to Mistress Culver's...'

'That was well done, Mother. And I shall, with your permission of course, open a bottle of Oporto.'

'I do not approve of strong drink, Mr...'

'Faulkner, ma'am.'

'Faulkner. It is the ruin of many but perhaps on this occasion...' She nodded to her son who briefly left the room.

'You are a seafaring man, Mr Faulkner? Nathan mentioned a rank, but I supposed that you might have served in the Low Countries.'

'I am a seafaring man, ma'am...'

'And a partner of Captain Strange?'

'Indeed, ma'am, I have a small interest in the affairs of Captains Strange and Mainwaring.'

At Mainwaring's name the old lady bristled. 'Of Captain Mainwaring I have no very high regard, sir. He was a pirate, I am told, and now lies close to the King in whose court untold evil is wrought. It is the devil's work, sir, and will bring down heaven's vengeance upon us all. I am fortunate in being old...' She broke off and stared beyond Faulkner who, for a moment, thought that the lucid moment had passed and she had lapsed into some senile reverie. He was wrong; a second later he too heard the rustling of skirts and the light trip of a feminine foot upon the stair. He heard voices too, the female tread followed by that of Gooding, returning with his bottle of port. The door opened and a young woman strode into the room with her brother behind her. Faulkner scrambled to his feet.

'My sister Julia,' Gooding said soberly.

Faulkner bowed again. 'Mistress Julia, your brother has kindly asked me to join you.'

She stepped forward and held out her hand. He took it and was about to raise it to his lips when he felt his own shaken vigorously. He looked up into grey eyes and a well-made, evenly featured face. A few pock marks lay on her cheeks but her mouth was wide and smiling, and her expression as open and candid as her brother's.

'You are most welcome, sir,' she said. 'Pray do not stand upon ceremony. I have ordered a beef pie from Mistress Culver's and it will be here shortly.' She took off her bonnet and Faulkner saw that, like her mother, her hair was dressed severely, drawn back and tucked into the nape of her neck in an unbecoming style that he had observed increasingly popular among the trading classes. Unlike her mother, however, there was a profusion of it and Faulkner was pricked by the curious question of what it looked like when it was unrestrained, for it was dark but, even in the poor light, betrayed hints of red. Her dress was also dark and unadorned, her collar as plain as her mother's, and he realized, with something of a shock, that he was in a household of Dissenters. His own modest splendour seemed raffish and even coarse, for all its pretensions to fashion. His sleeves overcapacious and his lace – though sober enough by the standards of those among whom he customarily moved these days – profuse. He thanked heaven that he had left his sword and baldric with his portmanteau, and was not obliged to swing it round the furniture in this crowded room.

'Megan!' the old woman cried and the wretched maid was sent to prepare the table for the imminent arrival of one of Mistress Culver's beef pies and a dish of cabbage. An almost self-effacing Gooding poured two glasses of port into two bumpers that he had taken from a shelf and, filling them, handed one to Faulkner.

'May we drink to business and friendship?' he asked, holding up his glass expectantly while his mother clicked her tongue disapprovingly.

'To friendship and business, I think, Nat,' Faulkner said, adding, 'with the ladies' permission, of course.'

'Reluctantly granted,' said Julia, settling herself on the stool beside her mother so that Faulkner was obliged to move and stand next to Gooding. The port warmed him and eased his attitude to these strangers, though he knew not what to make of them, nor what they made of him.

'He is a seafaring man, Julia,' her mother confided to her daughter in a stage whisper, as if this provided an explanation of the need for wine. She caught Faulkner's eye. 'I do not disapprove of seafaring men, sir,' she asserted, 'provided they confine themselves to their business of fetching and carrying. It is when they come ashore and disturb the peace of others' lives that I find them less attractive.'

'I am sorry for that, ma'am,' Faulkner temporized.

'You have sailed in Bristol ships, Mr Faulkner? In those belonging to Gideon Strange?'

'I have, ma'am.'

'But not lately, I think, else we should have seen thee hereabouts, or at least heard of thee.'

'I have not lately been in Bristol, no.'

'Mr Faulkner holds a commission from the King, Julia, as a lieutenant. He has lately been serving...' The light of hostility was plainly kindled in Julia's eyes at the mention of the King and clearly Gooding made the remark to make matters plain. Anticipating this Gooding changed tack. 'Mr Faulkner informs me he is minded to settle here and take a greater interest in the business, being a partner of Captain Strange.'

'I see,' remarked his sister icily.

The subsequent meal passed in silence and, at its conclusion, the hour drawing on and night approaching, Faulkner pleaded tiredness after his journey and retired to the bed the girl Megan had made ready for him.

He slept well, undisturbed by dreams. Gooding woke him and the two men broke their fast together before walking down to the counting-house to find Strange had passed a difficult night. Molly looked so drawn and exhausted that, after a day going thoroughly through the books with Gooding below, and apprehensive of another encounter with Mistress Gooding and her formidable daughter, he resolved to relieve her that night.

During the evening Strange rallied, sitting up with help from Faulkner, and for two hours engaged him in a conversation which, though desultory, was not without an enlivening spark or two, flashes of the former shipmaster he had known in earlier years. Towards one in the morning, Strange fell back on his pillow and for a while appeared to sleep. Perhaps Faulkner dozed too, for he next recalled feeling chilled and was suddenly aware that Strange had turned his head and wore a puzzled expression. As if forgetful of their earlier exchanges, he asked with a querulous anxiety, 'Mr Rat? Is that Mr Rat?'

'Aye, sir. It is indeed, Mr Rat,' Faulkner responded, leaning forward and offering a glass of water to Strange. 'Be a good boy, Mr Rat, and Henry and I shall look after you...'

'Of course...'

'Mind that you keep our secrets though ... and bury us both like decent gentlemen...'

146

'Of course,' Faulkner repeated, and then, summoning his nerve, asked, 'Do you wish me to send for a priest?'

Strange feebly shook his head and muttered, 'No, I have made my peace with God long since...' He closed his eyes and for several minutes the only sound in the room was his laboured breathing. Then he opened his eyes again and said again, 'Mr Rat...'

Faulkner felt profoundly moved. 'Thank you for your faith in me, sir,' he whispered.

Strange drew his lips back in a ghastly smile, his breathing a regular, steady labour of his ailing lungs. Faulkner must have slept again, for he woke with a start, cold to the marrow and aware of the first light of day entering the room through a slight gap in the curtains. Beside him Strange still drew breath but his efforts were weaker, shallower. Faulkner sat still for some time until, with a great effort, Strange lifted his body and raised one arm as if seeing something in the far distance. His breath now came in a spasmodic series of gulps and wheezes for some ten seconds as his extended arm wavered, and then he fell back dead. Faulkner waited for a few moments then rose, bent over the emaciated face and drew down the eyelids; then he walked across the room, opened the curtains and threw open the casements. Below, the street was stirring into life, and coming towards him he saw Gooding and beside him the figure of his sister. They saw the movement of the windows and hurried their steps. A moment later they stood beside the deathbed of Captain Strange.

'May God have mercy upon him,' whispered Mistress Gooding.

'Amen,' responded her brother.

Faulkner stood in silence, his head bowed. When he sighed and looked up his eyes met the candid regard of Julia Gooding. 'Have you nothing to say, sir?' she asked.

He shook his head. 'No, ma'am,' he answered quietly. 'I have said all I have to say long since.'

The three of them stood for several moments contemplating the dead man, then Gooding volunteered to go and see about the laying-out. 'Ensure Kit has some breakfast, Julia,' he added over his shoulder as he left the room. The matter-of-fact familiarity somehow broke down the remaining reserve between them all and Julia plucked delicately at Faulkner's arm, breaking his preoccupation.

'Come away, sir,' she said, her voice suddenly gentle. Without a word Faulkner took up his hat and followed her out of the room. On the stairs he paused.

'We ought not to leave him alone...'

'There is no need to, sir. Molly is here.' And Faulkner drew aside as the weeping Molly passed him, oblivious in the intensity of her grief.

A week later Faulkner received a letter from Mainwaring in which Sir Henry apologized for failing to attend his partner and friend's funeral. Gooding being about his business in the counting-house, Faulkner was sitting alone in the room he and Gooding had lately shared. Nearby Julia was talking – or perhaps reading – to her mother. Faulkner paid them no attention; Mainwaring's letter was distraction enough.

I received yours from Bristol only after it had been forwarded from Plymouth, where I was able, after divers distractions and difficulties, to send reinforcements to My Lord Duke. Thereafter I was plucked by the King's command to London where I find myself now, almost resident in the Trinity House, whereof I am lately elected a Brother and needs must call you hither on important business. Conclude, therefore, all matters you have in hand, leaving them to Gooding and meet me here...

Mainwaring's handwriting was eloquent of his haste and his exhaustion, and Faulkner crushed the letter after reading it. He was a damned fool for not making his intention in coming to Bristol clear to Sir Henry; now it had all become complicated by Strange's illness brought to its summary conclusion by his death. With a sigh he resumed reading the crumpled paper. Mainwaring was obscurely cryptic:

Things go ill in France. Very ill. Come as fast as you may.
  Yours Devotedly,
  Hy Mainwaring

When he had finished he looked up and started. Julia had noiselessly entered the room, and he got to his feet, aware that he was in his stockings, having kicked off his shoes and yet to pull on his boots.

'I am sorry if I startled you,' she said. 'Have you more bad news?'

'I am summoned to London.'

'Oh!'

'You will be rid of me.'

'Perhaps I do not wish to be rid of you, Lieutenant Faulkner.'

'Then your mother will be rid of me,' he said, smiling.

'On this occasion, it is not my mother's wishes that I care for.' Her sincerity stopped him from beginning to gather his things together; they had dropped the formal pronoun in the house, but now its absence gathered significance. She was closing the door behind her and dropping her voice. 'Shall you be gone long?' she asked.

'I ... I do not know.' He indicated the crumpled letter lying upon the bed.

'I thought that you were intending to occupy your future business in Bristol,' she said, pressing him for an explanation.

'Yes, that was my intention, but matters have overtaken me...'

'What matters?'

'Why, ma'am,' he explained, a hint of exasperation in his voice, 'business of state.'

'King's business?'

'Mistress Gooding, I am at a loss to know...'

'Is it to do with this war in France? Is that why you have been summoned by the King, your master?'

'And yours, ma'am, or so I believe,' he responded quickly, not liking her tone of asperity.

'I am a free thinker, Lieutenant Faulkner, and it disappoints me to learn that you are not.'

'Perhaps I am, ma'am, but not one whose opinion finds favour in your eyes.' He was irritated by her manner – what impertinence!

'But there is much about you that does find favour in my eyes, Lieutenant, and I would save you from your obedience to the King, by which means you may imperil your soul.'

He stopped what he was doing and stared at her. On the one hand her remark was exceedingly forward; on the other it was treasonous. It occurred to him that she was mad and something of this conclusion must have struck her. 'Sir, you may think me bold, even disturbed, but if you are going away so soon it is necessary that I communicate my sentiments, since my family relies so heavily upon you. With Captain Strange dead and Captain Mainwaring of some years, it is likely to be you with whom my brother will be most associated. As for myself, I have no time for convention and am thought of as headstrong, opinionated, unwomanly even, but you have made an impression upon me and I entertained for a little while the hope that you might have some feelings for me—'

'Mistress Julia, please I—' She waved aside his intervention.

'I am sensible that this outburst is embarrassing to you. I have no means of altering your intentions, nor would I seek to do so. All I ask is that after you have gone you do not forget us here. Quite apart from your business, you may be in need of true friends one day and I wish to assure you that I shall not forget you.' She stopped and gave him a steady look. Then she turned on her heel and was gone. An hour later, when he sent word by Megan that his horse was to be readied at the King's Arms and went to pay his respects to the old lady, Julia was nowhere to be seen.

It was only that afternoon, when he was in the saddle and riding hard to the east, that he realized that he knew little of women; that almost his entire knowledge of them centred on a foolish incident aboard the *Prince Royal* years ago and that although Mainwaring had encouraged every aspect of his education, the matter of women had been ignored. Sir Henry, he knew, took his pleasure of a lady of easy virtue from time to time; Gideon Strange had his common-law Molly, Harry Brenton pretended a knowledge of whoring, though Faulkner had privately doubted his capacity to fornicate as royally as he claimed. Those others among his seafaring acquaintances – Quinn, old Whiting, Ned Slessor – had been either married or spoken for, so that the tales of louche living, of sodomy and fornicating, had been associated with the court which he, busy about his and Mainwaring's affairs, had found repugnant. In short, whatever the predilections of others, his own continence had been complete; he had fallen – or so he had thought until making up his mind to return to his old life sailing out of Bristol – head-over-heels in love with Katherine Villiers and kept himself clean for her in some odd, almost perverse belief that if he did so, she would fall like a ripe fruit into his waiting arms. Was that not love, the romantic fever of which he had heard in the cheap songs sung in taverns? Now he found himself all a-pother over this lunatic but handsome sister of his new business partner. As the horse moved beneath him he found himself excited by wayward thoughts. Great Harry! He had had her panting with lust for him in his very bedroom! Why had he not flung the impudent wench on her back and had his way of her there and then? He knew what was required, felt the means stirred in his loins and she had been like a bitch in heat! He had heard men speak of such importunity but never previously experienced it, and now, like some crass loon, he had passed up a golden opportunity.

Stopping the night at an inn near Chippenham, he was tempted to carry one of the serving girls off to bed; though he had the money, he had not the nerve. Instead he fell asleep, his head whirling. Waking in the dawn he felt his erection and pleasured himself back to sleep. Much later, riding east again, he was full of a sorry mixture of self-disgust and apprehension. His ignorance of women, exposed by recent events, confronted him and reinforced the feelings of failure and inadequacy that he had thought to have thrown off since his return from Spain. But the freedom of recent weeks had combined headily with his contact with Julia Gooding whose image remained strong in his mind's eye. Had she been full of lust for him? Or had she merely expressed a trenchant view with unbecoming, if intimate, forthrightness? Reflecting on their several meetings gave him no grounds for considering her aflame with passion for him in the manner he had conceived in his fantasy; on the contrary, what she had shown was a sober regard for him, an offer of friendship. But was not that in itself promising?

And thus, unthinking of what might be awaiting him in London, full of lusty turmoil, self-loathing and awakening possibility, he arrived in the City in the early afternoon and repaired directly to the Trinity House in Whitehorse Street, Stepney.

Five

The *King's Whelp*

1627–1628

'Kit! How very glad I am to see you. By God, your arrival is timely. You have left your horse in livery?'

'I have, Sir Henry.'

'Come, I have to attend the palace and you may accompany me thither, after which we shall dine, but on our way I can acquaint you of matters touching yourself.' Mainwaring took his arm and turned him about almost as soon as he had arrived at the Trinity House.

'Sir Henry, I was engaged—'

'I know. In Bristol with ideas of a future there and sorry for the wretched state of things with Gideon dead, but all that is past. Affairs of state occupy us, Kit. And opportunity awaits.'

Offering no further explanation Mainwaring clambered into a waiting hired carriage and motioned for him to follow. Faulkner sank into the rough cushions wearily. He was saddle-sore, tired and hungry. He wanted a glass of something strong, a hearty meal and a sleep.

'I shall have to ask you to wait for me at Whitehall. I imagine that your arse is aching but there is much afoot,' Mainwaring said. The coach had moved off, an uncomfortable equipage, rolling like a ship at sea over the uneven road and frequently slowed as, with various imprecations and frequent cracks of his whip, the coachman forced its lumbering frame through the thronged streets. Faulkner had trouble keeping his seat and, despite his long journey, would have preferred to have ridden, even walked, rather than submit to this crazy mode of transport. Mainwaring pressed on and Faulkner was obliged to give Sir Henry his full attention. 'The expedition to La Rochelle has gone from bad to worse, as you may have heard. Richelieu's forces have the upper hand, M'sieur Soubise is in trouble, as is My Lord Duke of Buckingham, he being likely to be impeached. The Commons are in unruly uproar and the King...' Mainwaring let the silent inference hang heavily in the gloom of the coach. Then he lowered his voice into a confidential whisper, leaning towards Faulkner's nearer ear. 'The King is unreliable. Utterly. The conduct he manifested during his Spanish adventure was no aberration. All augurs ill and I am unhappy about what lies ahead.' Then he straightened up and resumed his conversational tone. 'However, whatever one thinks of My Lord Duke, he made the funds available himself for the construction and commission of the ten small vessels lately completed, one of which is presently readied at

Deptford, and tomorrow thither thou shalt go to take command of her.'

'I, sir? I command a King's ship?'

'You will sail with the King's commission, though the vessel of which you shall have charge is owned by My Lord Duke of Buckingham.'

'A letter or marque? Or,' Faulkner said, greatly daring but with his mind racing, 'am I to be a pirate?'

Mainwaring sat back with a chuckle. 'No, sir, a privateer at worst, but your commission will be from the King and your crew paid according to the new naval regulations.'

'I see.' Faulkner neither saw, nor understood. His mind was in turmoil as the unsprung coach lurched down Ludgate Hill leaving behind the vast bulk of St Paul's Cathedral, with its immense spire black against the sky. 'I had hopes that in Bristol—'

'Whatever plans you were cooking up, Kit, I must ask you to lay aside.' Mainwaring looked sideways at his young friend. 'Is this entirely contrary to your liking? Gooding is a good man – no pun intended – and I think that we must trust him, at least for a while.'

'Yes ... yes, of course. I am sorry; my mind has been much diverted by the death of Captain Strange and consequent events.'

'Is she lovely?' Mainwaring asked shrewdly.

Faulkner pulled himself together. The question was not serious; a joshing to jolt him out of his preoccupation. Sir Henry could have no idea about Julia Gooding's effect upon him. Nevertheless, he tested his patron. 'Is who lovely?'

'The woman you have obviously met in Bristol. I cannot think that you wish to suddenly become an owner of merchantmen, sitting in your counting-house all day, fossicking over your dusty ledgers. When a young man of your abilities even contemplates the possible attraction of such a thing there is usually a woman at the bottom of it.'

'You are wide of the mark, Sir Henry, on both counts. If I went to Bristol with any prospect in mind it was not to turn owner, but to take command of the *Swallow*, or another of the ships in which I have shares, but I had not considered those better experienced that presently hold command, and though I might have found a ship of my own, your summons terminated my adventure.'

'Well then, that is something in the favour of writing letters. And glad I am that mine was timely. Had there been a woman, it might have proved more difficult to persuade you to come.' Mainwaring slapped him affectionately on the thigh and lifted the window curtain with the handle of his cane. 'Nearly there. By God this thing rattles like a tumbrel!'

On their arrival at the rambling complex of buildings that in their entirety constituted the Palace of Whitehall, Mainwaring descended stiffly from the coach and waited while Faulkner followed him. It wanted about an hour to sunset and already the shadows were lengthening.

Waving airily along the thoroughfare of Whitehall, Mainwaring remarked, 'You may walk here awhile, I shall be gone about an hour. See, there beyond the Abbey and St Margaret's, the light of a tavern. That is The Grapes and I shall meet you there. Order yourself something, but save the best of your appetite for our joint pleasure.' And then he turned away.

Idly, Faulkner watched him go, walking with a vigorous stride towards the brick gatehouse of one wing where a pikeman leaned on the wall. The soldier straightened himself up at the approach of Mainwaring, and Faulkner saw another emerge, a courtier by his dress, who greeted Sir Henry and then turned back under the gate with him. Faulkner looked around, reviewing the crowded street. It would take him less than ten minutes to reach The Grapes so he began to saunter, pressed by the populace that inhabited the busy environs of the palace. He saw a girl selling oranges and was reminded of the apple-seller in Bristol who had initiated the fortuitous meeting with Mainwaring and Strange, and set him on this queer road. Odd, he thought, this business of cause and effect: who would think that a common trollop of a street vendor could metamorphose a starving boy into a gentleman? And never to have known the wonder of her agency! Was that the blind workings of luck, or of fate, or perhaps of God himself? He was, he considered in a moment of self-assessment, a virgin, innocent and rather unworldly gentleman; he also had to concede that he would have to – no *must* – do something to remedy that. He was no more than five paces from the orange-seller and noted she was pretty, in an ordinary way. He found himself measuring her against Julia. She had not Julia's looks, of course, but she showed a good deal of the other parts of herself that, on the evidence of their display, made up for the deficiency. He smiled at the thought and thereby caught her attention.

'Oranges, sir? Two for a ha'penny, five a penny...' She held one out and he felt, for one moment, like Paris. But his smile and his pre-occupation with the orange-seller had caught the attention of others; two tall-hatted, black-suited Puritan gentlemen walked past, tut-tutting with disapproval. Faulkner looked at them and wanted to explain that it was one such as stood expectantly beside him that had lifted him from the gutter. But the moment was as short as his explanation was long, and he was left foolishly next to the lass who had now convinced herself that he was about to purchase an orange or two, or even make her a better proposition.

'Sir...?' she said appealingly, so that he returned his regard to her big brown eyes and her grubby cheeks. He fished in his pocket for some coppers and was in this process when he heard his name called.

'Lieutenant Faulkner! Is that you, sir?' The voice was peremptory; he spun round and found himself staring into the exquisite face of Katherine Villiers; she was peering at him from an arrested sedan chair.

'Mistress Villiers!' he exclaimed. 'What a most fortunate turn...' He stepped forward and bowed over her extended hand.

'What a pleasure to see you, sir,' she said withdrawing her hand with a lovely smile. 'But pray do not let me interrupt your transaction.'

He shrugged and half-turned to the orange-seller. She was furious at her lost sale but he already had a penny in his left hand and tossed it to her before confronting Katherine Villiers.

'What brings you to London?' she asked. 'I imagined a lion like you would be with My Lord of Buckingham under the walls of La Rochelle.'

'My duties have taken me elsewhere, ma'am.'

'I hope that is not a euphemism to say that you were dismissed for the importunities of trying to teach a poor young girl the rudimentaries of seamanship?'

'It came close, ma'am.' He laughed, grinning widely. 'Heard you that I was in disgrace?'

She smiled and he felt ravished by the attention, and by the fact that she referred to that long-lost moment of intimacy. Did it prick her as much as it did him?

'No,' she said shortly. 'I heard quite the contrary; that you had impressed Sir Henry Mainwaring, that you had impressed My Lord Duke, that you had impressed Prince Charles and were like to ride higher in his favour now that he is King.'

'You mock me, ma'am.'

'I do. But you were not quite sure for a moment.'

He felt suddenly emboldened by her playful air. 'I have not been quite sure for a long time, Mistress Villiers. I had hoped that I might have exchanged a word or two on the homeward passage, after the admiral's untimely intervention.'

He thought that a cloud had crossed her face, a moment of uncertainty, but she recovered herself instantaneously. 'I thought the admiral's intervention was quite proper, sir,' she said archly, adding acidly, 'not that the Earl has proved much of a friend to the Villiers family...'

'I am sorry to hear it, ma'am.'

''Tis no matter. But –' she dropped her voice, causing him to lean in towards her so that he caught the odour of her perfume, the warmth and sweetness of her breath and noted the richness of her lace and the gorgeous silks of her ornate dress – 'I am glad to see you in good health. I am obliged now to attend His Majesty and must begone. I hope that fortune will play another pleasant trick upon us, Lieutenant. And before too long, perhaps.' Then settling back in the chair, she cried, 'Pick up!' and was at once lifted and disappeared into the crowd, heading towards the gatehouse into which Mainwaring had passed a lifetime ago.

'Amen to that,' he whispered to himself, his spirits suddenly soaring. He had not behaved like a milksop virgin, but with something at least of the dash of a cavalier.

'Oranges, sir? You never took any, sir...'

He turned to the girl. 'No, no thank you ... But

here, here you are for your pains. Get thyself a decent meal and a clean bed...'

'I got a clean bed!' she protested, insulted until she opened her fist and saw the dull gleam of a silver shilling. 'An' any time you want to share it, you'm welcome!' she added with opportunistic quick-wittedness.

For an instant he thought of bedding her, of losing his lack of experience that very night, and then, curbed by the sudden image of Milady Villiers, he thought better of the notion. Brenton's warning about the pox steadied him and he resumed his promenade towards the now glowing light of The Grapes. Already night was falling and the damp chill and stink of the street egged him on, so that once inside he called for a bottle of wine and two glasses, settling himself at a table in anticipation of Mainwaring's arrival and – more importantly – a good dinner.

He had drunk three glasses before Mainwaring puffed in, full of apologies as he removed his hat, tore his wig off and scratched his pate. 'God damn me, Kit, but I find playing the courtier a confoundedly tedious business.'

Faulkner filled the second glass and called for another bottle and two meat pies. After Mainwaring had quaffed a deep draught he sat back and blew out his cheeks. Faulkner waited and their eyes met.

'The King has granted you a commission but it is his wish that he presents it to you personally.'

'Personally...?' Faulkner was astonished.

'Yes. You will accompany me hither tomorrow afternoon. The King will grant you audience...'

'But why? I mean why on earth does the King...?' Faulkner broke off, dumbfounded.

'It seems he remembers you; besides he has despatches for My Lord Duke. It is a particular mark of His Majesty's favour that he has asked for you to carry them to the Île de Rhé.' Mainwaring stopped to take another mouthful of the wine, emptying the glass in the process. Faulkner refilled it, puzzled, confused, and aware that much of the royal favour was attributable not to him, but to Mainwaring. 'You have come a long way, Mr Rat.'

Faulkner felt an unmanly welling of emotional tears in his eyes. 'I know, Sir Henry ... I know.'

Seeing the young man's eyes brighten, Mainwaring smiled. 'Well, that was what was in our minds when we took you up, Kit. It was intended that you should be a King's sea-officer. It is well within your capabilities.' He paused then, seeing the approach of two steaming pies, he sat up, replaced his wig and smiled at the serving-girl. 'Thank you, m'dear.'

The following afternoon found the two men again approaching Whitehall in the rocking coach. Faulkner, his sword upright between his knees, was dressed in a fine suit of black slashed with grey that had – or so the tailor pressed that morning to provide and adjust it assured him – 'just that hint of fashion necessary to make an impression, without any pretension to dazzle'.

Certainly he felt a sensation of excitement which, partly due to the possibility of seeing Katherine Villiers at court, surmounted his nervous apprehension. He realized he was barely listening to Mainwaring's briefing.

'...should His Majesty extend his hand, drop to your right knee and kiss it lightly by briefly touching your lips to it. There, that is all you have to remember.'

Faulkner was appalled and his feeling of self-conceit was rapidly replaced by one of gut-wrenching terror. He had heard hardly a word Sir Henry had said yet could not possibly ask him to repeat it. In the end he simply sat still in a cold sweat and was shaking as though palsied when the coach stopped, and, just as he had watched the previous evening, they were met and conducted into the gloom of the palace. Faulkner never afterwards recalled anything about the maze of corridors and the brief glimpse of the sky as they traversed a courtyard only to plunge into more gloom on the further side. He did, however, remember the courtroom as heaving with people, of a canopy above them at the far end, its draped velvet parting above the backs of two ornate gilded chairs, both on a dais, one slightly higher than the other. Between the summit of the canopy where the gold-fringed velvet was gathered into a mock crown, yet above and behind the twin thrones, hung the Royal Coat of Arms borne by its golden lion and white unicorn. The room was hot and the air thick with sweat and perfume, the stink of tobacco smoke and rank breath, for everyone was talking at the tops of their voices. The fluted ceiling high above seemed as remote as heaven itself and the tall windows, ranged along one side of the large space, were grimy with the smoke from fires of sea coal. He caught Mainwaring's eye and Sir Henry made a face before jerking his head for Faulkner to follow, and they pushed forward, causing some disgruntlement in the process. Having reached what appeared to be the front of the assembly, Mainwaring took his station and Faulkner, his left hand upon the hilt of his sword, struck what he thought a pose suitable for the occasion and searched the serried ranks of the courtiers for the face he most wanted to see. He was thus vainly employed when three sharp knocks of a chamberlain's staff reduced the throng to almost instantaneous silence; a fanfare sounded from trumpeters in a gallery somewhere behind them. Then, in a wave of sibilance that was eloquent of submission and subservience, the gentlemen removed their hats, thrust their right legs forward and bowed, while the ladies sank in low curtsies. Faulkner followed suit in a deep bow, some of what Mainwaring had said coming back to him.

All eyes stared at the wooden floor as Their Majesties and their attendants entered the chamber. All Faulkner knew of their progress was the sound of the King's feet on the floor, followed by those of his gentlemen-in-waiting, while the swish of the Queen's gown entered and then left the circle of his vision. There followed another, one that he thought he recognized and yet could hardly believe, the embroidered roses of a dress he had seen but yesterday. He dared not look up until at some signal he entirely missed, the shuffle and flutter of the entire assembled court returning to the vertical, told him he could straighten up.

When he allowed himself to look he saw the King sitting on his throne, his vivacious French consort by his side, her round features pleasantly framed by dark ringlets. Faulkner could not recall anything that transpired in the next few moments with any clarity. The chamberlain seemed to draw several gentlemen from the assembly and lead them forward. Some presented their ladies, others did not. One or two knelt and kissed the King's hand, one man was dubbed a knight, the King standing for the short ceremony, the sword handed him by a courtier waiting ready behind the throne. The assembled court had begun to talk in low, respectful voices as these transactions took place and, from the same gallery that the trumpets had flourished their fanfare, there came now some light chamber music.

It seemed that the chamberlain worked a system as from the assembly he plucked – with great deliberation – those granted an audience of the King. After what seemed an age, during which Faulkner failed to locate any sign of Katherine Villiers among the bevy of ladies standing on the left of Queen Henrietta Maria, Mainwaring moved his head towards Faulkner and said in a low voice, 'Our turn shortly.'

Then the chamberlain stood before them, Mainwaring bowed his head to the chamberlain and Faulkner, almost by instinct, did the same. Then they were led forward and conducted down the empty spaces between the two sides of the thronged court. Faulkner could not tell whether they were being looked at or not, but he felt horribly exposed. Next to him Mainwaring dropped to one knee and he followed, keeping his eyes lowered, so that the polish on the King's square-toed shoes shone under his nose.

'Y–y–you have brought y–your protégé, I see, Sir Henry. You are most welcome, Lieutenant Faulkner.'

He felt a slight nudge from Mainwaring. 'Your Majesty is most kind,' he said.

'I would s–sp–speak with you privately. Pray follow when we leave, Sir Henry. Lieutenant Faulkner...' A strong nudge from Mainwaring caused Faulkner to look up and see the gloved, be-ringed hand. He straightened up and touched his lips lightly against it. The faint scent of soft leather entered his nostrils, then he was standing, following Mainwaring as he backed away from the two thrones with lowered head until the chamberlain, with a gentleman in a sober black suit, was being led forward, and then, quite suddenly, as though awakening from a dream, he was again standing amid the crowd and Mainwaring was smiling at him. He felt confused, flustered and gauche.

'That went well,' Mainwaring muttered.

'When the royal party leaves, fall in step beside me. You may look up once Their Majesties have passed us...'

They stood for another hour before the proceedings showed signs of winding up. The crowd fell almost magically silent, the King rose and extended his hand to the Queen before stepping down and leading her out the way they had come. As Faulkner raised his eyes after the royal pair had passed, two or three gentlemen followed, each leading a lady on his left side. Suddenly he found himself staring straight into the eyes of Katherine Villiers. Her lips showed that she appreciated his presence and he grinned foolishly back at her, a candid expression that instantly removed her own charmingly flirtatious half-smile. Faulkner felt the red invasion of his face, and then Mainwaring had stepped into the wake of the little procession and this time he knew everyone *was* staring at him. He could even hear the interrogative murmur of curiosity as to his identity.

In an antechamber the little procession dissolved and Faulkner, still smarting from Mistress Villiers's disapproval, was left to watch her withdraw with the Queen and the other ladies. Beside a table upon which lay some papers, pens, ink and sand, the King removed his hat and gloves. Faulkner noted again his smallness of stature but, in contrast to the young man whom he had encountered on the quarterdeck of the *Prince Royal*, he had acquired a polished hauteur conveyed in the expression of his face and the manner in which he carried his head. It was a fleeting but indelible impression that struck Faulkner – already sensitive over the bungled grin at Katherine – with considerable force, particularly as he recalled Mainwaring's earlier confidential remark that His Majesty was unreliable.

Mainwaring and Faulkner awaited the King's pleasure at some distance from the table at which the King now sat. Close to him, their heads bent in confidential discussion, were two immaculately attired courtiers, one of whom, he afterwards learned, was Sir Edmund Carleton, a private secretary to the King. Once, Carleton looked up and beckoned a waiting gentleman, who was for some moments included in the conversation before purposefully leaving the room. Then Mainwaring and Faulkner were summoned. For a moment the King discussed some matters concerning the ships-of-war at Plymouth with Mainwaring, about which a nervous Faulkner knew nothing. Then Mainwaring straightened up and stepped backwards, so that the King looked directly at Faulkner.

'M–M–Mr F–F–Faulkner,' the King said, passing his hand across a paper which bore a deal of close-knit handwriting under the King's signature, and to which was appended a heavy red seal, 'your commission as Captain.' Carleton handed the document to Faulkner, followed by a folded and sealed sheet of paper.

'Those are your orders, Captain,' the King added, 'and th–th–these –' again he waved his hand over the table, at which point Carleton picked up a bound and sealed packet and held them for a moment as the King concluded – 'are despatches for His Grace the Duke of Buckingham which you – at your peradventure – will deliver into his hands.'

Faulkner, almost faint from the importance of the moment in which he was not only promoted to Captain but personally charged with carrying the King's despatches to His Majesty's Commander-in-Chief in the field, muttered his gratitude, stepping backwards clasping the papers to his breast as he bowed and retired.

Before they had left the antechamber the King was attending to the next matter Carleton laid before him. Of Katherine Villiers, however, there was no sign.

The following day he was at Deptford to find that Mainwaring had anticipated everything. Quite extraordinarily his command, one of the ten *Lion's Whelps*, lay at the buoys stored and manned as fully as was possible – and which proved just sufficient. Even her officers had been appointed. Sir Henry had kept all this quiet, anxious, though Faulkner never knew it, that he might prove fatally reluctant to abandon his Bristol project. In a sense Mainwaring had indeed guessed a woman lay at the heart of his protégé's motives, though in a different direction to those originally ascribed. Though Mainwaring could not know it, Faulkner's acceptance of command of a King's ship rode entirely upon the encounter with Katherine Villiers that evening in Whitehall, which had entirely eclipsed all thoughts of Julia Gooding.

However, only Faulkner himself could know the queer twist this apparent good fortune had taken by his gaffe in the palace, extinguishing all hopes of making further acquaintance of Mistress Villiers just at the moment they had been rekindled. And now he was charged by King Charles himself to carry despatches to her cousin! In the circumstances he did what he had to and embraced the task to the exclusion of all else. He had no clear idea of the benefit conferred upon him thanks to Mainwaring's solicitude in readying the *Lion's Whelp*, thinking, if he thought about it at all, that Sir Henry had known that he must be off immediately, but he knew how to take advantage of it. Hardly had a dockyard boat taken him on board and an officer and side-party met him, than he sent for his first lieutenant as he made his way aft to the small cabin set aside for the commander. A moment later, to his surprise and delight, his second-in-command knocked on his door and, without awaiting leave to enter, did so.

'Welcome aboard ... sir.'

There was just sufficient of a delay before the term of respect, and just a mocking and familiar tone in the voice to cause Faulkner to spin round. 'Harry! By Heaven 'tis indeed you!'

'I think, Mr Brenton more becoming, Captain Faulkner, now that rank separates us.'

'You are not bitter?' Faulkner asked, suddenly

172

concerned at a future riven with bad blood. 'I had no idea...'

'No indeed, Kit,' Brenton said. 'In fact I solicited the post from Sir Henry when I got wind of the possibility and probably knew before you did yourself.'

'Well, I am damned glad to see you. Now look, we are under orders, special orders, to sail at once. The ebb starts in four hours, can we be away on this tide?'

'If you don't mind dropping down river in the dark.'

'What about the hands? Are they...?'

'In accordance with Sir Henry's orders I mustered them three days ago. We have stood-to at stations twice and manned the great guns once. The sails are in the buntlines...'

'I noticed that. Sir Henry seems to have done more than I could have asked.'

Brenton was grinning at him. 'If I may presume upon our old friendship, Kit, it is you we have all been waiting for. We've poached some damned fine seamen and if we don't cast off tonight my guess is that half of the damned rogues will have run by tomorrow morning.'

'What about food? When did they last eat?'

'They have dined today. All you need is a pilot; that I could not order, not being able to guess your requirements.'

'Sir Henry promised me a pilot from Gravesend. I shall send him a note at the Trinity House whither he has gone. You and I can surely manage the river, it's the estuary I am more wary of.'

'I'll get young Eagles – he met you at the entry – to take your note to Ratcliffe.' Brenton was already making for the cabin door but he turned with it half-open. 'Where is your baggage? And do you have any cabin stores?'

'Cabin stores? No, damn it, I never...'

'No matter. I have enough if we are not bound far, enough for a fortnight or three weeks if we are careful.'

'That is civil of you, Harry.'

Then he was gone and Faulkner called for pen and ink from the purser; his was in his portmanteau just then arriving in his cabin attended by a one-eyed seaman who stood silent until noticed.

'What is it?' Faulkner looked up from the portmanteau.

'I'm Crowe, sir. Your servant.'

'Very well. As you can see, Crowe, I travel light. We shall have to make do...'

'Make do; aye aye, sir.'

A moment later Lieutenant Eagles was knocking at the door. Faulkner had the note ready for him. 'To Ratcliffe in all haste, Mr Eagles...'

'To Sir Henry at the Trinity House?'

'Indeed, yes.'

The night was cloudy and the moon had yet to rise as they slipped the mooring and began to move downstream under topsails filled with the light westerly breeze and the thrust of the ebb tide. Faulkner posted Eagles forward to see them safely past the tiers of lighters, the moored colliers and five huge Indiamen lying off Blackwall. They dodged among a handful of swim-headed lighters ghosting along under their sprit-rigs, and so down to Gravesend where a grizzled old pilot who stank of tobacco clambered aboard, stared at the compass and introduced himself as 'Nairn, Cap'n.'

Faulkner fell to pacing the deck, sending Brenton below with the off-duty men and leaving the deck to the pilot. He had to confess to a nervous thrill; his vessel was small enough, a pinnace of little more than 120 tons burthen and sixty feet in length, but she bore ten guns: eight culverins and demi-culverins of iron, and two brass sakers as chase guns. What was more, her rig was powerful for her size, her three masts reaching up into the darkness, upon the fore and main of which the pale oblongs of the topsails drew manfully. They had set two headsails and the water chuckled along the side as, aided by the tide, they sped down through the Lower Hope before turning through a right angle and headed a little south of east down Sea Reach and the vast estuary of London's River.

Faulkner could not have slept, even had he been able to, for the notion of sole command, notwithstanding the presence of the pilot, caused his heart to beat with a mixture of pride, anxiety and zeal. He had read his orders and knew his business; once clear of The Downs sometime tomorrow forenoon he must press to the westward with all speed, avoiding contact with the enemy until after he had delivered his despatches to the Duke of Buckingham.

He wished Katherine Villiers might see him now – *Captain* Christopher Faulkner; a man enjoying the particular favour of his Majesty King Charles I. Might he not grin to his heart's content, by God? Most certainly he might! And then, just as he was feeling mightily pleased with himself, the thought entered his head that he had yet to get the pinnace out of the estuary which, though seamed with channels, was equally strewn with extensive sandbanks, and although he had brought larger ships out of the Medway bound for Plymouth, he had himself not taken charge of the navigation until beyond the Kentish Forelands. Now the Nore and Knob, the Pansand, the Spaniard, the Last, the Girdler and the Tongue had still to be negotiated. Thank heavens the *Whelp* drew only a few feet. But should not the pilot have put a man in the chains to sound? The question clawed at him; would the pilot tend to the matter without prompting, or should he take the initiative himself? He was, after all, the commander and the responsibility lay entirely with himself. He walked purposely forward.

'Mr Nairn?'

'Cap'n?'

'I, er, I was considering a leadsman...' He was almost ashamed of the tentative note in his own voice.

'Aye, sir. By my reckoning the watch changes in a few minutes. I was holding my hand until then. We'll be down by the Nore by that time and...'

'That is well, Mr Pilot. Do as you will.'

A few minutes later the bell struck and he saw the flit of dark shapes as the watch changed, the men exchanging remarks with their reliefs before going below to the warmth of their hammocks. Eagles came aft from his duty at the knightheads and Faulkner ordered him below too. He was content to keep the deck himself on this, his first night at sea in command.

Suddenly the leadsman's cry came from forward. 'By the deep four!' Every few minutes the call pierced the night air which, apart from the gentle rush of water along the *Whelp*'s side, the creaking of the gear and the low murmur of voices as the watch huddled out of the way forward, was silent. The pilot was a dark figure lit faintly by the pale light in the binnacle next to which he stood, while the helmsman occasionally leaned upon the great curved tiller, making some minor correction to the ship's heading. Faulkner did not interfere with the pilot, who from time to time held a small sandglass to the light of the binnacle. Faulkner could hear him muttering, probably subconsciously, as he did his calculations and adjusted the course. Now and again he would move forward and peer ahead on one bow or the other, then march aft with a modestly triumphant air to resume his station beside the binnacle. A few seconds later Faulkner would see the pale shape of a buoy or sometimes a beacon slide past them, and knew that they were holding true in the south channel,

bound for the North Foreland and the Gull
Stream which led to The Downs off Deal.

The hours passed and they carried the ebb
eastwards; the wind backed a little into the
south-west and they braced the yards accordingly. At about three in the morning the pilot
cast about and, seeing Faulkner, came over to
him.

'You'm lucky, Cap'n. We'll have the ebb
round the Foreland, though it'll likely die afore
we reach The Downs. Are you intending to
anchor?'

'No, Pilot. I'm for the westwards...'

'In this wind? It may freshen from the sou'-
west.'

'Then we shall have to beat; stretch over to the
French coast.'

'Huh! You mind them French corsairs, Cap'n.
They'd like to snap up a handy little man-o'-war
like this'n...' He paused, then added, 'Well, you
can hang out a flag for a punt off Deal an' I'll
take my leave o'you.'

They were fortunate in carrying the ebb
almost as far as Deal before the flood began.
With her fore and main yards braced sharp up,
the forenoon found them signalling for a boat
and by noon they had discharged the pilot, cleared the danger of the Goodwins and stood offshore, the white cliffs above Dover receding
astern. Only then did Faulkner hand over the
deck to Brenton and go below to where Crowe
had prepared his bed-place. Throwing off his
doublet, with Crowe pulling at his boots, he

rolled himself in his blankets and fell instantly asleep.

He had no idea how long he had been sleeping when he felt himself being rudely shaken.

'Cap'n, sir! Cap'n!'

'What the devil...?'

'Cap'n.' Crowe ceased shaking him. 'Mr Brenton's compliments, sir, and he thinks you should be on deck!' No further explanation was needed. Faulkner tumbled out and drew on his boots. Grabbing the cloak Crowe held out for him he drew it round his shoulders over his shirt and ran out on to the quarterdeck.

'What is it?' The question was superfluous. Both Brenton and Eagles stood at the taffrail and stared at the man-of-war three miles astern of them. She was not of the largest class, but something equivalent to an English fourth or fifth-rate. Nor was there need to ask what nationality she was, for even though her three masts were in line, they could see the fly of the large white ensign fluttering just beyond the edges of her sails – the white colours of Bourbon France.

Faulkner felt his mouth go dry and cleared his throat. 'Is she gaining on us, Mr Brenton?'

'Aye, sir, I am afraid so. And we're on the larboard tack, full and bye. She's almost as weatherly as we are with new sails...'

'And if the wind gets up any more, we'll be labouring...'

Faulkner thought a moment, casting about the horizon. He could see the English coast, a faint blue smudge on the northern horizon. How far away was it? Eight, ten miles? An idea occurred to him. 'Hoist our colours,' he said briskly, 'then run the jack up to the fore-truck. Send the men to stations. We'll ease the braces and run her off a little...'

'Won't that allow her to—'

'Do as I say, Mr Brenton, and look lively.' There was an edge to Faulkner's voice that he was not conscious of but both Brenton and Eagles noticed. Brenton met Eagles's eye and he gave an imperceptible shrug.

'Aye aye, sir.'

'Mr Eagles!'

'Sir?'

'Be so kind as to go below and fetch my glass. Crowe will know where it is stowed.'

A few moments later Faulkner was staring not astern at the man-of-war which had followed them round on to their new course, but ahead to where the coast of England took a damnably long time to look any nearer. Closing the telescope with a sharp snap he fell to pacing the deck, attempting to divert his mind and let time prove whether his gamble would pay off. He conceived the idea that if he did not stare at the chasing enemy he would not find it growing larger, a crazy fancy, but one which allowed him to appear composed. One thing, with the enemy so close dead astern, she would have to veer off her course to open fire and it all depended upon whether the French captain would reserve his fire until he had drawn almost alongside, or whether he would attempt to knock their rig about and disable their quarry so that she fell quickly into their hands. The problem with that was that in order to do so, the French man-of-war would lose ground and there was no guarantee that a quick shot – unless it was extraordinarily lucky – would achieve the objective. Better to hold the chase, which in any case was in the larger ship's favour, allowing overwhelming force to be brought to bear with the inevitable consequence of Faulkner's surrender.

The thought made his blood run cold. The wind was increasing, a chill shower of spray burst against the bow and swept aft, stinging the face as it hit them. Surrender? If he was pushed to that extremity he must destroy the King's despatches. Whatever happened to him, it was most important that nothing of the King's communication with Buckingham fell into French hands. He was about to call Eagles to find the sealed package, but then thought better of it. He looked along the line of the deck. He had forgotten all about the crew and now he saw them all, some of the complement of sixty-three men whose stations required them on the upper deck in action, most crouched about their guns, awaiting the word to cast off the breechings.

'Cast off the breechings, Mr Brenton, and load with grape and ball.'

He watched the men stand to their task and then raised the glass again. 'Stand by the braces, Mr Eagles! Steer nor'west a quarter north!'

The *Whelp* steadied on her new course and the men trimmed the yards a little. It was not a large alteration but just sufficient to ... Had he got it right? He must allow for the tide which was against them, but there was a chance and it was the best they had, given sufficient time. He allowed himself a glance astern and was shocked how the enemy had gained upon them. He turned away again and, to calm himself, raised his telescope and peered ahead. Was that...? No, it was only a tumbling wave-cap, one among innumerable white horses that danced over the sea which, here in the Channel, was a deep blue. He looked up; above them a cloudy sky told of a steady wind and no change before dark.

Faulkner could feel the sweat running under his shirt, yet he felt chilled. He made himself pace up and down, up and down, stilling his nerves and resolutely refusing to look astern again. Damn the Frenchman! Damn him to hell! Up and down: think of something other than black disgrace, possible death, certain imprisonment and dishonour at having to ditch the King's despatches. Why did this have to happen to him? Why did he capitulate to the thought of gaining some regard from the lovely, flirtatious and doubtless faithless Katherine Villiers? Why did he not have the good sense to eschew the court, stay in Bristol, marry Julia Gooding and grow fat and prosperous as a Jamaica merchant? God, what a bloody fool he was! Anything was better than this slow torture, this slow road to obloquy! Why had Mainwaring and Strange lifted him out of the gutter? To be taken on his very first day at sea in independent command by some foul dog of a Frenchman?

Faulkner allowed himself another look astern. Above the heaving rail of the *Whelp* the bow-sprit of the Frenchman seemed to loom. It was so close he fancied he could see the cranse iron on the end of the Frenchman's bowsprit itself. He spun and stared ahead. How far now? The coast was perceptibly nearer, but it was still miles away and though there were three or four brown lug-sails under the land they were only fishermen and of no potential use to the harried *Whelp*. Then he thought he could see what he was looking for. It was not yet clear and the tide was high but, nevertheless, they had a chance! He spun round and addressed the man on the tiller.

'Keep her steady now.'

'Steady as she goes, sir,' the seaman respond-ed, although he had been tending to his duty assiduously for the last forty minutes as Brenton hovered nearby.

'What d'you mean to do, sir?' Brenton asked, anxiety written across his usually carefree face.

'Stand on, Mr Brenton, stand on!' Faulkner replied. 'Another ten or fifteen minutes...'

Brenton turned to Eagles, his expression quiz-zical. Eagles frowned, stared ahead then shrug-ged with incomprehension. If Faulkner noticed anything, he ignored it, leaving his officers none the wiser. There was no time for explanations; if his ruse worked, well-and-good; if not it would not be necessary to explain what he was trying to do. For twelve long minutes the chase ran on.

The tension was palpable. The men stood patiently to their guns, every now and then one of them would stand up and stare astern, then crouch down again and report the progress of the Frenchman. Only their commander seemed relatively disinterested in the mighty nemesis creeping up on them from astern.

Faulkner was expecting it, but Brenton noticed it first: a change in the *Whelp*'s motion as she dashed over the seas which caused her to roll gently on the new course. Suddenly there were more breaking wave-caps and as others realized something odd was happening, few quite understood. Then someone looked astern and saw the Frenchman turn away from the wind, his yards coming round as he stood off to the north-east, leaving the *Whelp* to run on to the north and west. They had outwitted their enemy and the distance between them rapidly increased. Ten minutes later they watched the French man-of-war put up her helm and head away, back towards Boulogne in the far distance.

'My congratulations, sir,' said Brenton.

'Thank you, Harry,' Faulkner said quietly. The relief that flooded through him made him feel strangely light-headed, almost weak at the knees. 'Stand the men down, but mind you keep her going on this course until we're under the land before we tack. Short legs to the westwards until after dark. I'm going below.'

Brenton nodded and watched Faulkner as he left the deck. Then Eagles was beside him.

'Harry, what the devil did we do?'

Brenton looked at the younger man and grinned. 'You don't understand?'

Eagles shook his head. 'No. One minute we were about to be overtaken and the next the whole thing is over.'

'I must confess, I didn't comprehend it at first but Captain Faulkner took us over the Varne Bank. We draw only nine feet while that fellow will draw nearer twenty...' He let the explanation sink in and Eagles's eyes widened with appreciation.

'The devil,' he breathed, admiringly.

Although the wind remained contrary for the entire passage, it did not freshen and by keeping under the English coast until they were well to the west, the *Whelp* beat her way down Channel, tack by patient tack and using the tide when it served. The encounter with the Frenchman also affected morale for, although the decks were wet and water found its way below so that the pinnace became a thing of damp misery, the mood of the little *Whelp* was sustained by the outcome and men began to mutter that Faulkner was a 'lucky' man. It would have surprised him to have heard how his cool nonchalance was admired among the simple souls who manned his ship, but all unknowingly he had established a name for himself in a modest way during that anxious hour or two.

Ten days later they had doubled Ushant and, having stood some leagues further south, turned in towards the land, hoping to make a landfall on the Île de Rhé.

Six

Buckingham

1628

'If I may speak frankly, Kit, I like this not at all...'

Faulkner looked at Brenton who sat opposite at the table as they finished off a postprandial bottle. The necessity of having to heave to for the night in order to close the French coast in the light of morning suggested to Faulkner that he should invite Brenton to dine with him. So, with the deck left to Eagles, the two old friends relaxed after their meal, the air grew thick with tobacco smoke as the *Whelp* gently breasted the incoming swells from the broad Atlantic and the wind, not more than a gentle westerly, soughed in the rigging.

'What don't you like?' Faulkner asked, diverting his mind from its preoccupation with his coming meeting with the Duke of Buckingham and the light in which it would cast him. At the bottom of his thoughts lay the troubling image of the lovely Mistress Villiers.

'These policies of the King's,' Brenton said. 'Do not mistake my meaning, I beg you. I am as loyal as the next man, but he is in deep trouble with Parliament who resist all attempts to force tax-raising measures through. I have heard that money has been demanded in the form of forced loans and refusal to pay has meant imprisonment for those gentlemen unwilling to comply with the royal will. As for the troops and the seamen, both are ill-paid and word comes from Buckingham's forces that they are mutinous, they hate the Duke, and could not care a fig for the Huguenots, wanting only to get back home. Truly little will come of this policy other than that His Majesty will blight the fortunes of the Palatinate abroad and cause terrible dissent at home.'

During their acquaintance aboard the *Prince Royal* Faulkner had developed a respect for Brenton's independence of thought. Brenton owed his position and commission to the fact that he came from a good family and he in turn had rapidly determined that Faulkner, though a thoroughly able sea-officer, possessed no patronage beyond that of Sir Henry Mainwaring and had no family. Consequently Brenton saw the technically-able but somewhat politically naïve Faulkner in part as a sounding board for his own political opinions, but also as a malleable accomplice, while at the same time being one who was likely to rise in the sea-service. Brenton had no clear objective in thus cultivating Faulkner, but he sensed the rift between the King and Parliament was serious, and knew, far better than either Faulkner or Mainwaring, the mood of the greater part of the English people.

Faulkner frowned. He did not understand the political point of English support of the Palatinate beyond a vague comprehension of the King's sister being the Elector Palatine's wife. As for domestic politics, he was apt to think of them attaching solely to the Court, entirely forgetting the rising power of Parliament, though he recognized well enough the attachment of the Puritans and the Dissenters – like the Gooding family – to the Commons.

'Dissent? How mean you?' he asked.

'Did you not detect it in Bristol?' Brenton paused. 'You spoke of your people there being sober and somewhat dull Puritans, I thought.'

Faulkner frowned. 'Yes, but I cannot recall expressions of dissent ... though Sir Henry...' He broke off, recalling that Mainwaring's remark about the King's unreliability had been in confidence.

'Sir Henry...?'

'Oh, 'twas nothing and likely I misunderstood.'

'Sir Henry expressed a disloyal opinion did he?' Brenton asked, leaning forward with a smile on his face. 'Then he is shrewder than I thought,' he said, adding in a slightly cynical tone, 'I had marked him for a King's man, through and through.'

'I have no doubt but that he is, utterly,' Faulkner said hurriedly. 'I am no political beast, Harry, preferring to leave those matters to those better equipped to deal with them.'

'Like My Lord Muckingham with his open purse and tight fist, revelling in the King's high opinion and seducing him from his proper regard for the good of his people. You cannot surely think that Buckingham's policies, which the King follows as a dog does a bitch in heat, will lead to any advantage. The King is bankrupt of funds and damn nigh bankrupt of friends.'

'And in consequence we are defeated in France,' Faulkner responded. 'Against which you must allow our ships have done much execution among French shipping in the Channel. It was with the intent of revenging themselves of that disadvantage that we met our friend of the other day.'

'That is true, to be sure, but to hold the sea you must maintain a fleet and we shall find that increasingly impossible, if indeed, it is not already impossible.'

'I think you are too gloomy in your prognostications, Harry. We shall see what state our arms are in tomorrow.'

'We will indeed.'

The following morning they sailed into the Pertuis Breton and the fleet anchorage off the Île de Rhé to find all was in confusion, as what seemed like hundreds of boats were pulled industriously betwixt the ships and the shore. The English standard still flew above the fortress on St Martin but as Faulkner learned within moments of stepping ashore, Buckingham had given orders for the withdrawing of his forces. Faulkner asked the whereabouts of the English commander of an officer of foot who was cursing a motley and ill-disposed mob of men whose semblance to an infantry regiment was negligible as they almost fought their way down to the stone harbour and the waiting boats.

'My Lord Duke? God knows. Are you from England?'

'Aye, with despatches for the Duke of Buckingham.'

'From the King?' the man asked, lowering his voice. Faulkner nodded. 'If I were you, I should keep that quiet.' He was about to resume herding his men, but added, 'Unless they bring orders to withdraw, you are wasting your time. This has been a disaster; Richelieu has outfoxed us, the Rochellais despair of us and are treating with the Cardinal, we have little food and the islanders hate us. The sooner this lot are back on English soil, the better. To be truthful, there have been moments when I feared for my own life, not from the enemy but my own men, for God's sake!' At that he turned away and marched down to the harbour. None the wiser as to the whereabouts of Buckingham, Faulkner began to walk inland, past more groups of men bearing pikes and arquebusses making their way down to the boats of the fleet. No one seemed interested in the location of their commander-in-chief and several intemperately expressed their devout wish that he was in hell.

The hostility of the dishevelled and retiring troops increased the further he walked away from the landing up the rising ground. Every-where the tents were coming down and cooking fires were being extinguished and bivouacs cleared. The sparse villages and settlements of the fisher-folk and subsistence sheep-farmers looked neglected, as though the mere presence of the English army had blighted them, while of their inhabitants and their domestic livestock there was scant sign. After an hour Faulkner had made his way to the outer works of the fortress at St Martin. It took him a further half-hour to make his way into the citadel where he was assured Buckingham had his headquarters by the milling soldiery. The lack of direction was palpable, an air of confusion prevailing every-where. No one seemed interested in the fact that he carried the King's despatches, a fact he was compelled to announce in order to make any headway at all. In due course, however, his dog-ged persistence paid off and he encountered an elegantly dressed young man wearing half-armour whose very appearance, in such contrast to the rest of the dishevelled army, hinted strongly that he was part of Buckingham's per-sonal suite. After explaining his mission, Faulk-ner was finally led into the Duke's presence.

In the company of several other high-ranking officers, Buckingham sat behind a table upon which the remains of a meal, some empty bot-tles and a few papers lay littered. Although Buckingham was dressed as elegantly as ever, his doublet was undone and it was clear that a deal of drinking had accompanied what Faulkner took to be a council of war. The young officer bowed and introduced him.

'Your Grace, Captain Faulkner, newly arrived from London with His Majesty's despatches.'

It was clear that Buckingham had need to pull himself together. This was reflected by the conduct of the others. A gleam of recognition entered Buckingham's eyes as Faulkner stepped forward and presented his sealed package and the covering letter.

'Faulkner ... You were aboard the *Prince Royal*, were you not?'

'I was, Your Grace.'

Buckingham grunted, shaking off the lassitude of overindulgence as he fumbled with the buttons of his doublet. 'Pen and ink!' he ordered, and his military secretary brought both. Buckingham scribbled his signature against the receipt Faulkner handed him with the sealed packet. Then he tore at the seal and began unwrapping the contents, looking up briefly at Faulkner. 'Very well, Captain. You may go.'

'Your Grace.' Faulkner bowed. 'May I enquire whether you have any orders for me?'

'Orders? Why, pick up as many of these damned dogs as you can, and convey them to Portsmouth,' he said dismissively, at which point one of the officers rose.

'With your permission, Your Grace, I will embark with Captain Faulkner.'

The move seemed to galvanize Buckingham who suddenly enquired, 'What is your ship, Captain?'

'The *First Lion's Whelp*, Your Grace.'

Buckingham's face visibly brightened. 'A *Whelp*, by God! No, Goring, you may not. She is mine and I shall reserve her for myself.' He smiled at Faulkner. 'Pray refresh yourself, Captain, while I digest His Majesty's wishes.'

Faulkner withdrew with the young staff officer, who introduced himself as Captain Charles Aylwin, and accepted a glass of wine and a slice of sausage. After a few moments the man identified as Goring led the other senior officers out and Aylwin went in to see the Duke, emerging a few moments later to beckon Faulkner inside. Buckingham stood, his doublet fully buttoned, all trace of his former *déshabillé* eradicated.

'Captain, you have doubtless seen the state to which we are reduced and that the army is under orders to embark. The commands that you have brought are quite impossible. I shall come aboard your *Whelp* at daylight, by which time the embarkation will be completed and we may weigh and proceed home.'

'I shall make the necessary preparations, Your Grace.'

If Faulkner expected any personal advantage to accrue to himself for the conveying of His Grace the Duke of Buckingham on his homeward passage, he was to be, yet again, disappointed. No flag flew at the *Whelp*'s main-truck to reveal the presence of the Lord High Admiral of England: that remained at the masthead of the flagship.

The Duke's passage in the *Whelp* allowed him to enter England quietly without ceremony so that he was at the King's side before the reports of the extent of the military disaster reached His Majesty. Being alongside the King enabled Buckingham to smoothly explain the losses of men and *matériel*, usually by blaming the conduct of others. The consequences of this were to be dire: the King learned nothing about military operations nor ever lost the habit of foisting the blame for his own later military incompetence upon the shoulders of other men.

Unaware of all this, the departure of the Duke left Faulkner with a false sense of his own importance and orders to take the *Whelp* out on a cruise and – within the limits of his stores – wage war upon French commerce before laying her up for the winter at Deptford.

In this, however, Faulkner achieved a modest success, enhancing his own growing reputation by taking four French coasting vessels off the island of Marcouf before escaping over the horizon, only to make a brief appearance at Harfleur where he put the local fishing fleet to flight after taking three of their number. He was most lucky in discovering a laden merchantman at anchor off St Valéry en Caux which he carried off under the noses of the French ashore. Thereafter, and fearing the pursuit of a ship-of-war such as they had encountered on their outward passage, he headed for the Thames where the *Whelp* was paid off and the evidence of his prizes entered before the Prize Court. With Buckingham owning the *Whelp* he anticipated no problems in securing favourable adjudications and before Christmas he was able to pay those men who answered his summons to Deptford the monies due to them. His officers, Brenton and Eagles especially, all pocketed sums which, though modest enough, pleased them mightily. As for himself, he was some two hundred pounds better off, though he had enriched Buckingham by three times that amount.

Though no great exploit, the cruise of the *Whelp* under Faulkner was sufficiently known about to persuade the Court of Trinity House to take notice of him. Mainwaring advised him to invest in a London ship, and Faulkner purchased the majority shareholding in a 200-ton snow named the *Perseus*, all of which caused his election as a Younger Brother of the Trinity House.

Early the following year Faulkner's new ship was among those chartered to convey to the newly established colony of Maryland – named in honour of the Queen who was thus known at Court – some of the fifteen hundred orphans and homeless children found on the streets of London. The business detained Faulkner in London for several months and in this manner he took no part in Denbigh's resumption of operations from the Île de Rhé in support of the Huguenots of La Rochelle that year. Denbigh had married a sister of Buckingham's and thereby obtained the chief command. However, his stay in the Pertuis Breton was short-lived – a mere seven days – before he returned home, to the fury of the King who had given his word to support the Protestant cause.

These circumstances enraged the public, many of whom were inflamed at the King's treatment of Parliament over the Petition of Rights, which he first approved and then, entering Parliament in person, promptly repudiated. The populace of London, always sensitive to political turmoil, began to appear on the streets in a bloody mood. Milling crowds called for Buckingham's impeachment even as the Commons solemnly attributed all the ills of the kingdom to Buckingham's malign influence on the King. The Duke was reliably reported to have brushed aside the powers of Parliament, claiming that neither the House of Lords, nor the House of Commons, could touch the hair of a dog if it lay under the King's protection. The implication was clear: he was, alongside the King, above Parliament. The matter came to a head when a mob murdered the Duke's physician, Doctor Lambe, attaching to the corpse a placard which asked:

Who ruled the Kingdom? – The King.
Who ruled the King? – The Duke.
Who ruled the Duke? – The Devil.

Meanwhile, in taverns and ale-houses the doggerel was roared out that:

Let Charles and George do what they can,
The Duke shall die like Dr Lambe

Only vaguely aware of these disturbances, Faulkner's preoccupation with his Maryland venture was abruptly ended when he received orders to recommission the *Whelp* and join a squadron then forming at Deptford where Buckingham would embark for Portsmouth. Yet another expedition was intended to sail for France, a move widely regarded as stupid and designed solely to recover the King's reputation in Europe, of which no one anticipated success, except Buckingham and the King himself.

Though thought to be concerned about the Duke's safety, the King accompanied Buckingham to Deptford where the Lord High Admiral once again embarked. Faulkner, keen to ensure that nothing went wrong with the firing of salutes and the getting under way of the squadron, took no part in the ceremonials of embarkation. Indeed, he was not happy until the ships had cleared The Downs and stood down Channel where the cool breeze blew away the complications of the shore. He was beginning to loathe the predominance of political argument that seemed about to tear the country asunder; it seemed that every street corner produced its orator, even in the purlieus of Wapping and along the Ratcliffe Highway. Even the Brethren of Trinity House – good seamen to a man – whose main concern was the regulating of pilotage on the Thames and the dispensing of charity to the wretched wounded and incapacitated seamen of the King's ill-run navy and their widows and orphans, were not averse to falling into violent argument over the rights of the King versus those of the Parliament.

From time to time he encountered Mainwaring there and his old protector seemed bowed under the weight of his duties and responsibilities. 'We must hold together,' Mainwaring had asserted, 'else our legitimacy will be compromised.'

To which another of their number, a Younger Brother named William Rainsborough, had interjected, 'Aye, Sir Henry, you are right, but does our legitimacy derive from the will of the King, or is it for the benefit of the poor? His Majesty had left us in our beneficent goodness to attend to the abuses he promotes under His Grace of Buckingham...'

'But these differences are passing, Rainsborough,' Mainwaring had maintained.

'Let us hope so, Sir Henry. Let us hope so,' Rainsborough had responded.

The Duke's squadron joined the other men-of-war and transports assembled at Spithead towards the end of August. Again the season was late and within a month the equinoctial season would be upon them, but still Buckingham delayed, almost as contemptuous of the weather as he was of the common people of England. He sent orders for his captains to join him ashore for breakfast on the 23rd and Faulkner received his summons the night before, ordering a boat for early next morning. He was fortunate in having again secured the services of Brenton and Eagles, along with many of his former hands who, hearing of the hot press sent out to round up all available seamen for the new expedition, had chosen to volunteer with the 'lucky' Captain Faulkner.

That morning Faulkner arrived at the Sally Port early and made his way to Buckingham's quarters, where he learned the Duke was in conference with Monsieur Soubise, the Huguenot representative. After a confused buffet with some two score of captains and officers jostling for viands in a small room in which Soubise's own suite were also milling, Faulkner heard his name called. Summoned to Buckingham's side as he made to leave the room, the Duke introduced him to the King's secretary, Carleton, whom Faulkner recognized from the audience at Whitehall Palace. They had left the main room and were in the entrance lobby, approaching the door to the street where a coach waited for Buckingham. Having attended to the formalities, the Duke drew on his gloves, saying:

'Captain Faulkner, be so kind as to conduct Mr Secretary Carleton to your *Whelp*, weigh anchor and carry him through the fleet, so that he may convey a report of our strength and preparedness to the King.'

Buckingham did not wait for an acknowledgement for he turned immediately to an officer on his far side. Faulkner was in the act of addressing Sir Edmund Carleton when he was shoved rudely aside. Losing his balance, he stumbled and swung round as a powerful man, having pushed Faulkner aside, plunged a knife into Buckingham's chest.

'Villain!' cried the Duke, plucking the blade from his own body and falling back into the arms of those behind him as blood started from his breast and mouth. Cries of 'Murder!' and 'Assassin!' alerted the others, including the Duchess of Buckingham in the rooms above, so that she and her sister, the Countess of Anglesey, rushed on to the landing. Their screams added to the pandemonium below where Buckingham lay in his own gore, the life ebbing fast from him. As someone slammed the doors closed, others cried out for the whereabouts of the murderer and a man stepped forward.

'I am he,' he said calmly, from the open door of the adjacent kitchen. At first few heard him in the hubbub and then Carleton grabbed Faulkner's arm.

'Seize and hold him!' he said and, as others realized the man had confessed to his crime, the rasp of swords being tugged from their scabbards added to the uproar. Swiftly Faulkner, Carleton and several men surrounded the assassin and denied others the presumed right to summarily execute the murderer, who remained quiet and self-possessed throughout, until in due course, his victim having been declared dead, he was taken away in irons.

'He did not deny it,' Faulkner subsequently told Mainwaring. Soon afterwards La Rochelle capitulated, only four of its fifteen thousand inhabitants remaining, most reduced to living skeletons thanks to their trust in King Charles and the Duke of Buckingham. As for those English seamen who had taken part, none held their heads high except perhaps John Felton, Buckingham's executioner.

'He was a gentleman, a lieutenant owed arrears of pay for his services before La Rochelle and, so I am told,' explained Mainwaring, 'a man who confessed the crime without torture, claiming he had killed the Duke so for God and this country...' Mainwaring shook his head. 'They say that when brought to the Tower the people cheered him and set him up as David as opposed to Goliath, and when imprisoned in the Tower the Earl of Dorset threatened him with the rack if he did not reveal his accomplices. Do you know what he said?'

Faulkner shook his head.

'"I am ready for that. But I must tell you that I will then accuse you, my Lord of Dorset, and none other."'

'I heard he was hanged at Tyburn,' Faulkner said.

'Aye and is gibbeted at Portsmouth. The King wanted him racked but the Attorney-General demurred – he was too popular.'

'What make you of such a man and such a deed, Sir Henry?' Faulkner enquired.

Mainwaring looked at Faulkner and saw in the question the deficiencies of the education that he had conferred upon his protégé. 'John Felton preceded the executioner, Kit. Buckingham had far over-reached himself and his death by Felton's hand only puts off a day of coming evil.

Parliament already had its hounds on My Lord Duke's trail and it was only a matter of time...' For some moments Mainwaring stared at Faulkner and then asked, 'Are you still minded to make something of Bristol?'

Faulkner looked up. He had not considered the matter of his future since again laying up the *Whelp* at Deptford. 'I do not know. I have connections here with the Trinity House and yourself, not to mention the *Perseus*...' The image of Katherine Villiers floated into his mind's eye. Almost without thinking he asked, 'What of Mistress Villiers? Have you heard of her?'

'Mistress Villiers? Do you still yearn after her, Kit?'

'I entertained some hopes...' he said in a low voice.

'I understand that her cousin's fate has ensured that she stands high in the Queen's favour.' Mainwaring paused. 'I think, Kit, she is beyond your grasp.'

'I fear so.' Faulkner caught Mainwaring's eye. 'In that case I shall make my way to Bristol, if the Trinity House will approve my decision.'

'I have no doubt but that can be arranged. I am being pressed to stand for election as Master...'

'And I hear that you are betrothed, Sir Henry,' Faulkner said with an assumed cheerfulness, 'in which case allow me to drown my sorrows and drink to your health.'

'Over a good dinner, Kit, after which you shall meet my bride-to-be.'

'That I should very much like.'

Part Two

A Ship for the King

Part Two

Seven

High Barbary

January – September 1637

'Is that Captain Faulkner?' Faulkner peered from beneath the wide brim of his hat from which the torrential rain poured as from a downpipe. Driven by a strong westerly wind the winter rain lashed the two men cruelly as they met in the narrow street. 'Who asks?'

'Captain William Rainsborough. It is Faulkner, is it not?'

'Indeed it is, though one is like to meet the devil on such an evening.'

'Aye. God help sailors on such a night.'

'Amen to that. Do you have business with me, Rainsborough?'

'I do...'

'Shall we then adjourn; the King's Head is hard by.'

'By all means, Faulkner, by all means. Anything to get out of this damnable rain.'

Inside the tavern Rainsborough threw off his sodden hat, gloves and cloak, shaking his long dark hair as he kicked out a stool from under a table. He was a well-made and imposing man whom Faulkner recalled from the Trinity House. They shook hands. 'What brings you to Bristol, Captain?'

'Please call me William. I know you to be a Younger Brother of the London House and that is partly why I am here.'

'I am indeed, as I know you to be too. And, by the way, I am known to my friends as Kit.'

'Well then, let us have a glass before I answer your question...'

'Allow me, I am known here...' Faulkner called for wine and food as the two men drew up chairs as close to the fire as they could, though the tavern was not crowded that wet evening.

With a tankard in front of each of them Rainsborough said, 'I am come to see you and ask you to join our expedition. I will be frank with you, I would rather have stayed in London where I have much to occupy myself, but in deference to Sir Henry Mainwaring's wishes I am here to solicit your assistance.'

'I know of no expedition,' Faulkner replied. 'Indeed the very word is like to numb me since I was associated with Buckingham's ill-fated expeditions to La Rochelle.'

'Well this is no repeat of Buckingham's policy, though it is something that man might have undertaken with better effect upon the country and his own standing therein. No, we are intending an expedition to Sallee, to attack the pirates' stronghold there and break them so that they no longer terrorize our coasts. We have petitioned the King and he is in favour but, and with Our Gracious Majesty there is usually a but, there are insufficient King's ships ready, though two may be made available. This is a mercantile venture, an armed mercantile venture, though we will sail under the King's commission and therefore make of ourselves his servants for the purpose.'

'And I assume the King wishes us to subsidize this expedition ourselves,' Faulkner said ruefully.

Rainsborough smiled and took a swig of his ale. 'Not quite,' he answered after wiping his beard, 'we provide the ships, the officers and men, but a portion of Ship Money will be placed at our disposal to fund contingent expenses plus the commissioning of such men-of-war as the royal dockyards yield.'

'Ship Money is not a phrase to be talked of here in a loud voice.'

'I was not aware of using a loud voice,' Rainsborough rejoined.

'In a manner of speaking, I mean,' Faulkner said, aware that Rainsborough's bonhomie was conditional. 'Though much of Bristol sides with the King, there are those who do object to such a tax. But what of me, William? Why dost though come all the way to Bristol to see me? Just because Sir Henry Mainwaring wished you to?'

'In part, but also because the *Perseus* mounts twenty guns of heavy metal, we know you have her properly manned with a gunner and competent mates and we would have her in the squadron. As she is presently lying in the Pool I wanted a quick decision.'

'Surely there are plenty of London ships mounting such artillery?'

'Aye, but not many are owned by Brethren. Besides, she is a fine ship and we wish to charter her, preferably with you in command since her present master is unwell and has had no previous naval experience.'

'I know him to be unwell, though not sufficiently indisposed to be replaced, which he will not like...'

'Come, Kit, are you willing or no?'

Faulkner smiled. 'Did you think that I was so rooted in this place that you could not winkle me out?'

'I had heard you were comfortably placed. When a man has amassed a fortune he is reluctant to leave his hearth and his fortune in the hands of others. Besides, you are married, are you not? When a man marries he is less predictable.'

'You have come a long way for a rejection, William, so out of fellow feeling I shall agree to join you, though I must contact my agent and arrange for such lading as is intended for the *Perseus* to be loaded aboard another vessel.'

'Is that problem insuperable?'

Faulkner shook his head. 'No. I have shares in a small brig named *Pegasus* and if I do not delay, matters may be satisfactorily arranged.'

'I can take letters for London myself, if you

wish.'

'Good. Then that is settled. Now, tell me more...'

They fell to discussing details and were thus occupied until about nine o'clock, when the tavern door opened to reveal a sodden wet Nathan Gooding, anxiety writ large upon his face.

'Kit! There you are; we were all wondering where on earth you had got to on such a night.'

'Ah, Nat, I was on my way home when I encountered Captain William Rainsborough come especially from London to see me on business. William, this is my partner and brother-in-law, Nathan Gooding.' Rainsborough stood and the two men shook hands.

'Julia was anxious about you,' Gooding said when they sat again and had ordered ale for him.

'Julia worries overmuch,' Faulkner said.

There was an awkward silence and then Gooding, looking between the two men who showed little sign of moving, asked, 'May I ask the nature of your business Captain Rainsborough?'

Rainsborough looked at Faulkner. 'I think it best Kit tells you himself, Mr Gooding.'

'Please, call me Nat.'

'As you wish.'

Gooding now stared expectantly at Faulkner. 'It concerns the London ship, Nat...'

'The *Perseus*?'

'Aye. Captain Rainsborough wishes to charter her as an armed merchantman on an expedition intended to punish the Sallee Rovers for their

209

temerity in attacking our coasts.'

'That is good news indeed. They have long been asking for a lesson and for too long have used Lundy Island as a lair.'

Faulkner explained the nature of the operation and its quasi-private status, pricking the bubble of Gooding's enthusiasm when he remarked at his conclusion that: 'I shall myself be taking command...'

'You...?'

Faulkner nodded.

'But I thought ... Julia will not like this, Kit...'

'Maybe not, but this is an important service and I am determined.' Faulkner made to rise, inviting Rainsborough to lodge the night with them but he demurred.

'I think, if they have a room here, I shall remain. Besides, clearly you have matters to resolve and my presence would be a hindrance. I shall call upon you tomorrow for your letter for your man in London, thereafter I shall expect you to follow as soon as you are able.'

'Very well.' The three men rose and shook hands. Then Faulkner and Gooding stepped out into the lashing rain and made their way home.

Julia's anxiety for their whereabouts was plain on her handsome face and Faulkner silenced her protestations with a kiss.

'Heavens, you are both sodden,' she cried, taking their cloaks and spreading them over the backs of two upright chairs, then placing them before the fire.

'Julia,' Gooding said, 'Kit has some news. It is

best that I retire and leave you to discuss matters. Goodnight.'

When he had gone and Faulkner had drawn off his boots and stockings so that he wriggled his toes comfortably before the hearth, Julia came and knelt at his knee. 'Nat's tone was ominous, Kit. What is this about?'

He looked at her, his right hand toying with a stray lock of her hair that, at the end of the day, had escaped its confinement. His feelings towards her, even after six years of marriage, were still strong. She was a lovely creature, a mass of contradictions that kept him in thrall: prim, proper, yet well read, self-assured and opinionated by day, but capable of a physical love that had transformed him by the depths of its passion. For her, he was strong and handsome; a man of substance rather than great wealth, steady, reliable but possessed of some unfathomable quality over which she had long fretted in the privacy of her own thoughts. Her sense of this encouraged her to exert herself in their private life, binding him as close to her as she knew how, for she worried that what she sensed was a restlessness in his spirit that she could never satisfy.

They had not had children and she worried that this was God's judgement, for she was aware that the strong physical attraction that had drawn her to him was in opposition to the wishes of her late mother who had warned her of violent passion, especially for one 'who was not of their kind'. And while Nathan approved for

211

reasons of business, he too was less happy on grounds of religion. Kit Faulkner rarely accompanied them to Sunday worship these days, though he had done so in days of his brief courtship of Julia and during the first years of their marriage. True he bore more of the appearance of a Puritan than he had formerly done; his dress was less flamboyant than when in Mainwaring's service, but he was insufficiently interested in the deep scriptural debates that preoccupied many of the Goodings' fellow Dissenters to take much notice of them. This distressed Gooding himself, though Julia made light of it.

'He has a sound, true and loyal heart, Brother,' she had said when Gooding raised the matter. 'That is much to be encouraged in this uncertain world.'

'Aye, but I can never quite forget that he was among Buckingham's men...' he had responded.

'I think that unfair; certainly he was close to Mainwaring and he to the King's service, but that is far from becoming Buckingham's man. Besides, Buckingham has been dead near ten years.' Gooding had said nothing in reply, but his expression betrayed his dubiety. 'That he is not fulsome in the practice of our religion,' Julia had rattled on, trying to convince her brother, 'may be a matter of time. Let God do his work, Nathan.'

Gooding had turned to look at his sister. 'I fear you are besotted with him Julia. I have seen the carnal gleam in your eyes...'

'Nathan!' she had risen, outraged at his presumption. 'How can you speak so? Perhaps if you were yourself married you would understand love—'

'Love? I do not doubt Kit's sincerity or his honesty, but he remains closely allied to Mainwaring and we know the old pirate to be close to the Court, and not to our principles. The news from London is all about the assumption of power by the King to the detriment of Parliament. There is much talk of an imminent rupture between the two—'

'There have been those before—'

'Yes, and each succeeding schism is worse than that which preceded it. I fear a permanent division that will precipitate strife of an altogether different kind.'

'And how does this affect Kit and I, Brother?' she had asked.

To which Gooding had replied, 'Much will depend upon which way your husband will jump, Sister.'

Now she stared at her husband full of foreboding, for the tone of his last remark had caught at some apprehension deep inside her.

'Dost love me, Julia?' Faulkner asked as he cupped her cheek and she pressed his hand against it.

'Why ask, husband?'

'Because the news of which Nathan spoke will not be to your liking.'

She drew back. 'What is it?'

'I am to go to sea again...' He watched the import of his words sink in. They had been talking of relinquishing their old lodgings above the haberdasher's shop and buying a larger house. It was a pleasing prospect, and the more so since the possibility existed that Julia had conceived, but this was not the first such occasion and she thought best to wait before telling her husband, having several times previously miscarried.

'But Kit, you promised ... You are a shipowner of some standing; it is unnecessary...'

'It is necessary, my darling. Listen to me and I shall explain. The King has no ships and has received a petition from the Brethren of Trinity House to mount a punitive raid upon the pirates of Sallee. You know enough about the villains to understand that they must be extirpated and to this end I was visited tonight by William Rainsborough, a fellow Brother of the London House, who wishes me to make the *Perseus* available as an armed man-of-war – a service for which she is ideal – and sail under his flag.' He paused, allowing her to digest this information. 'This is an important public service, Julia. It is no foolish tilting at France, as Buckingham was wont to do, nor is it a voyage made for profit alone, but one which will put an end to the wholesale rape and kidnap and God knows what foul consequences of these raids upon our coasts. It is shameful that we have tolerated them for so long...'

Her fine eyes were full of tears and she nodded. ''Tis a noble enough venture, I see, but must *you* go?'

Faulkner smiled. 'Old Morris is unsuitable and

while his mates are staunch enough fellows, they will need a steady hand. Besides, it will not be for more than three months.'

'Three months,' she said wistfully, thinking of the possible quickening in her womb. In three months she would be certain and the matter would be beyond doubt.

'Well?' he asked. 'I would rather go with your blessing, than without it. What do you say?'

'That you will go whatever I say, for I have never tried to rule you, Kit.'

'Only in the matter of religion,' he said with a wide grin.

'And I failed there,' she responded. She laid her head on his knee, whereupon she was struck by a terrible thought. Suppose she successfully carried their child, only to lose her husband on this noble quest. She looked up at him. 'What if you were to be killed?' she asked sharply.

'What if I were to be despatched by an encounter with a brewer's dray tomorrow? Would you have me in a rush basket to preserve me from harm?'

'I would have you in my bed, husband,' she said, giving up. 'You may go with my blessing and I shall pray to God to preserve you, and if he does I shall require that you devote yourself to my religion and path of righteousness on your return.'

'I rather think that depends upon Archbishop Laud and his attempts to make us all of one church,' he said, smiling.

Julia shook her head. 'Why does the King

promise one thing and then place himself under the influence of yet another with a stronger will than he possesses.'

Faulkner raised an eyebrow. 'Aye, and then claim his rights are divine. You would think that one who sat close to God would know his own mind and stick to an honest policy.' He sighed. 'Sometimes I do not know what to think or who to believe.'

'But you know *what* to believe, Kit,' Julia said with an intensity of meaning that he disliked.

'Do I? I am not so certain...'

'But,' pressed Julia, thinking of the possibility of their changed familial prospects in three months, 'you must promise that when you return you will take some instruction for the safety of your immortal soul.'

Faulkner grinned at her again. 'Then you had better pray that I am not taken prisoner, nor forced to turn apostate, become circumcised and embrace the Mussulman religion.' And before she could determine whether or not he joked, he bent and kissed her, his right hand freeing her hair with a twist so that it tumbled about her heaving shoulders.

A week later Faulkner was in London where, under a lowering mid-February sky, he found matters moved apace. Rainsborough had acted with commendable speed, in marked contrast to the slow deliberations of the formal Admiralty. He had presented his petition to the King in January and by the end of the month had both

216

approval and funding from the third levy of Ship Money to fit out several ships for war. To two regular men-of-war, the 36-gun *Leopard* and *Antelope*, were added the armed merchantmen, *Hercules*, *Mary* and *Perseus*, and two former *Whelps*, each of 14-guns, now renamed the *Providence* and *Expedition*. Rainsborough was appointed admiral and, with the single exception of the vice admiral, George Carteret, in the *Antelope*, all the commanders were experienced mercantile shipmasters and members of the Fraternity of Trinity House.

Faulkner threw himself immediately into the business of fitting the *Perseus* for war, securing a requisition of powder and shot, extra small arms and, on promise of a generous bounty, a crew. He was pleased to note several of the *Perseus*'s regular crew answer his call to muster, and even more gratified to see three men who had served with him in the *Lion's Whelp* ten years earlier. Captain Morris was persuaded to leave his ship and retire, at least for a while, and Faulkner addressed the ship's two mates, a sturdy Yorkshireman named Lazenby and a Londoner named Norris.

'Well, gentlemen, you shall be commissioned lieutenants for the duration of the commission. Some matters you may find a little different, and your skills in keeping station may be taxed, but otherwise your experience will stand you in good stead. I understand from Captain Morris that both of you are doughty fellows and I shall expect nothing less. Are you willing?'

'Aye, sir,' they both replied.

By the end of February the *Perseus* was ready for sea and she dropped downstream to join the squadron, then at anchor in The Downs. Here Rainsborough joined his flagship, the *Leopard*, a new vessel of over 500 tons, built only three years previously to a design in which Sir Henry Mainwaring had had a hand. On 4th March Rainsborough gave the signal to weigh anchor and although they ran foul of a south-westerly gale and the *Hercules* lost her mainmast, being obliged to put into Lisbon for repairs, the majority of the squadron brought to their anchors off the Moroccan coast on 24th March, where the *Hercules* rejoined them on 18th April.

The speed of the departure of the ships was to ensure that they were in a position to blockade the pirates before the customary date of their departure for a cruise in northern waters, and in this they were entirely successful, for from the mastheads some fifty vessels could be seen lying ready in the Bou Regreb River, a fact confirmed by a reconnoitring boat sent from the *Leopard* shortly after the ships had anchored and prior to Rainsborough calling for a council of war.

Faulkner joined the other captains assembled in Rainsborough's cabin that stretched across the stern of the *Leopard*. A stiff onshore breeze made the ship lurch and roll at her anchor, occasionally tugging uncomfortably at her cable, but this did not deter the assembled company who gathered round the large sheet of paper that bore a roughly sketched plan of the Bou Regreb estuary. On either side of the defile cut by the river lay the two twin towns of Old and New Sallee. They were divided by more than the river, for both were occupied by opposing forces, a fact discovered by the commander of the *Expedition* who had been sent in pursuit of a fishing boat by Rainsborough. News of this rebellion proved much to the admiral's satisfaction and he sought now to exploit it in order to obtain the liberty of all those Christians presently enslaved by the pirates.

Among those aboard the *Leopard* was a former slave of the Sallee pirates, a man named Hopkins who had been ransomed some years earlier and had petitioned Trinity House for alms. He had been attached to the expedition on account of his knowledge of both the local geography and of the local tongue. With pecuniary inducement, the fishermen had roughly outlined the situation ashore and this intelligence was now laid before the council of commanders.

'It would seem,' Rainsborough told them, 'that those loyal to the local holy man occupy the old city, and these people are, in a general sense, not directly engaged in piracy, though all profit from it. Opposing these is the main body of the pirates who, we are informed, are our quarry. These men are under the domination of a man called ... what is he called, Hopkins?'

'His name is Abdullah ben Ali el-Kasri, sir,' Hopkins advised. 'He is a rogue whom I recall well. He is proud and obstinate, a man grown

219

rich and powerful on piracy. He and his men have fortified the ancient *kasbah* of Rabat, making it the citadel of New Sallee, where lie his headquarters and the place where he will have at least some of his captives, though most I suspect will have been sold long since.'

'Thank you, Hopkins,' said Rainsborough. 'Now, gentlemen, I propose that we make our intentions clear by opening a bombardment of the port, here...' He indicated the rough position on his crude chart. 'The *Leopard, Antelope* and *Perseus* will move closer inshore and use their great guns to this end. The pinnaces will search and destroy all local craft along the coastline – the *Expedition* to the northwards, the *Providence* to the south – while the *Hercules* and *Mary* will guard our flanks and – when they receive the order, and not before – open fire on any movements ashore that would seem to threaten the centre. Should any of the three bombarding vessels require support or assistance for any reason whatsoever, the commanders of these two vessels will provide it. Is that understood?' Rainsborough looked about him and was met by assenting nods and murmurs of comprehension.

'Good,' he went on, resuming his briefing. 'Now before we open operations against the pirate fleet, I intend to send Mr Hopkins ashore under armed protection on the conclusion of this meeting. He will seek an audience with the chief holy man in Old Sallee and attempt to secure some sort of accommodation and an agreement to desist from raiding our coasts. My intention is to make our purpose known to be against piracy, not against the population, or at least, that portion of the population under the, er...'

'The *marabout*, sir,' put in Hopkins helpfully. 'His name is Sidi Mohammed el-Ayyachi.' A few sniggered at the impossibility of the foreign name. One or two made notes.

'Very well. That is all.'

The captains walked out of the cabin on to the quarterdecks in groups, discussing Rainsborough's orders. Several stopped whilst awaiting their boats and stared at the coast which lay a few miles to the eastwards. It had a dun-coloured appearance, with occasional patches of grey-green and the darker green of palms. They could clearly see the cleft of the river valley, and a curve of sand-spit extending from the northern bank behind which the Bou Regreb wound inland unseen. The pale flat planes of the ramparts and towers of Old Sallee rose conspicuously on the north bank, above which protruded domes and minarets, the pale sunshine twinkling on the crescents of Islam that sat atop their summits. To the south the further works of the *kasbah* of New Sallee extended closer along the river, sheltering the masts and yards of the pirates' ships. Beyond, the walls climbed over the low hills and all faded into the immense distance that contained the unknown and terrible Atlas Mountains.

'Give them bloody hell, Kit,' a voice said in Faulkner's ear as he swept his telescope along the shoreline. Lowering his glass, he turned to find Rainsborough's flag-captain, John Dunton, alongside him. 'Give them hell,' he repeated, 'they can expect no quarter from me...'

'Ah, I recall you were a slave...'

'Aye, at Algiers, and only ransomed last year.' Dunton ground his teeth. 'My son remains there,' he said, his tone grim. 'He was taken out of the ship with me and is only ten years old. I hope that he is dead by now, though his mother would hate me for saying so.'

'I am sorry...'

'Just give them hell! That is all we can do.' Dunton moved away, his face unhappy, his eyes gleaming with the prospect of a kind of revenge. Though this was Sallee and not Algiers, a rain of death and terror seemed meet for pirates of any colour.

The following morning the ships worked their way cautiously inshore under easy sail and with their leadsmen in the chains. Having taken up their assigned stations and anchored with springs upon their cables, they awaited further orders, a wait that extended into several days, though Hopkins sent out reassuring messages that all was well and that he had made contact with some English merchants in the old town and was hopeful of meeting the *marabout*.

Matters stood thus for several days, until Hopkins sent a request that Rainsborough himself went ashore and, with Hopkins interpreting, met the *marabout*. Two days went by and George Carteret, the vice admiral and the only purely naval officer in the squadron, betrayed his anxiety by pulling round the anchored ships and soliciting the opinions of the other commanders as to Rainsborough's intentions. Captain Harrison, who was acting as rear admiral and happened to be dining with Faulkner that day, remarked that 'Carteret probably hoped William would be cast into Sidi what's-his-name's dungeons in order that he might take over the command, for he's as green as grass with jealousy and riled at serving under a merchant captain!'

'From what I have seen of Rainsborough's methods,' Faulkner remarked, refilling Harrison's glass, 'they are far superior to my experience of regular naval procedures.'

'What, even Mainwaring's?' Harrison asked, surprised.

'When Sir Henry is left to his own devices, there is none to match him for organization and efficiency, but when we flew Rutland's flag in the *Prince Royal*, there was a deal of confusion and wasted time. As for the expeditions to La Rochelle, why, not one of them left early enough in the year to achieve anything worthwhile and the waste was incalculable.'

'The rulings of commerce sharpen a man's wit, wouldn't you say?'

'Absolutely.'

'Still, I would hate to lose Rainsborough at this juncture, if only because serving under Carteret we might fall into such evils. Let's drink to his safe return.'

Two days later the *Leopard*'s boat was seen

pulling out from the shore, the oar blades flashing in the sunshine of a fine spring morning. Immediately on regaining the *Leopard*'s deck, Rainsborough again made the signal for 'All captains' and again they all repaired aboard the flagship, where Rainsborough gave Hopkins the freedom to open the explanation of what had transpired.

'I was initially admitted to the *marabout*'s presence after three days wait, which indicated a quite uncustomary haste that, I think, marks his surprise and possibly apprehension at our warlike appearance. Early negotiations also showed that the presence of our admiral might speed matters to a conclusion, so I requested Admiral Rainsborough joined me, explaining that from the perspective of Sidi Mohammed, our arrival could prove timely.' Hopkins conceded the floor to Rainsborough.

'With the assistance of Mr Hopkins, gentlemen, we soon confirmed that it was imperative for Sidi Mohammed to suppress the rebellion of the pirates in order to retain his own position and influence...'

'And probably his life,' put in Hopkins.

'Indeed, probably his life,' said Rainsborough. 'In consequence of this he agreed to an alliance with us, in earnest of which he has released seventeen slaves. We must, however, seek ratification from London and must therefore lay here quietly, only denying the passage of any ship inwards or outwards until I have permission to treat with this holy man.' Rainsborough paused, then added, 'This may prove difficult for us; onshore winds, if strong enough, may cast us on to a lee-shore, so we must be vigilant. We must also keep up the spirits of our men, who dislike inactivity and are always the devil near land, and that I confide to yourselves, bearing in mind that exercising in dumbshow drills may seem like time wasting, but may prove invaluable as we shall certainly go into action before we leave this place.'

It was an unsatisfactory situation, as they all agreed, but little could be done until the *Expedition* returned with permission to proceed as Rainsborough, with unexpected statesmanship, proposed. Happily, however, the King's sanction arrived by mid-July, along with the reinforcement of two ships, including the frigate *Swan* with two months' victuals and money for the squadron to purchase fresh meat from Tetuan. Matters now moved to a swift conclusion. Rainsborough and Hopkins again went ashore and presented Sidi Mohammed with the fait accompli. With the English ships offshore, the *marabout*, whose levies had already invested New Sallee, summoned Ali el-Kasri and his besieged garrison to surrender. El-Kasri responded by firing guns, whereupon Rainsborough hoisted the signal to his squadron to open fire.

The weeks of dumbshow practice paid off and aboard the *Perseus*, as with the other vessels close by, the fire was slow, measured and deliberate. Faulkner had sent two of his young officers aloft from where they remarked the fall of shot, as far as was possible, but once they had the range and were able to fire at the base of the walls along the waterfront quay, where a number of the pirate ships were moored in tiers, they began to see the result of their handiwork as spars fell and the first coils of smoke rose from a burning ship.

The *Leopard* was firing over the walls and dropping her shot into the town itself, while the *Antelope*, close inshore, plugged away at the defences, her balls ploughing up clouds of sand and rock as they scoured the foreshore and prevented any response from the garrison.

'My God, see the fires the *Antelope* has started,' Faulkner remarked to no one in particular on the *Perseus*'s deck, as he peered through his glass. He could see miniature figures, black-robed women for the most part, running from the danger, small shapes alongside them that might have been children or perhaps goats or other small livestock. At one point a troop of horsemen came dashing along the sand. Although they were probably Sidi Mohammed's troops, they were thrown into confusion by the bombardment and very largely destroyed. It was a grim business and one which was kept up by the exhortation, made by Faulkner and the other captains, to: 'Remember the men, women and children these people have taken from their hearths!'

The gunfire ceased at darkness, but resumed the following morning when Rainsborough ordered the two shallow-draughted pinnaces

226

closer inshore. Both entered the river itself and anchored against the stream, from where they were close enough to shoot fire pots at the pirate ships lying board-and-board along the water-front. By noon they were all ablaze, a great pall of smoke lifting over the walls of New Sallee and disfiguring the sublime and perfect blue of the sky. Such was the hatred among the English for the humiliations and losses to these pirates, that they exacted a terrible vengeance.

Day after day the bombardment went on until the stocks of powder aboard the English ships were running low. Apart from the appearance of the Moorish horsemen on the beach, the rest of Sidi Mohammed's troops, said to number twenty thousand, successfully reached the waterfront area, setting fire to warehouses in which El-Kasri had stored a year's corn. Three weeks later they stormed the ramparts and were soon in the city, whereupon ferocious hand-to-hand and house-to-house fighting ensued.

During this protracted period a few escaped slaves began arriving alongside the English ships. English, French and Dutch were either swept up by the pinnaces scouring the shore, or found their own way out by swimming or in stolen boats. Gradually resistance in New Sallee crumbled and ebbed, and the green standard of Sidi Mohammed, flying conspicuously from minaret and tower, proclaimed those parts in the hands of the allies. Offshore, more and more escaped slaves were picked up, and on 28th July Ali el-Kasri surrendered.

Rainsborough now began negotiations for the formal release of more enslaved Christians with the Sultan through Sidi Mohammed. These were forthcoming, and by the 8th August the squadron was crowded with some three hundred and fifty men and a score of women, all hungry and in want of food and shelter. With the onset of autumn gales now imminent, and their stocks of powder exhausted, the admiral ordered Carteret to withdraw with all the released captives and to take with him the *Antelope*, the *Hercules*, *Providence* and *Expedition*. He was to lie off the Spanish coast west of Gibraltar for as long as supplies permitted, before returning home. Prior to following himself, Rainsborough ordered Faulkner to proceed south, towards Safi, the port for Marrakech. Here he hoped to secure the release of a further thousand slaves who, so the negotiations with Sidi Mohammed had revealed, had been sold on to the *mastabas* of Tunis and Algiers. Faulkner was to make contact with an English merchant named Blake and await Rainsborough's arrival, while he concluded his treaty with the Sultan of Morocco and waited for expected reinforcements from England.

Faulkner was glad to be detaching. They had been too long moored off Sallee and he ordered the anchor weighed with a light heart. In a stiff west-south-westerly breeze they hauled their yards sharp up and stood along the coast. It was all but deserted, the English blockade having proved singularly effective. Inshore, an occasional fishing boat was descried, but little else until, that is, Faulkner and Lazenby were staring under the curve of the foot of the fore-sail, trying to make out the walls of Safi in the noontide glare.

'That is no minaret, Captain Faulkner,' Lazenby remarked, his face screwed up as he stared out on the larboard bow, 'that is a ship.'

Faulkner levelled his glass again and took pains to better focus it. 'You are right,' he said without removing the telescope from his eye, adding, 'and she is square-rigged, which means she is either a European trader or a pirate. I am not minded to leave whoever, or whatever that ship is in any doubt as to who commands on this coast. Send the men to quarters, run up our colours and run out the guns.'

'Aye, aye, sir.' Lazenby went off, shouting orders for all hands.

Faulkner added with a shout, 'And an ensign at the main masthead too, Mr Lazenby.'

When he eventually lowered his glass he found the slightly stooped figure of Walker, the gunner, at his elbow. 'Well, Mr Walker, you have come to inform me how little powder we have remaining, no doubt.'

'I have, sir. And precious little it is if you are seeking an engagement.'

'It may be a Frenchman, or a Dutchman, or a Spaniard or Portugoose...' Faulkner remarked. Walker stared out over the deep and heaving blue of the Atlantic.

'That's a Moor, sir. No self-respecting Dutchman, nor a damned Spaniard or Portugoose would set a topgallant like that. We've taught them much but not quite how to set a top-gallant...'

'It could well be an undermanned merchant-man, Mr Walker,' Faulkner said.

Walker sucked at his teeth. 'It *might* be,' he said with such emphasis on the conditional, that its negative quality put the matter beyond doubt.

Something caught Faulkner's eye and he again raised his glass. In response to their own en-signs, one flying from the peak and the other streaming from the main-truck, the approaching vessel had hoisted a large red flag, bordered in blue, the crimson field of which bore blue discs. Faulkner knew it for the colours of Sallee – here was a pirate that had not been mewed-up and blockaded by their arrival but had probably been lying off Safi awaiting the turn of events further north.

'You are right, Mr Walker. We shall have to fight. You had better repair to your magazine and make up as many cartridges as you are able, and please send Mr Lazenby and Mr Norris to me.' A few minutes later the two lieutenants stood beside him. Faulkner snapped his glass shut. 'Yon ship is a Sallee Rover; we have only a few rounds left, so hold your fire until you can make every shot tell. I would have you go round the guns and tell the captain of each that is my wish, and if they value their lives they had better attend to the order. Also make certain that every man has arms of some sort. They will likely try and board and will probably outnumber us. You

230

are used to the Jamaica trade but you, Mr Norris, have served in a slaver, I think...?'

'Aye, sir, I have.'

'Then you know what to do. No quarter is to be given, no quarter whatsoever, or we shall end up enslaved.'

'No quarter, aye aye, sir.'

As they moved away Faulkner resumed his study of the enemy. She was, he thought, Dutch-built; a prize perhaps, or the possession of a Dutch renegade – he knew there were a number of them, alongside Englishmen turned Muslim. She could be well handled, or she might not be: that topgallant looked well-enough set to him. After a few minutes he lowered his glass and took a turn about the decks, then rattled out orders.

'T'gallant sheets, there! Clew-up!'

When the topgallants were hauled up in the bunt, and the yards had been dropped down to the caps, he ordered the fore and main courses likewise clewed-up. The *Perseus* slowed her headlong rush and under topsails quietly bobbed upon the swell, instantly manoeuvrable and awaiting the other to reveal her intentions. Within a few minutes the oncoming ship had done the same and done it well; it was clear that they were meeting a ship of some force and expertise.

'Stand to your guns, men!' he called, so that those men released from the guns to handle the sails returned to their action stations. That was one drawback of hiring armed merchantmen as commissioned ships: they always fell short of what the Royal Navy considered an adequate complement. Faulkner doubted if his opponent suffered any such deficiency.

Under reduced sail the two vessels were approaching one another on opposite courses. Relieving the *Perseus* of her press of sail enabled her to manoeuvre on a more even keel and he guessed that the enemy, still on the lee bow, would brace up sharply, cross ahead and rake them. Faulkner walked across to the two men at the helm. From there he shouted to Lazenby, who was commanding the starboard guns, 'Starboard battery! Double-shot your guns, knock out the quoins and aim high, but wait for my word!'

Lazenby lifted his hand in acknowledgement and Faulkner waited only long enough to see the flurry of activity round the guns in the starboard waist. He had a ruse, but it depended on his men holding fire and the enemy holding his nerve long enough to close the range. In this he was not disappointed as the two drew closer and closer. Whoever the enemy commander was, he was an experienced fighter and this led Faulkner to conclude he was probably a renegade, rather than a native Moor. The latter were less willing to take on an opponent not easily dominated, because their business was piracy, not annihilation. An apostate Dutchman, or Frenchman, or Englishman, come to that, would be unwilling to fall easily into the hands of a European, still less his former countrymen.

'Stand by to put your helm up,' Faulkner said quietly to the helmsmen, who swiftly grasped his meaning. They could see the shrinking distance between the two ships and watch the relative vertical motion between them rising and falling with the swell, as the wind, steady enough, drove them down towards each other.

'Keep her full and bye,' Faulkner added, anxious to maintain speed and steerage-way for the disarming manoeuvre. His heart was pounding in his breast and it came almost as a shock when Lazenby called out that the starboard guns were all ready.

'Thank you, Mr Lazenby,' he said, remembering those long agonizing minutes off the Varne ten years ago when he had run from the Frenchman. Did a man have a quotient of luck, like a cat's nine lives? If so, how did one calculate where one stood in Dame Fortune's regard?

Faulkner crossed the deck, raised his glass and steadied it against a stay. He could see something like movement in the waist of the enemy, a slight density of darker hue above the foreshortened rail. 'He's sent his hands to the braces,' he muttered to himself, then turning his head he called to Norris, 'Send your larbowlines to the braces, Mr Norris, trim the yards as and when we swing!' Then he shouted: 'Stand-to, Mr Lazenby!'

'All ready, sir!'

Faulkner no longer needed the glass but he was undisturbed by the movement of Norris's men which was heard rather than seen. Someone forward called out, 'They're swinging the yards, sir!' and he saw the enemy ship – now no more than two hundred yards away – swing to larboard, across their bow. The enemy captain had to move his ship some seventy yards ahead before he commanded the length of the *Perseus*. As Faulkner ordered his own helm put up to swing the *Perseus* to larboard he would shorten that distance, but also the time, perhaps catching his opponent out by a few seconds, perhaps delivering his own ship to perdition by as much. He watched the two rigs, each of three masts, move against each other and as they did so selected his moment, praying that it would come on the upwards roll.

'Fire!'

As the concussion of her starboard broadside rolled over her decks and the *Perseus* shuddered to the thunder of the discharge and the recoiling gun-trucks, lurching to leeward in reaction, Faulkner observed the cloud of smoke from the enemy's own guns. A second later the air was rent by the tearing noise of the passing shot: a few holes appeared in the sails and a rope under strain parted with a twang, so that the fore topgallant yard swung unconstrained by its severed brace. A thump or two told where a few balls had hit the *Perseus* and an explosion of splinters came from at least three places along her starboard rail. Someone amidships staggered back and another seemed to disintegrate as a gobbet of scarlet blossomed and then spread in a wet and lurid stain across the white planking. A sharp laceration ripped across his own cheek and he felt first the warm wet blood pour down his face and then the sear of the pain as the splinter passed him like a thrown knife-blade.

He experienced a moment of hesitation and doubt, his left hand flying up to his torn cheek. Then, as the flare-up of pain subsided, he heard the ragged cheer and stared through the smoke. The corsair had lost his main and fore topmasts, but was fast dropping astern.

'Wear ship!' he roared. 'Wear ship!'

Already the helmsmen were heaving the helm up again, allowing the *Perseus* to pay off. In the waist Norris was dashing about, shouting to men to man the lee braces and rushing to the starboard pins to cast off those a-weather. Despite his flesh wound Faulkner grinned; no naval lieutenant would have used his initiative and done that. They would lose ground to leeward but might yet come up to cross astern of the corsair and rake him. It all depended...

But once round on the larboard tack they found they could not lay a course sufficiently hard-up on the wind to pass across the stern; the best they could do was rake her from an awkward angle as they passed ahead. The guns would have to fire independently, losing the crushing effect of a broadside, but Faulkner hoped that his disabling broadside had had a demoralizing effect, if nothing else.

In the event, the leeway of the disabled pirate caused her to drift rapidly so that, instead of passing ahead, the *Perseus* was obliged to pay off and, in the lee of her enemy, further lost way. Faulkner could see the enemy crew mustering in the waist, readying to board: there must have been sixty or seventy of them.

'Fire when you can, Mr Norris! Clear away those boarders! Mr Lazenby, starbowlines to the larboard rail and repel boarders!'

Faulkner put his hand to his sword hilt and realized with a shock that he was unarmed. He could not leave the deck at such a juncture and cast wild-eyed about him, suddenly terrified. Amid the sudden, renewed and now continuous discharge of the guns, near muzzle-to-muzzle, the image of Julia came to him in a flash of self remonstrance. What a fool he had proved! Christ, what a fool! Then he saw Walker on deck, approaching him purposefully with a worried look on his seamed face. 'Get me a sword, Walker,' he shouted, 'a cutlass, anything, for the love of God!'

A moment later Walker was pressing a heavy cutlass into his hand and shouting, 'We've no more powder, Captain. The last cartridges have gone to the guns!'

'Arm thyself then, and fight for your life!'

The words were hardly out of Faulkner's mouth when he felt the jar as the *Perseus* and the pirate vessel collided and then ground together in the swell. The *Perseus* possessed the higher freeboard, which gave his men a slight advantage as they poked and prodded at the Moors attempting to clamber through the gunports as the discharged cannon recoiled inboard, while others sought to gain advantage by scaling a few ratlines and then launching themselves across the gap with savage cries of *'Allah akbar!'*

Faulkner hefted the cutlass; it was a brute weapon; unbalanced, crude and difficult to handle, but it was sharp and its blade, given a slashing momentum, was irresistible. Of the bloody carnage that followed, he recalled only small, shocking impressions accompanied by powerful sensations of fear and triumph, which followed one another in bewildering sequence and drove his reactions as he parried and slashed, thrust and parried. He remembered the rent in a bare brown-skinned belly that was girded by a scarlet and gold sash over which a wobbling, twisted and almost liquid stream of intestines suddenly emerged. He remembered also the whistle of a scimitar blade, the noise of which seemed to attest to its extreme sharpness, and the wind of its passing as it shaved his shoulder. (Later he discovered the right shoulder of his coat to be missing.) He also recalled a man's hand, its fist still grasping a sword, pass under his line of vision and thinking only that he must not tread upon it and thereby slip. What of this damage he himself executed, he did not know, though he recollected with perfect clarity the look in the eyes of a man into whose midriff he had plunged the cutlass, before remembering to twist and withdraw it in time to parry the thrust of a pike. He also remembered – would he ever forget? – a moment of pure terror when someone behind him pulled at his long hair and jerked his head back violently, exposing his throat and causing him to topple backwards. The man who had grasped at him may have been in the act of falling, wounded, for as Faulkner himself fell, he felt his hair released and he rolled sideways, somehow regaining his feet and still in possession of the cutlass. But he was bleeding from several cuts as well as the deep gash on his cheek and could feel his strength ebbing. He began to long for the madness to end, but was aware that even as this detached desire flooded him with an infinite weariness, he was hacking and stabbing at what seemed like wave after wave of pirates attempting to gain the deck of the *Perseus*.

Then, as if a curtain lifted slowly, it seemed as if the enemy withdrew; the pirate ship appeared to slowly detach itself and move away, a gap opening up between the two vessels so that the killing was suddenly one-sided, as those Moors left aboard the *Perseus* were murdered in what was rapidly turning to cold blood. Faulkner was to learn later that Lazenby had set the sprit topsail and drawn the two vessels apart, and thereby saved them after a brisk fight of no more than twelve minutes duration.

As Faulkner came to, faint with loss of blood but aware of what was going on about him, and propped himself against the binnacle, Lazenby approached and spoke as though from a great distance.

'There are twenty-eight of them dead on board

and at least half a dozen lost between the ships, sir ... Are you hearing me, Captain Faulkner?'

Faulkner nodded.

'And we've lost seven men for certain, with eleven wounded, five of them badly and probably mortally.' Lazenby paused. 'We lost Ephraim Walker, I'm sorry to say.'

'Oh, that is sad,' Faulkner muttered. 'And what of our late friend?' he raised his head in an attempt to catch sight of the corsair.

'Licking his wounds, sir. I think we should get you below, and get those scratches dressed.'

After being bandaged and taking a draught of wine, Faulkner was back on deck. Norris was among the dead, but Lazenby had proved invaluable and had done what knotting and splicing was necessary to get the *Perseus* under command again. When Faulkner found him he was staring at the pirate ship through Faulkner's own telescope.

'I took the liberty,' he explained, and Faulkner brushed the apology aside as Lazenby handed the glass over.

'It is of no matter; what do you make of her?'

'Little activity on board, sir. I think we might take her if we had powder to stand off and scour her deck of those infernal blackamoors...'

'He does not know we have no powder,' Faulkner said. 'Suppose we were to bear down upon her boldly...' He left the sentence hanging and Lazenby picked up its meaning.

'I'll stand the hands to and see just how many guns we could load,' Lazenby paused, a calculating look on his face. 'Small shot, I think,' and with that he made off, calling to the men, many of whom had slumped on the deck in the hiatus, exhausted with the bloody business of murder. Faulkner rallied himself and called for a man at the helm and for two or three others to clear the decks of the dead. After a few moments of activity, the yards were braced round, the helm put over and, with a few buckets of water thrown over the worst of the bloodstains, three guns were loaded with langridge and primed, their crews spiking them round and anticipating the best angle at which to fire as the *Perseus* bore down upon her disabled quarry.

There followed several long minutes of silent suspension as the full topsails drove the *Perseus* forwards with an inexorable progress, her two ensigns still flying bravely. Faulkner studied the corsair. She seemed inert, no sign of activity on her deck, indeed no obvious awareness of approaching nemesis. Was this an ambush? Faulkner felt the prickle of sweat as apprehension took a cold grip of his gut. There was no doubt that she had initially possessed a far larger complement than the Englishman, but despite those left dead or dying aboard the *Perseus*, she might still overwhelm them if they got close enough to attempt a second boarding. The near-silence grew as the distance shortened and Faulkner, weak from loss of blood, felt his knees buckling and his hands shaking. He gritted his teeth and growled at the helmsman, 'Steer small...'

Then a shout of alarm went up and Faulkner realized he had achieved surprise. A second later and men were lining the pirate's rail, one or two of whom fired their long arquebusses. The balls passed harmlessly, though several sank themselves in the *Perseus*'s stout planking. Their speed, relative to the wallowing pirate, her waist encumbered by the fallen spars from which her crew had been trying to free her, seemed to increase as they now rapidly closed the distance. Then they were sweeping past and the sparkle and pop of small arms rippled along her rail. Faulkner was spun round and knocked off his balance as a ball struck his shoulder, but otherwise passed him without leaving more than a severe bruise, by which time Lazenby had discharged his three guns with cool deliberation and swept the pirate's deck, scouring it with iron and reducing it to a bloody shambles at pistol-point. Then the *Perseus* had swept past and Faulkner, who had regained his balance and his composure, ordered the men to the braces and put the helm over again, quite forgetting that they had no powder left at all.

It took them some minutes to put the vessel on the wind and only when they did so did Lazenby have the time to remind him of the deficiency. 'Whatever small arms we have, every man to line the rail and...' He had no need to say more; Lazenby again scurried off, kicking the inert and generally exhorting the tiring crew with a torrent of foul language to which they responded with curses of their own. As Faulkner approached to make a second pass a solitary figure stood above the pirate's taffrail and raised a white cloth, calling in heavily accented English, 'I am your prisoner!'

'Hold your fire!' snapped Faulkner, moving swiftly to the rail as the *Perseus* again passed the corsair. 'Have you a serviceable boat?' The man with the white cloth shook his head. 'Then I will tow you, stand by to take a line forward ... Mr Lazenby...'

'Aye, sir, I'll make all ready.'

When Admiral Rainsborough arrived off Safi three days later in the *Leopard*, he had with him the *Mary Rose*, commanded by Captain Thomas Trenchfield, like Rainsborough an Elder Brother of Trinity House, and the pinnace *Roebucke* under Mr Broad, both reinforcements that had reached him off Sallee. Here he found Faulkner's *Perseus*, her guns run out and commanding her prize. When Faulkner reported aboard the flagship, Rainsborough shook him warmly by the hand and congratulated him.

'Well done, Captain Faulkner,' he said, nodding towards the anchored prize, 'now we have some additional bargaining counters here to add lustre to our cause.'

Faulkner had made contact with the Arabic-speaking English merchant Blake, and now Rainsborough entered another tedious period of negotiating through Blake, who had been appointed the Farmer of Customs by Sultan Moulay Zidan and had access to His Highness.

242

On 19th September, having embarked another two hundred and thirty manumitted Christian slaves along with Blake, some merchants and an envoy from the Sultan, Rainsborough's ships weighed anchor and two days later took their departure from Morocco. Faulkner had lost his prize in the negotiations, but had the consolation of carrying over a hundred of the liberated Englishmen home in the *Perseus* and the action had increased his reputation. Those men among his crew who complained were swiftly silenced by others among their number whose zeal for the Lord of Hosts ensured them that their repudiation of Mammon ensured a state of grace.

Faulkner took no part in the celebrations attending the arrival of the Moroccan envoy in London. He had long broken his promise to his wife of a three month absence, but was anxious to make amends, and only heard later of the procession through the streets which, although conducted by night, were lit as though by day. The Moroccan ambassador, Blake and his fellow merchants, all wearing gold chains and extravagantly dressed, rode into London on Arab horses. Behind came a large number of the freed slaves dressed in white, some of whom had been captive for thirty years. They were met by the Lord Mayor and Aldermen in their robes. Finally, on Sunday 5th November the ambassador was received by King Charles and presented to the King several saker falcons and four richly caparisoned Arab stallions, led by red-liveried Moorish grooms.

Faulkner was in Bristol the same evening. It was a black night of wind and sleeting rain such that it occurred to him that nothing had changed since the day he had left. He was tired and saddle-sore as he stumped up the stairs. Seeing the light under the door he paused a moment, puzzled by the unfamiliar noise of the squalling cry of a baby. When he came into the room he saw first Gooding and another man of his brother-in-law's acquaintance, a member of his congregation, Faulkner recalled. The two were bent over a printed bill which they had been reading in silence until interrupted by the sudden, unexpected opening of the door. Both men looked up in surprise. Faulkner had not intended to startle them and apologized.

'It was thoughtless of me, Nathan; I am sorry.'

Obviously preoccupied by the bill he had been reading, Gooding picked it up in a fury and waved it in Faulkner's face. 'This is your King's doing!' he said, taking no notice of his brother-in-law's unannounced arrival, nor making any comment on his overlong absence. He was beside himself, such as Faulkner had never previously seen him. 'It is infamous! Infamous!'

'What the devil do you speak of? And what do you mean by "my" King?'

'Are you not a King's officer?' Gooding's co-religionist asked, as if seeking not to be omitted from this vilification of a man lately arrived home from God-alone knew where.

Faulkner was taken aback by this welcome and met it with a rising anger of his own. 'What if I am? And what are you doing here? I barely know you, so by what right do *you* have to accost me thus on my arrival in my own home?'

Aware of Faulkner's temper and that he himself had behaved shamefully in the manner of their greeting, Gooding let his breath out in a long, exasperated exhalation. 'I am sorry, Kit. That was unforgivable of us both; please forgive us but we are outraged by the contents of this bill.' He waved the paper and then slapped it down upon the table.

'Prynne, Burton and Bastwick have been not merely been pilloried but mutilated!'

'What is that to me, for Heaven's sake? Or to you for that matter? Who is Prynne ... do I not recollect hearing his name before, for causing trouble and criticizing the court and Archbishop Laud? And who are the others?'

'Good men, Kit, good men. Men who speak truth unto power...'

'What is their offence? They cannot have been mutilated for nothing, not even by "my" King, who I increasingly hear called a tyrant.'

'He *is* a tyrant, Captain Faulkner,' Gooding's friend put in, his tone now moderated and indicating a desire to put the newly returned mariner in the political picture. 'A black and bloody one. You probably recall Prynne having been fined and thrown into the Tower, his ears cropped, for seditious writings three years ago. Well, he has – thank God! – been at it again despite his incarceration and has been fined a further five thousand, ordered to lose the remainder of his ears and to be branded on both cheeks...'

'He is a Puritan,' Faulkner said with an edge of sarcasm, as that explained the matter and cutting this lengthy peroration short.

'And bears witness, Kit,' put in Gooding.

'That's as maybe, Nat, but for myself I care not. I came here to see my wife and on the stairs I heard—'

The noise of a baby's loud and fractious crying came again and then was abruptly cut off. A light dawned on Gooding's face, as though the noise recalled him to the reality of the present moment.

'Kit, I am so sorry! I had quite forgot!' He was laughing and held out his hand to Faulkner to shake the now thoroughly bewildered man's hand. 'I am sorry. We made you the King's whipping boy and all the while we neglected your timely homecoming! Thank God you have arrived safely, we had almost given you up for lost. Come ... come, Julia is within...'

Gooding backed away towards the door of the bedroom which he indicated, almost bowing to Faulkner as he realized the truth. He was across the room and flung open the door in a second, to find Julia, sitting before a fire, with a child suckling greedily at her breast.

Eight

Civil War

1638–1645

It was by such cumulative degrees that England descended into civil strife. While war raged in Europe between Protestant and Catholic, England fell into factions of a more political complexion, though religion lay at the root of them. A King of unwearying duplicity whose French and Catholic Queen caused suspicion as to the King's true allegiance to the Protestant Church of England – itself ruled by an Archbishop of strong political views and a hater of Calvinism who owed his position to the late and hated Buckingham – found himself pitched against an increasingly intransigent Parliament whose members were opposed to the King's assumption of powers that he conceived he received directly from God and argued that no policy could be enacted without the consent of itself. Those in Parliament most affected by this zeal for the rights of the House of Commons were largely Puritans whose sober dress, strong principals and convictions that, contrary to the King and Royalist party's belief, God was of *their* opinion.

Like most of his fellow countrymen, Faulkner continued his own life, following his own interests. The steady expansion of the new colonies in North America enabled the Bristol ships owned by Gooding and himself to return handsome profits, while his participation in the expedition to Sallee had persuaded him to try the *Perseus* in the Mediterranean trade – sailing to Oporto, Leghorn and Smyrna. It had also widened his acquaintance with the Brethren of Trinity House, and early in the following year he was persuaded by several others, Rainsborough included, to invest in two Indiamen and thereby he was inexorably drawn towards London, removing himself there with Julia and their son Henry Gideon, named after Faulkner's patrons. Here, soon afterwards in the summer of 1639, their second son was born at their new home in Wapping, and named Nathaniel in compliment to his uncle who remained in Bristol.

'It is right that we should leave Nathan to manage affairs in Bristol,' Faulkner told his wife, 'for he must surely marry and settle himself, and while we all occupy that old lodging nothing will change.' Julia did not like London. Unlike Bristol the rain and wind did not scour it clean; rain brought soot from the sky and wind kicked indescribable muck about the streets. It was a huge and filthy place, a veritable warren of narrow alleyways, of running ordure and manufactory stinks, of soap-works and tallow-makers, its river an open sewer, its inhabitants mixed, its daily turmoil endless and without rhythm or regulation.

In the following eighteen months Faulkner's affairs prospered; his weekly assemblies at the Trinity House where the conviviality of his companions in both arms and commerce flattered him, so that it sometimes seemed inconceivable that he had risen from the gutter. He never forgot it, however, and became known for his casual generosity to the street fruit-sellers, in tribute to that unknown – and probably long-dead – girl who had first sent him in pursuit of apple cores. London for Faulkner was all absorbing, and while he regularly encountered Sir Henry Mainwaring at the Trinity House, neither man sought to disturb the tranquillity of their respective lives. If Mainwaring was disappointed that Faulkner had failed to become a naval officer, he rarely referred to the matter, nor to Faulkner's lack of political colour. He, perhaps better than others, was aware that a man's life took unpredictable twists and turns. As for himself, Sir Henry, a widower after only three years of marriage, was now an admiral and seemed content that his protégé had made a success of his life. Once or twice, out of a solicitous and natural interest in Faulkner's affairs, Mainwaring would refer to their past association.

'What a pity,' he once remarked with a sigh after a meeting of the Trinity Court, 'that George Villiers did not act as he should have done and, indeed, *could* have done to reform the navy. You have regulated things so much better in the Indiamen...'

'We make a profit, Sir Henry,' Faulkner responded quietly, as they took a glass of wine with their fellows before dispersing. 'What is a deficit to the state is as something that makes a deficit in commerce – not to be tolerated.'

'But what of defence? The Dutch are a nuisance to us as you well know in the Indies – you recall the bloody affair at Amboyna when all our people were massacred? They are to be watched and do not like our expansion. Our trade is increasing, our colonies need guarding, even our coasts are still not entirely safe, for the corsairs from Algiers are about their damnable work again and those from Tunis are said to be as bad. Damn it, I would not be surprised to hear those from Sallee have broken their treaty...' Mainwaring broke off and then, perhaps divining Faulkner's thinking, added, 'We cannot defend ourselves by such means as the expedition to Morocco, relying on the goodwill of those about us this morning. Their pockets are generous and some are said to be deep, but not deep enough.'

Faulkner nodded. 'No, but you are right, Sir Henry, it is just that the means of paying for a fleet are so imperfect. If the ships are fit, the men are in want; if the men are provided for, the ships or the victuals – or usually both – are rotten and the men will not serve. But you are almost alone in speaking of grand strategy,'

Faulkner said with a rueful irony. 'Everywhere else I hear the noise of faction. These present troubles with the Scots—'

'Tell me, Kit,' Mainwaring interrupted, dropping his voice and suddenly speaking with some intensity. 'Tell me, if matters warranted it, would you come back and serve under my flag?' Faulkner hesitated and the hesitation goaded Mainwaring. 'We may have need of good men, competent men at sea. I cannot insist, but...'

'I know, Sir Henry, I know.' Faulkner shook his head and looked down. He was silent for a moment and then looked Mainwaring directly in the eye. 'I am bound to you by more than gratitude and loyalty, Sir Henry. I am conscious that our paths have diverged through circumstance but, if you are worried about the Dutch you will find me as ready as the next man to stand in defence of my country and my own.'

Mainwaring put his hand on Faulkner's arm. 'Well said, Kit. And God bless you for it. Let us hope that it never comes to such a pass but who knows? The world turns and turns – perhaps it will not be the Dutch...' and with that Mainwaring patted Faulkner's arm again and moved away. Faulkner stared after him, feeling distinctly uneasy. Mainwaring was an enigma to him no less than to others, despite their years of intimacy. Sometimes Faulkner thought him capable of divination, or necromancy, or some black art that foretold the future, for he knew him to have rarely been wrong in his judgements. He left for home feeling disturbed by the exchange and the mood had not left him when he arrived after a short walk.

'Husband, you look tired,' Julia had remarked as he cast his hat aside and crossed the room to take her hand and kiss her. She touched his cheek lightly. 'Something troubles you...' she said.

He shook his head and laughed. 'Nothing more than a flight of geese over my grave.'

'Please do not speak thus.'

'Oh come, 'tis only a figure of speech...' She remained silent, though her eyes wore an expression of reproach.

'It is politics, I suppose,' she said with an air of resignation, and he caught at the hint, telling her of news he had also learned that morning.

'The word is that Parliament is being recalled.'

'Does the King want more money, or is it the Scottish war?'

'Both. I cannot conceive of the latter without the former...'

'No.' Julia fell silent, and he smiled and sought to withdraw, but she held him back. 'I have news, Husband...'

'News?' He frowned. 'Of a ship? Nathan writes that the *Garvey* is near overdue...'

'No, not a ship. A child. I am with child again, Kit.'

He knelt quickly beside her, seized both her hands and looked up into her face. How strong she seemed, her handsome, even features still remarkably unmarked by age, at least to his

252

eyes. 'That is wonderful,' he breathed. 'Oh, Julia my dearest darling...' He paused, then collected himself. 'Are you quite well and feeling strong?'

'Perfectly,' she responded with an ironic smile.

'And do you hope for another son, or a daughter?'

She shrugged. 'I am content with what the Lord has in store for me.'

He nodded. Henry and Nathaniel were fine, active boys and another son would be delightful, but a daughter would, he thought to himself, be quite wonderful. But Julia had not finished with him.

'Will you come and worship with me. I have yet to settle with the local congregation and I cannot continue to go alone, without my husband...'

He sighed, reluctant to commit himself to her faith. He had gone frequently with the Brethren to church and was by the nature of his oath bound to attend services and respect the liturgy of the Church of England. However, he was aware that there were those among the Brethren who were irked by the preaching of Archbishop Laud and spoke warmly in favour of some Parliamentary speeches opposed to the King's policies. 'Julia, you know how I am situated...'

'I do not like our life here in London,' she said without heat, as a matter of plain, unequivocal fact. And then she rose and left him standing in the middle of the room.

'Damnation!' he breathed. 'Hell and damnation!' And again the mood of uncertainty that he had felt since leaving Mainwaring and the Trinity House settled on him. He sat before the fire and pulled off his boots, and stared moodily into the flames, watching as they slowly died and all that was left were glowing embers. Night was upon them and he was hungry. He had not heard anything of the boys and his heart was full of a dark foreboding.

The coming upheaval was preceded by events which, in the manner of portents, did not seriously impinge upon the lives of the Faulkner household. In due course, Julia was brought to bed and presented Faulkner with a bonny baby girl who was christened Hannah and baptized into the Church of England at St Dunstan's, Stepney. This family event went hand in hand with increasing good fortune in Faulkner's shipping enterprises. Events on the Indian coast, though not without cost, returned intermittent profit which showed every sign of settling into a steady return, while the West India and colonial trade improved year by year.

But these private and successful speculations were gradually overshadowed by events elsewhere. The massacre of Protestants in Ireland was followed by a rebellion of Catholics, while the man widely held to be the architect of these troubles, Thomas Wentworth, Earl of Strafford, entertained the London mob by his execution, having been abandoned by his late master, the King. Matters finally flew out of hand in the following year, 1642, when the King entered Parliament with the intent of arresting several members who had been inveterate in their opposition to the King's imposition of taxes without the sanction of the Lords and Commons. This foolhardy and intemperate act on the part of His Majesty was, in the opinion of many who would otherwise have been loyal, a provocation. Tipped off, the five members escaped and the King was left to look foolish, and in the deteriorating atmosphere in the capital even the Brethren at Trinity House began to divide in their opinions, especially as, that summer, they were approached by Parliament for a loan of money 'for these great occasions'.

With the news that King Charles had raised his standard in Nottingham and declared his intention of regaining control of London by armed force, Julia presented her husband with an ultimatum: for the sake of the children, she claimed, they must remove at once to Bristol. Julia's hatred of the capital had not lessened since she had given birth to Hannah and her daughter's christening into the established church had troubled her conscience and added to the widening rift between herself and her husband.

'You are too troubled by your affairs to take notice of my wishes, still less to take notice of your sons' welfare,' she had stormed at him one night.

'It is precisely for you and my children that I labour, Julia,' he responded angrily. 'In these unsettled times something must be laid down for the future, whatever that turns out to be...' Dissent between them had been unusual but the sense of impending disintegration that had sent tremors through London in those weeks was palpable and several families of their acquaintance had migrated to the country.

'Confound it, Julia, these are not easy times. The boys are well enough and I rely upon your good sense and character to see them set in the right path. They have nurses and can have a governess when you judge it right for them and we shall see—'

'Husband, you do not understand! There is more to all this than the education of our children and our happiness. The Temple is being destroyed—'

He rounded on her then. 'You think I do not understand, that I do not hear the noise of collapse? Why, God damn it, the noise is deafening. I would not expect you to comprehend the consequences but even at the Trinity House we have hardly elected Sir Henry our Master but the Commons declare him a delinquent!'

'And what are Sir Henry's misfortunes to me, Husband? He is an old man and not likely to much affect us here ... Where are you going?'

At the door Faulkner turned. 'I am going to cool my heels. Nothing is profited if you and I argue like this.' And with that he left her.

Matters simmered thus for a day or two, but the row had unsettled Faulkner more than he cared to admit, for there was justice in Julia's complaint. His promise to Mainwaring was brought into sharp focus by events at Trinity House. He had heard that Mainwaring had joined the King and he was certainly not in London where, in early November, he was declared by the Commons as a person debarred to serve as one of the Brethren. This was an unwarranted and illegal intrusion into the Brethren's affairs and provoked even deeper resentment when it was followed by the placing of the Corporation's affairs in the hands of a Parliamentary Commission. The purpose of this was clear: access to the funds of the Brethren, which were held in trust for the relief of the poor, and several of the Fraternity concurred with the resolution of the Commons and thus allied themselves with the Parliamentary faction.

Faulkner regarded these events with sorrow. His own life, though bound up with the Fraternity, was not contingent upon it and he, among others, attempted a neutrality which proved unsustainable. One night, towards the end of that month, he received a visit from Rainsborough.

'It seems I am fated to come to you by night, like Nicodemus, Kit,' Rainsborough said as he settled himself by Faulkner's fire and gratefully accepted a glass of mulled wine. 'I apologize for disturbing your household.'

'My wife has retired,' Faulkner replied. 'On the last occasion of your coming to see me I had no idea why, now I fear I do...'

'We are in desperate straights, Kit. War will ravage this country, ruin trade, wreck our lives, and it is no longer a question of possibilities, as you well know. By all accounts the fighting at Edgehill was prolonged and bloody, and the Earl of Essex's forces are now, happily, secure hereabouts.'

'I hear the King makes his headquarters at Oxford,' Faulkner remarked. 'Is that where our late Master now is?'

'Sir Henry? I have no positive knowledge of his being there. Certainly he has fled London, but what of you, Kit. I do not know what the fleet's position is, but if the Parliament requires sea-officers...' Rainsborough left the implied question hanging. Faulkner preferred not to address it, since he had guessed the purpose of Rainsborough's visit.

'The fleet will declare for Parliament,' he said, 'of that there is little doubt, for it was so ill-served by the King.'

'What, entirely? I can understand resentment among the men but what of the officers?'

Faulkner thought of Brenton. 'Many of them will repudiate their loyalty to the King's Majesty, William. Of that I have little doubt...'

'Well the argument is clear: the King has by his actions, forfeited their loyalty, any oath being bound by conditions of lawfulness, but I am surprised that you think this movement towards Parliament so wholesale.'

Faulkner shrugged. 'It is only an opinion.'

'And what of you? You are a man of loyalty, I know, and firmly attached to Sir Henry, but your wife is of Puritan stock and known for her capacity to think for herself, and you would not have allied yourself with such a woman had you not been in some sympathy with her.'

Faulkner looked at Rainsborough. 'I know you have come here to discover my allegiance but, to tell truth, I have none other than to myself and my family. The matters of principle lately debated and now tearing our land apart seem altogether too violent, too disruptive to be worthy of espousal if all they achieve is civil war, and that is what we are at the start of...'

'There is no doubt of that,' Rainsborough agreed, a tone of exasperation in his voice.

'I do not come from land, or money, William,' Faulkner pressed on, though baulking at the prospect of explaining to Rainsborough that he came from nothing. Instead he said, 'What I lose, I lose irrecoverably. That is not consonant with my duty to my wife and children.'

'Will you go to America? There are those who think that is the thing to do.'

Faulkner shook his head. 'No, I have no purpose there, and besides, I hear your own family are deserting America to fight here alongside Parliament.'

Rainsborough nodded. 'Many think the principle worth fighting for,' he said pointedly, adding, 'I neither think you are capable of sitting on the fence nor really want to; were I inclined to it, I would wager you will become embroiled before long.'

Faulkner shook his head. 'Not if I can help it,' he answered. 'Perhaps you would wish to lay

259

odds on whether I shall favour the King or Parliament.' It was a foolish conclusion to the conversation, but he wanted an end to it. Rainsborough was importuning him and his own domestic turmoil did nothing to incline him towards Parliament which, if the truth be told, he thought acted with as high a hand as the King, especially in the manner of their condemning Mainwaring, a man to whom the nation owed much.

Sensing this Rainsborough rose and picked up his hat. Faulkner picked up the candlestick to light him to the street-door, where he turned. 'You are a valuable man, Captain Faulkner,' Rainsborough said with a rasping formality, 'a well-regarded and competent sea-officer. You are wasted as a ship-owning merchant – London is full of them. Indeed the place stinks of them and their attachment to Mammon. There are weightier things abroad. Mighty workings. The Lord of Hosts is roused and summons those of us with the courage to do his bidding to cleanse the Kingdom and to establish a quiet, Godly and good governance among the people of this England. All this, so long deferred, so long wanting courage to its accomplishment, is now come to its ripe term. If you do not join us, you will be against us and so will your wife and family.' Rainsborough paused. 'You are not a fool, Captain Faulkner; you perfectly understand what is at stake. The Queen has already fled to The Hague and France is so embroiled in her own troubles that she can expect no assistance; in short, the King's arms cannot prevail.' Then he turned, opened the door and was gone into the night.

Faulkner returned to the fire and sat staring into it for some moments. Nothing, not even Rainsborough's valedictory diatribe came as a surprise; he had heard the arguments deployed, incessantly it seemed, over the past year or so, perhaps longer. Their intensity had deepened and with what consequences! Civil War was an ugly thing and a man who knew the precarious nature of survival would fight to prevent his success being lost to the squabbles of others.

He leaned forward, picked up a poker and stabbed at the fire. 'Principles!' he growled to himself.

'He is right.' Julia's voice startled him and he spun round. She stood in her nightdress by the door.

'Is he? Well, well. You and the good Captain Rainsborough are in agreement. Would you have me join the forces of Parliament?'

'I would have you do what was right.'

'Which as far as I am concerned means remaining here to attend to my family and my affairs which, by the by, provide for other families. Now let there be no further argument upon the matter. I am a seaman and I served the King in that capacity, otherwise I know nothing of war on land. I sit a horse ill and I possess neither a pike nor an arquebuss. If the King—'

'You would not answer a summons from the

King,' Julia said in a sudden, indignant assumption.

'I doubt that the King has the time to sit and write an appeal to me, Julia. Besides, why all this zeal for action, eh? Men are killed and maimed in war; is that the prospect you delight in for your husband?'

'Of course not! I do not want this war any more than you but...'

'But what?'

She shook her head, remaining silent.

'But what?' he persisted.

'I just know that you will be unable to avoid commitment before all this is laid to rest. I do not ask you to fight, I only ask that you stand for the right cause in this unhappy matter. You do not understand that I, as a woman, must needs have my interests declared by you as my husband. If you declare for the King, I am by association also attached to the King and that is not my inclination. I do not believe the King rules by divine right, that his decisions are infallible and that he is responsible only to God. His decisions are patently fallible, even pretending that he knows his own mind which, by all accounts, he rarely does. You yourself admitted that he is not to be relied upon and that his word is given too lightly, that he promises whatever is expedient and does whatever is in his own interests. That is not kingly.'

'Go to bed, Julia,' he said in a low voice.

'Promise me—'

'I will promise you nothing beyond allowing

you to go to Bristol, if that is your wish, with the children. Is that what you wish?'

She nodded. 'I think it may be for the better, perhaps for a year, until matters are clearer.'

'I pray that the matter may be clearer in a year, though I doubt it. And what if Bristol declares for the King? You will be caught there like a rat in a trap, whereas here, in London, it is more certain that, as the home of Parliament and the mob, it will remain resistant even if the King's arms triumph. He would have to negotiate a peace with London, not take it by storm. Bristol's fate is less predictable.'

'I had not thought of that,' she admitted.

'No. You had not thought of that.'

'But...'

'Go to bed. I need some time to think.' He bent and again poked at the fire. 'Goodnight,' he said as she withdrew. Whether or not she replied he did not hear.

The glowing embers of the fire were mesmerizing and he sat staring into them for an hour, fancying he saw odd scenes, all hellishly red and edged with the grey accumulation of ash. Faces, horses, forests came and went before his tired eyes. What was to be done? He felt neither cause of sufficient magnetism to require his devotion, and indeed he had little need to provide further for Julia and the family, for he was of sufficient means for them all if he fell into the arms of death this very night. Perhaps he could send Julia and the children abroad, following the Queen to Holland. He had contacts enough in

Lisbon, in Oporto or distant Leghorn. He shook his head; she would not go and he knew the detachment from her religion that he had effectively forced upon her, without serious intent, inclined her to obduracy.

Perhaps, he thought, inverting the problem, that since she was well provided for it was he who should go. She was not intimately party to all his affairs, but she was master of some capital and aware of aspects of his business that, without much awkward formality, she was more than competent to take over. The idea grew until he realized that its impracticality made it a mere fantasy. That he could fantasize tonight was admitted, but how many such nights might be left to him, and in thinking of nights he was aware that they had not lain together for some time, and an ache and an itch was awakening in him that he had not yet sensed in her after the birth of Hannah. After a while he rose and fetched pen, ink, sand and paper, set another candle, made up the fire and wrote at length to Gooding.

When he had finished and had heard the watch call that it was past midnight, he sealed the letter and added a superscription. Then he stared once more at the fire. The letter to Gooding was a form of insurance, it was true, but it ensured some provision of financial stability, at least as far as he could then devise, and it was more than generous to Gooding himself. Faulkner stood and stretched. He was tired, but not yet ready for sleep. He looked about the room, at the sturdy furniture and the dark panelling – not bad for Mr

Rat, by God! And now poor Mainwaring was running like a hunted fox – how strange and impermanent were the ways of the world.

He picked up the candle and, as he made his way towards the door, its light fell upon the portrait of Julia that hung close by the door in complement to his own on the other side. It was a fair likeness and he recalled how he had first been stirred by her, yet had known little of her body under her dark and modest habit. Now he knew and the thought pricked his lust. He mounted the stairs content at last with his night's work, which had advanced matters as far as they might and for which the unknowing Julia ought to be grateful.

He pushed open the bedroom door with its familiar creak and heard her stir before he held the candle to her head. She was asleep and he kicked off his boots and removed his outer garments, and then stripped himself of his small clothes. Then he blew out the candle and lifted the coverlet, lowering his weight on to the mattress. Julia moved at the disturbance and rolled towards him. There was insufficient light for him to see more than the pale form of her face under its lace cap to which he reached out and deftly untied. This woke her and he moved towards her, his hands sliding down so that she quickly divined his intentions and was fully awake.

'Husband?' she said. 'This is not the time...'

'I have a need of you,' he responded, 'now.'

'I think not, Kit. I am neither in the mood nor

the season, and I do not wish for another child.'

'Forgive me, but I am not in need of another child either, but I would have you for my pleasure.'

'Please, no...'

'Come...'

'No!' She thrust him aside so that he lay back and for several moments stared at the ceiling. Beside him Julia's breathing slowly subsided. Then, just when he sensed she might be about to speak, and without a word himself, he rose, fumbled for his clothes and boots and left the bedroom.

For several months matters stood still in the Faulkner household, relative to events in the country at large. Julia had second thoughts about an immediate removal to Bristol, not least because Faulkner declared that he would remain in London, probably until the end of the New Year. He had become withdrawn and though neither of them referred to the incident in the bedroom, its unprecedented nature had nevertheless caused a rupture in their former intimacy. She, uncertain of his temper, therefore preferred to remain in the capital and await the outcome of events. The war meanwhile gained momentum: among the Parliamentary field officers a new name was emerging alongside that of Essex and Fairfax, that of Cromwell, and success crowned the endeavours of this former member of the House of Commons. But the Royalists, though defeated at Newbury, took

Bristol and effectively cut off Julia's retreat. Difficulty was experienced in getting letters through, though a communication of sorts was kept up by sea, and it was soon clear that Gooding and his co-religionists were themselves besieged within the city limits of Bristol. It was a far from easy time, though there were hopes of a peace when negotiations began at Oxford, though these swiftly broke down. Trade faltered and economic recession began to bite; Faulkner was obliged to call upon his reserves, securing, at Julia's insistence, the services of a tutor for Henry. The young man, a zealous Puritan of her choosing, ought to have been in harness but he seemed sickly and his appearance caused Faulkner some anxiety for fear that he imported some contagion into the house, but it was not a matter he could do battle over and no ill effects seemed to ensue; both Harry and his siblings seeming robust in health despite the air of the city.

At the year's end, despite the distant horrors of the war, it seemed that Faulkner's middle road might ensure a tranquil family life. The following June told of a battle at Cropredy Bridge, which was swiftly followed by a more serious blow to the King's forces at Marston Moor in July. The Queen was reported to be intriguing on her husband's behalf in France, and York was taken by the Parliament's army. Only in the West Country were the King's arms successful and a Parliamentary force surrendered at Fowey, while a second action at Newbury in late October proved indecisive.

Despite these upheavals Faulkner might have remained relatively unaffected by it all, other than having to accept dwindling profits and the rising costs of ship-owning. The schisms in the country had rent the Fraternity of Trinity House where the senior Elder Brethren took sides, those inclining to the cause of Parliament included several of the Sallee commanders led by Rainsborough, and William Batten, a former colleague and friend of Mainwaring. Many of the Younger Brethren withdrew their presence and looked increasingly to their own affairs. Much saddened by the breakdown in amity among his fellow seafarers, Faulkner was one of those who adopted this course of action, particularly as Sir Henry had disappeared. Thanks to his origins Faulkner lacked the driving political background of many and his unwillingness to engage in the political process was due more to ignorance than disinterest. Ever since Mainwaring and Strange had set him upon his way, his endeavours had been entirely directed to learning the business set immediately before him and, if he imbibed anything of politics, they were the opinions of Sir Henry and chiefly directed at his country's naval and mercantile might. With this in abeyance – for he had proved quite correct in assuming the 'Royal' Navy would abandon the King and declare for Parliament – and the nation turned inwards in search of the answers to its dilemma in civil war, Faulkner had felt himself somehow redundant. Besides these considerations, there were those of Julia and the three children; his wife's views were well known and generally he deferred to them, except in the matter of religion where he pretended to an adherence to the Anglican faith, though he had as little time for bishops as any puritan. He knew that deep fractures were appearing in his own marriage but Julia was obedient to him and with that he was content. While she ruled within, he continued with his affairs, maintained correspondence with Gooding and between them their ships both from Bristol and London managed to make the occasional profitable voyage.

Nevertheless, convinced that the Parliamentarians would emerge victorious, there were times when Julia attempted to goad him into throwing in his lot with them.

'Husband,' she lectured him on one occasion, as they sat late over dinner after the children had been sent to bed, 'there are men rising in the land. Does not your own ambition prompt you to wish to rise with them?'

'Men rise and fall, Wife,' he replied abruptly. 'Look at Buckingham, look at Laud, look at Strafford.'

'Things are changing now, changing ... What of this man Cromwell who is said to be raising a new army?'

Faulkner shrugged. 'Let us wait and see. Thus far we have been preserved...'

'You are worthy of greater things than all this,' she said, her argument taking a different direction. 'You are well known to many as a man competent enough to provide ships...'

'I am content, Julia. We have much to be thankful for,' he snapped, her remark pricking his conscience, for if her arguments stirred anything within him, it was a sense of having somehow abandoned Mainwaring in his hour of need.

Towards the end of 1644 it seemed as though Faulkner had done the right thing. Both sides in the war appeared, at least from what Faulkner gleaned, to have worn themselves to a standstill. There were rumours of peace talks, notwithstanding others of a new force raised by General Oliver Cromwell, and these auguries were confirmed when delegates met at Uxbridge. This news came as a relief to Faulkner who, in recent weeks, had been troubled by visitors from among the captains who had taken part in the expedition to Sallee. Although it was never admitted, it was clear that they had been sent by Rainsborough and they sought Faulkner's services in the organization of the navy.

The first of these was Trenchfield, who had been blunt in his recruitment. 'You are an experienced surveyor, Captain Faulkner, you know Mainwaring's works and his publications and we would employ these in the country's service. His *Seaman's Dictionary* has been published, you know, and we wish to use it as a manual for the fleet.'

Disturbed, Faulkner promised to consider the proposal, hoping that matters would be settled at Uxbridge before he had to commit himself, but, even as the delegates met, another Trinity House man who had served under Rainsborough off Morocco, Captain Brian Harrison, called on him, urging him with similar reasons to return to the fold where he was sorely missed.

Knowing of these visits, Julia again attempted to persuade him to declare himself for the Parliamentary cause, but he refused. 'They want to plunder my purse, Wife, that seems to me the chief purpose of the Parliament here.'

But on a frosty morning, late in the month of February 1645, a man arrived at Faulkner's warehouse asking for him. He was brought into the counting-house where Faulkner was in consultation with Harris, his chief clerk, and old Roger Godwin, a master mariner who deputed as ship's-husband.

'There's a fellow arrived wishing to speak to thee, Cap'n Faulkner,' one of the junior clerks said respectfully, interrupting the three men. Faulkner looked up. The man wore a large hat which obscured most of his face. Faulkner could see a long beard and hollow cheeks but the eyes were in shadow. He was cloaked against the cold and his boots were bespattered with mud. In deference to the clean-swept floor he stood just inside the door.

'Ask him his business,' Faulkner said, turning to Godwin. 'We must, I fear lay the *Phoenix* up then. See to the matter, Roger.' The old man nodded and collected his papers with a sigh. Faulkner turned to Harris. 'At least the India-men are employed.'

'Indeed, sir. At least for the time being.'

'Things should improve, I am sure. The *Phoenix* will not, I think, be idle for long ... What is it?'

The junior clerk coughed and said, 'He insists on seeing you alone, sir, and asks that you will walk with him.'

Faulkner looked up at the man and then turned to Harris. 'Well, there is little to detain me, Harris. I shall see what this fellow wants. Perhaps a cargo for the *Phoenix* is on offer.'

'I pray that to be the case.'

The two smiled and Faulkner picked up his hat. As he approached, the stranger turned away and walked towards the door that let on to the narrow street and the stink of the river. A thin mist coiled off the silver streak of the Thames glimpsed down the alleyway. The man waited next to the warehouse doorway for Faulkner to catch him up. At that time of the tide the alley was less crowded than the street, and less cluttered by barrows, though it led down to Wapping stairs.

'Captain Faulkner...'

He thought the voice vaguely familiar, though could not at first place it, then the man briefly lifted his hat before his face was again shadowed by its brim. Again he had that sense of familiarity without clear recognition.

'You do not recognize me, sir...'

'No, I do not.'

From a satchel slung about his shoulder, the stranger removed a package and held it out to

272

Faulkner. 'Perhaps you recognize the hand hereon?'

Faulkner needed only a quick glance and his heart thumped. 'Sir Henry Mainwaring.' He looked directly at the man who this time removed his hat entirely. It took a moment for Faulkner to realize that the lined and hollow-cheeked features and the haunted eyes into which he looked were indeed familiar.

'Eagles? James Eagles ... By heaven! I ... I apologize ... you are much changed ... older, I mean, I intend no offence...'

'None taken, Captain Faulkner, but is there somewhere we can go?'

For a moment Faulkner did not understand, though the sense of apprehensive urgency in Eagles's voice was plain enough.

'I am come from the West Country...'

Comprehension dawned on Faulkner. 'You are with Mainwaring and he is with the King!'

'Very like, but here is not the place...'

'No, no, of course not.' Faulkner felt a quickening of his pulse, a rare excitement stirred him. Fear mixed with a deep longing that confused him for a moment until his thoughts cleared and he seemed, at least to Eagles, to remind him of the man who commanded the *Perseus* in the fight with the Sallee rover off Safi. 'Come,' Faulkner said, taking his elbow and turning him round, 'let us to my house, it is only a short step. Walk leisurely and talk of ships. My ship *Phoenix* – a stout vessel like the *Perseus* – is lately in from the Mediterranean and discharged, but we have no lading for her.'

Eagles fell into step beside him as they ascended the alleyway, turned into the street and began shouldering their way through the crowd. 'I am sorry to hear that.' He paused, negotiated a dray being backed by a rough waggoner, and asked, 'What is her armament?'

'Fourteen culverins and a brace of sakers; she is ship-rigged and handy, and faster than the *Perseus*, though she was no laggard, even on the wind.'

'No, indeed. And what of the old *Perseus*? Does she still turn over a florin or two in your favour?'

'Indeed, though not as many as I should like.'

Within a quarter of an hour they had reached Faulkner's house to be welcomed by Julia and the children. After formal greetings, during which young Henry showed some social polish that was reciprocated by Eagles, who was equally flattering to little Hannah and Nathaniel, the three of them were packed off with their mother. As she left, Julia's expression betrayed her apprehension at the purpose of Eagles's intrusion and Eagles himself was less happy when they had gone.

'Forgive me, Captain Faulkner, but your wife ... she is of Puritan family?'

'You need entertain no fears. She is headstrong but loyal. Come, sit down and let me see what Sir Henry has to say.'

Eagles's slight air of reluctance prevailed as he sat and handed over the packet which Faulkner rapidly opened. The two men sat in silence whilst Faulkner read the long letter. When he had finished, he looked up at Eagles. 'You know the contents?'

Eagles nodded. 'I do, and I bring you other, more immediate, intelligence that is just now reaching London but which bears heavily upon what you have just read and your response may – indeed, I think, will – be contingent upon it.'

'Oh? And what, pray, is that?'

'The so-called treaty of Uxbridge has failed. War is broken out again, hence my presence here. As you see from Sir Henry's correspondence, we are anxious to hire or purchase ships to augment those already secured for the King's service, for which we have funds and in which I am commissioned captain.'

'So Sir Henry says,' Faulkner responded drily, 'but it was not money that was concerning me. There are those who depend upon me; my family are among several others in my ships...'

'Employment for the *Phoenix* or the *Perseus*, Captain,' Eagles persisted. 'Moreover the Queen is in Paris and help from France is imminent, all of which will ensure the King prevails.'

'How is Sir Henry?' Faulkner asked.

'Well enough, but anxious that you should join us.'

'And expecting me to do so,' Faulkner said flatly.

'Indeed, as he confided in me that you are bound to do so.'

Faulkner sighed. 'He is no longer my master,'

he said in a low voice, 'but I am obliged to him ... mightily obliged.' He paused before adding, 'If I am to do as he wishes then I must first secure my family in a place of safety.'

'There is little time. I can make you an offer for those of your ships in London now. I beg you send the *Phoenix* at once to Jersey...'

'I shall go to Bristol, Husband. And take the children.' Julia's voice startled the two men. Eagles rose and Faulkner followed suit. 'I am resolved,' she went on. 'If the fighting has begun again then there will be no peace for this country until either the King or the Parliament has a victory, and God alone knows what misery that will cause.'

Faulkner looked from one to the other and suddenly made up his mind. 'You are right, Wife...'

'It is not safe, Madam, for you to travel as you wish,' said Eagles. 'You are better off here in London...'

'Let us eat,' Faulkner said, 'and while you eat I shall write. Come, sit, James; and Julia, bring the boys.' He rose and left the room, leaving Julia and Eagles to stare with ill-concealed hostility at each other until he returned with pen, ink and paper. 'I have prevaricated too long. Go! Fetch the boys, Wife; I would speak with them.'

Faulkner sat and began writing. With a short expression of exasperation Julia left the room and they could hear her calling for bread, ale and meat, and summoning the two boys from their studies. A few moments later Faulkner looked up to see his two sons standing before him. Henry was a tall lad, growing fast; Nathaniel his junior and a smaller likeness. They both had Julia's strong, handsome features and his own stature.

'Hal, go to my chest and fetch me my glass.' Faulkner bent again to his letter-writing while a disturbed Julia fussed at the table as the maid brought in the food. When the boy returned, Faulkner laid down his quill, took the glass in one hand and drew towards him a platter on which lay cut slices of fresh bread.

'My boys,' he said with great deliberation, indicating the sliced bread. 'Sir Henry Mainwaring gave me the means to put this on our table, and the King gave me this –' he held his hand out for the telescope which Henry handed him – 'when he was Prince of Wales, that I might better execute my office at sea.' He handed the telescope back to Henry. 'I cannot in all conscience spurn the call now made upon me. Captain Eagles here is lately come to summon me to the King's colours and I must, perforce, answer the call that loyalty demands. You shall stay here with your mother, assisting her and continuing your studies. God grant that this war will soon be over and that we all live to see its end but, if not, you are to obey your mother in all things. Do you understand?'

'Yes, Father.' Both boys nodded obediently, suddenly aware of the seriousness of the moment, if not the consequences.

'Now, eat. Feed Captain Eagles, Wife. I shall

finish these letters and soon return. You and I, James,' he said to Eagles, 'will embark in the *Phoenix* this evening...'

'Can we not come with you, Father?' Nathaniel suddenly asked.

'No!' Julia's resolute tone brooked no argument, nor was Faulkner of a mind to dispute the matter.

'This is no game, my lads,' he said, 'as Captain Eagles will testify. 'This –' he put his finger to his cheek that bore the livid scar of his wound – 'was a lucky escape. Jousting with death is not a matter for boys, though there will be plenty like you swept up in this dreadful business. It is my wish that you stay here and learn your lessons.' He tapped one of the letters. 'I have here instructed Harris to take you under his wing as soon as you are able, Harry. You Nat, may follow in due course but I hope by then that all this will be over.'

Julia had stood throughout in silence, and now Faulkner indicated that Eagles should eat with the family whilst he went about his business.

'I shall be back in an hour but I must first attend to these letters.' And with that he left Julia confronting Eagles across the table, and the two boys, much subdued, standing in the no-man's land between them.

When he returned he found Eagles alone at the table asleep, his head resting on his arms. The room grew gloomy in the encroaching twilight. He found Julia with the children in the parlour, the atmosphere cold with foreboding, pain and hostility. It was clear she had attempted to get the boys to read, but while Hannah played happily enough, neither Harry nor Nathaniel were falling in with the diversion and Julia herself could barely staunch her angry tears.

'We both knew this moment must come in due course, Julia,' he said in a low voice, ignoring the children.

'But why the *King*?' she asked, keeping control of herself with the greatest difficulty.

'You know why the King,' he said softly.

'For a telescope?' she cried, exasperated.

'Yes, perhaps for a telescope,' he responded quietly. Curiously his decision, whether it had been made for right or wrong, had brought with it a kind of inner tranquillity that he was unable to explain. Perhaps it arose from the years of anxiety and uncertainty; perhaps it was the long-delayed consequence of the death of physical love between them.

'I loved you,' she said in a low voice. 'I loved you for the man I then knew and thought of as a constant character. I love our children but...' He said nothing, sensing what was coming, and prepared himself for the humiliation that he felt inevitable and which was Julia's right to inflict upon him. It stung nevertheless. 'But you have no backbone and are swung so very easily...' She was almost sobbing as she uttered those last words.

He nodded. 'Perhaps,' he said quietly, 'but you know not from whence I came, nor have you never asked beyond believing, as was correct, that I was an orphan. I know privation, Julia, you do not; I have striven to avoid it all these long and wearying years—'

'Then why submit now? Why give in to the weaker party whose cause is broken, discredited and damned? Why side with the King?' Her voice had strengthened as it gained conviction. 'Fight if you must, but fight on the side of justice and right! But why, in God's name, fight for Charles Stuart?'

It was a question he could not adequately answer. His response was visceral not rational. Did it come from that natural cunning that had led him to seek the apple cores dropped so long ago on the quayside at Bristol? Was that the root of his self-preservation?

'You will do well enough. The letters that I have written will see to that. If you cannot go to Bristol and your brother, you may remain here as long as you like. You are made master of most of my fortune for the sake of yourself and the children. I shall ask Eagles to witness those documents that are necessary before I go. Now, I must make my own preparations. I hope that we may meet again but, whatever happens, I charge you to look after the children.' He looked briefly at the two boys. Tears coursed down Nathaniel's cheeks and he was wracked by sobs as he pretended to lose himself in his book. Henry stared at him over the spine of his. It was already too dark to read and the pretence of the thing added to their mutual distress. It was shaming to argue thus in front of them but it was now the only thing they had in common. 'You had better find flint and tinder, Harry,' he said, 'or you will ruin your eyes.'

He hoped the boy would hate him for that remark, for he did not wish Henry to see him in heroic mould, nor conceive foolish ideas of emulation. He wanted the boy to cleave to his mother, and he only realized much later it was because Julia was correct in her foretelling of the future – it was very likely that the King's cause was doomed.

Below in a room, now almost completely dark, he found Eagles astir. Realizing the two men were alone, he coughed and said, 'I brought something else, a separate missive from Sir Henry that he specifically charged me with delivering to you in absolute privacy.' Eagles took a folded and sealed letter from his satchel and handed it over.

Faulkner took the letter to the fire, which he kicked into life until it gave out sufficient light, then sat beside it to read what Mainwaring had written. It was an informal note, clearly written in haste and bearing neither date nor location of origin.

My Dear Mr Rat,
Eagles is about to leave and there is one further thing that I must confide in you. There is a lady here anxious for your safety and welfare. Spare her a thought in her distress, for there is little I can do for her

and her fortunes are low. She asks after you in tender terms.
Yours affect'ly,
Hy Mainwaring.

Overwhelmed with emotion at his leave-taking of his family, Faulkner read the letter without comprehension, looking up at Eagles, who was watching him with some interest. Then something began to burst inside him and he reread it, at the conclusion of which he sat back in the chair, his chest heaving and his heart thundering as if it would explode.

'Are you well, sir?' Eagles asked anxiously.

Faulkner nodded, unsure what to feel. Eventually he managed to ask, 'Do you know the contents of this letter?'

Eagles shook his head. 'No, I know nothing beyond the fact that Sir Henry told me that should you seem unwilling to answer his summons, I was to show it to you. In the circumstances, I had almost forgotten it.'

'I am glad that you did not,' Faulkner said. 'I am also glad that you did not show it to me earlier. It would have had quite the contrary effect to that intended by Sir Henry!'

He stood, and leaving a thoroughly puzzled Eagles waiting again, went to gather his effects, noisily stumping about the house to deter enquiry from either Julia or the boys. Had one observed him at this time one would have thought him mad, for his face worked excessively, torn, it would seem, between laughter and tears. Moving with almost manic energy, he executed his task in a vacillating mood of high excitement and self-loathing. He was at once spineless and vindicated, a weathercock, a fool...

There was only one possible lady to whom Mainwaring could have referred and she, he had long ago concluded, he was never likely to see again.

Nine

Pendennis

1645

'Kit! By God, you are most welcome! A glass, a glass, my dear fellow, a glass.' Faulkner wrung Mainwaring's outstretched hand. 'And you have brought a ship.' Mainwaring turned and greeted Eagles before pouring both men a glass of wine. Mainwaring peered through the stern windows of the *Saint George* at the *Phoenix* which, not half an hour earlier, had dropped her anchor in Carrick Road off Falmouth town, under the looming presence of Pendennis castle.

'The King has a fleet again,' Mainwaring said, handing them each a glass, 'mustering fifteen armed merchantmen and now yours. Is she chartered, or purchased outright?'

'I have chartered her, Sir Henry,' Eagles put in.

'And her people?'

'Men signed for a voyage,' Faulkner said. 'They will stay if they are paid. Trade is fallen off mightily now the war has resumed and they mostly have families.'

'Hmmm,' Mainwaring grunted, 'money does not buy loyalty except in the short-term. Still, the ship's the thing. There are King's seamen enough here in the West Country.' Mainwaring turned to Eagles. 'What news did you glean in London?'

Faulkner studied his old master and mentor. Mainwaring was much altered, a man on the threshold of old age, careworn and lined by anxiety, thinner through poor living and over-work, his once heavy features fallen away, giving him the lugubrious appearance of an old hound.

'And what of matters here?' Eagles asked, re-capturing Faulkner's attention.

Mainwaring shook his head. 'The Prince is presently at Pendennis and is mustering men.'

'We saw the standard as we came in by the Black Rock,' Eagles remarked.

'Aye, a fine lad sent thither by his father to raise forces...' Mainwaring's voice tailed off.

'But...?' prompted Eagles.

Mainwaring blew out his cheeks. 'But while men come in we have news that Fairfax is on the march.'

'Black Tom!' Eagles shook his head.

'Aye. And he is expected in Truro within a day or two.' Mainwaring turned to Faulkner. 'You are come just in time, Kit.'

'So it would seem,' he replied, ruefully. Were it not for the fact that a question for Sir Henry burned in him, he might have felt the clutch of fear and despair in his gut, but from some foolishness he felt instead a surge of pure elation.

'Fairfax will invest Pendennis,' Eagles said. 'And what then?'

Mainwaring sighed again. 'The arguments range from Ireland to France, but my advice is Jersey, which is the most practicable, opens up a communication with the Queen.' He paused reflectively, adding, 'And with ships we may yet come to the King's aid.'

Faulkner sensed that Mainwaring's optimism was recurring, making the best of disaster and always as resourceful as ever. Eagles seemed privy to the contagion, for he reminded them cheerfully that, 'They have yet to take Pendennis, gentlemen. Let us drink to its defence and its stalwart garrison.'

'Well,' said Mainwaring after a moment, turning to his table on which a litter of charts and papers lay scattered. 'We have work to do. James, you shall relieve me in command of this vessel and here is your commission to that effect.' He handed Eagles a sealed document. 'She is not in good condition, James, and, as you may hear from the noise of the pumps, requires constant attention. Nor are her sails or ropes much better, alas, but she may be used in defence of the castle and we shall presently remoor her to command the approaches. You may take over this cabin.' Eagles took the commission and nodded as Mainwaring turned to Faulkner. 'I shall hoist my flag aboard the *Phoenix*, Kit, thither we shall go now with my effects, such as they are. James, I am likely to return here by nightfall when, I hope, to have better intelligence of Fairfax.' Mainwaring saw Eagles to the cabin door, engaging him in a brief, private conversation, before returning to the table, calling for his single manservant and gathering up his papers.

When his effects were ready, they descended the *Saint George*'s side, into the *Phoenix*'s boat. Reading Mainwaring's mind, Faulkner held his peace until they reached the privacy of his own cabin aboard the *Phoenix*. 'There is little space here, Sir Henry, she was not designed as a flagship.'

'Needs must, Kit, and necessity is the mother of invention. I shall not trouble you unduly but I require agility. The Prince of Wales is a fine but very young man, much influenced by those around him, all of whom have vested interests. We have had word of a conspiracy by the Cornish gentry to seize him and hold him hostage against the King's conduct. I tell you, we are in desperate straights and much will depend upon these few ships.'

'I see,' Faulkner said ruefully.

Mainwaring was watching the younger man

whose character he knew well. 'No moment is well chosen in war,' he said consolingly, 'and nothing is more uncertain than the outcome until its end.'

'Do you hold out hope that the King's cause is not lost?' Faulkner asked.

'No, but the Prince's isn't...'

'The Prince's...?'

'I conceive it my task in life to think of the future. The present I leave to the fools who inhabit it. That is why I have shifted my flag into the *Phoenix*, Kit.' He looked at Faulkner expectantly.

'You are providing for retreat.'

Mainwaring nodded. 'Let us call it retirement.' He watched the younger man nod and then waited for him to ask the question that lay between them. It was to Faulkner's credit that he did not blurt it out immediately. There were those about the Prince, as about his father, whose every move was governed, not by their monarch's cause, but by their own self-interest. Moral qualities were as rare in the King's party as they were superabundant in the Parliament's. And the quality of personal reticence was a tribute to Mainwaring too, for the manner of his bringing-up and schooling Faulkner seemed now justified, and the more so since Eagles had told him that he had not needed to tempt Faulkner with the lure of Mistress Villiers.

'I am glad to see you, Kit, and you will be wanting to know of Mistress Villiers.'

Faulkner gazed back at him, his eyes steady.

'Did you think I would not have come hither were it not for her?'

'You have a wife and family...'

'I have.'

'It may have been necessary...'

'To tempt me?'

Mainwaring shrugged. 'Perhaps, but I know that you came of your own inclination.'

'Eagles informed on me?'

'Of course. This is *civil* war; brother turns against brother, father against son. It is easy to embrace a spy and easy to turn one's coat. Perhaps we shall all have to turn our coats, kill our fathers and maim our sons; certainly enough of it has been done already. If the Parliament wins it will itself fall foul of faction; that is why we must stand by the Prince. He is young, persistent, possesses the courage of his father without, it seems, his lamentable want of common sense. It is not a question of divine right, but legitimacy. The present King will go down in the mud like Richard at Bosworth, but no mixture of righteous brothers-in-arms will ever rule this country without legitimacy. That is what kings confer. Had Charles seen the sense of this he would have seduced Parliament with the charm he endows on so many. Were he to choose the right men, instead of the likes of Villiers, Goring and all the other self-serving wastrels who, whatever their abilities, have not the integrity and military ability of a Fairfax or a Cromwell, King Charles's cause might have prospered, but Eagles tells me this latter has

288

mustered a new army; that is bad news.' Main-waring broke off and sighed, shaking his head. 'You and I must play a longer game, Kit. You are young enough to see the end of it, I shall not.'

Faulkner could think of nothing to say. Main-waring's words had made a deep impression on him, the arguments obviously the product of serious consideration. They had driven thoughts of Katherine Villiers from his mind and, in a moment of almost Damascene revelation, he realized why he had abandoned his family at Mainwaring's summons. It was to him that Faulkner looked, as a son might to a father. He had not yet come of age, a rum thought for a man in his mid-thirties, in the midst of a war, but it was true. The underlying security of a past, of roots, of family and tradition had never been a part of him. An English gentleman could not grow up without these essential foundations. The realization marked at once his coming of age and his despair at his failure as a father; how could he imbue his sons with any a sense of belonging, of self-worth? Now he knew why all he had found to concentrate on was his business, and simultaneously how this must have dis-appointed Mainwaring.

He looked up. Mainwaring's tired eyes gazed at him with unmistakable affection and, for a fleeting second, Faulkner thought the old man could divine his thoughts. Flushing, he turned to the locker in his cabin, drew out a bottle and two glasses.

'Here's to the long game, Sir Henry.' He handed a glass to Mainwaring.

'And to your homecoming, Kit.'

A moment of companionable silence descended upon the two men. 'Mistress Villiers,' Mainwaring suddenly said, 'is in Pendennis with the Prince. You will find her much changed from her former state. It is said the Prince, a precocious young man, has already stolen that without which a lady is ... well, just that, though I am unsure of whether he is the only one, or even the first. She has a child ... a bastard, naturally, and but for the charity of Lady Fanshawe, wife to the Prince's military secretary, Sir Richard, she would, I fear, have been left in Bath and ere now become the whore of a Crophead colonel ... It is not a pretty tale, Kit, and I tell you now only because I feel someone better provided for than myself should assume her welfare. Buckingham was a vain, rapacious, self-serving man but he was not without talent, talent which we might have harnessed to the good of the navy had we been able to curb him. Were you to feel some charity towards her, mindful of our common interest in the fortunes of the poor...' Mainwaring left in the air the reference to the workings of Trinity House and the oaths of loyalty that Faulkner might feel for its twice Master. Faulkner nodded. Mainwaring finished his wine and looked about him.

'See that there is a bed-place and a desk of sorts for me here, Kit. Meanwhile, with your leave and your boat, I shall ashore and to the

Prince, and try and glean some intelligence of Fairfax – if anyone has had the forethought to send out a patrol.'

'I shall be perfectly happy to take the lady under my protection, Sir Henry.'

'I shall seek to make the lady aware of your offer. Tongues will wag to their own conclusions, of course,' Mainwaring added, smiling.

'So be it. Some will be wagging already, but I have made my bed and must like lie upon it.'

'Very well.' Mainwaring nodded, held out his hand and Faulkner saw him to the boat. After he had gone Faulkner gave orders for the red cross of St George to be hoisted to the main-truck. 'We are a flagship, Mr Walker,' he said to the first mate. 'And you are now commissioned a lieutenant in the King's service.'

Faulkner did not sleep well that night and was abroad early, pacing the deck long before the cook was stirred from his slumbers. The night-air was chilly and the watch were only too pleased to keep out of his way. He guessed the news that they had become a man-of-war had unsettled them and had, before going to his uneasy bed, summoned them aft to tell them that any man who wished it could go ashore in the morning. The little assembly, half-seen in the twilight, had been disturbed by the news and he had sought to retain them with a promise.

'The ship is mine, my lads. She is on charter to the King and under the charter-party we are entitled to a share in any prizes. With matters so uncertain ashore, you must give due consideration to your fates. Stay with me and I give you my word that I shall do all I can for you. Ask yourselves: would I have brought you here and thrown in my lot if I thought the act foolish? Now go below and make up your minds. From tomorrow you will be ruled by articles of war, not commerce.'

Only Mainwaring's analysis had made that speech possible and he was glad that he had not attempted sooner to reveal to them what was afoot. How they would react, he must wait until later to learn. For the moment he had other matters to think on. He stared about him.

The ship lay quiet on the still waters of the harbour. To the west, a cable's length distant, lay the *St George*. In the stillness he could hear the starting of the pumps, and guessed the men had been called early to empty the well. Four other ships and a bilander lay at anchor, two of the former being commissioned. Beyond the furthest lay the town of Falmouth, nestling under rising land and tailing off to the southwards, where a narrow isthmus connected the mainland to the high ground that lay directly south of the *Phoenix*. This was crowned by the round keep and the outworks of Pendennis before falling away to the south-east, where lay the entrance to the harbour with, on the far side, the promontory named after St Anthony. Between, in mid-channel, lay the Black Rock, forcing ships through a narrow passage commanded from the north by the guns of another castle, directly east of the anchored ships, lying at the tip of another peninsula at St Mawes. In the great half circle that swept then through north round to the west and back to the town of Falmouth, lay dark wooded hills into which inlets wound, seemingly swallowed up by the land. All was sunk in a deep, fragrant tranquillity but, as he watched the gradual lightening of the cloudless sky beyond St Anthony's Head spread slowly, the first coils of the smoke of cooking fires rose from unseen and distant cottages. The world was waking.

Something moving caught his eye, and a small boat – a fisherman, probably – detached itself from a dark finger of land and began to pull out across the harbour from where the River Fal itself disappeared into trees. Faulkner recalled the lie of the land; the Fal ran up to Truro and the reflection brought him back to reality with a start. Was Fairfax yet in the town? There was little doubt the Parliamentary forces seemed better organized than the King's. He abandoned the troubling thought and turned on his heel, staring up at Pendennis wherein lay Katherine Villiers. He tried to imagine her as Sir Henry had described her, 'much changed and with a child'. How would she seem to him now that the first heat of youth had passed? How would he seem to her? He shied away from any sentiments of gratitude. She was a Villiers, proud and haughty; perhaps he would want nothing to do with her. She was defiled, a wanton. No, worse, if Mainwaring was right: an abandoned wanton! Did 'much changed' mean her beauty was ravaged by time and dishonour? How did a proud spirit, such as she possessed, cope with humiliation? Would she even accept what charity he could offer? And what charity *could* he offer? Oh, he had means enough for his own purposes, to be sure, but he could hardly despatch her to Julia with a note for his wife to take her in like a stray cat! And yet that was exactly what she was – a stray cat!

He scratched his head. In the cold and growing light of morning, Sir Henry's request seemed unrealistic. He could not keep her on board. No captain could keep a woman and discipline in the same vessel. Nor would endless protestations that she was merely kept for her own safety convince the hands that he was some philosophically, altruistic gentleman. What *was* he to do with her? He could, of course, simply palm her off with money and let her take that and her chance, but that was not Mainwaring's intention. Alternatively, he might pass her off as Mainwaring's woman. That would not please Sir Henry, but it might placate the crew. What was clear was that if she was allowed on board, her status must be made clear at the outset and she must assume the character of a passenger. But what as? The Prince's mistress, perhaps?

He took another turn up and down the deck. The boat he had noticed earlier had not stopped, as he had anticipated, to cast or tend net or pot, but came steadily onwards. He watched it for a moment before resuming his preoccupation, unable to make any conclusion beyond acquiring a growing certainty that the King's affairs, and now presumably by extension those of the Prince of Wales, were in a disastrous muddle.

The sun suddenly rose above the land and, in an instant the high ramparts of Pendennis shone with an ethereal splendour. He stared at the castle with a curious air of superstition and rationality. An omen? Of course not. A matutinal phenomenon? Of course. He almost shook his head to clear it, drawing in the sweet dawn air. God, how beautiful were the mornings!

There was more activity in the harbour now. A few boats were putting out from Falmouth where the smoke from cottagers' fires could now be clearly seen rising grey against the distant greenery. The sunshine fell upon the splendid façade of Arwenack House, home of the Killigrew family, which lay upon the isthmus connecting the mainland with the rising massif upon which Pendennis stood. The boat he had first seen setting out from the vicinity of St Mawes was no longer a silhouette, but he could quite distinctly see two oarsmen and, in the stern, the large hat of a passenger: a gentleman, no less. He stared a moment longer. The boat had emerged from the Fal on an ebb tide – had it come directly from Truro, or some place close by? He could see little more detail, but something about the man in the stern gave Faulkner the impression that he was in a hurry, and long before it proved to be the case, he knew the man brought news, and that news was not good.

An hour later came a formal note from Mainwaring. He was to prepare for action and to pass the order to the other vessels in Mainwaring's name. The Royalist force in Truro had surrendered to Fairfax and the Parliamentary forces had now left Truro and were marching south to seize the Prince or, if that failed, invest Pendennis. All thoughts of Mistress Villiers were again driven from Faulkner's mind as he put the ship in a state of defence. Although she had not been laid up in London, all his endeavours prior to their departure had been in the mustering of a crew and the storing of the vessel for a short voyage. While he had sufficient stores for two months, the urgency with which Eagles had pressed him to leave the Thames and his own inclination not to tarry meant that he had little enough powder and shot on board. He discovered a small store of powder in one of the anchored merchantmen and purchased it immediately, but he was still in want of balls and sent a party ashore to pick up suitable stones. All the guns were scoured and a muster was made of small arms, reinforcement of which was sent across from the *St George* by a thoughtful Eagles. He was fully aware of the condition of the *Phoenix* and it came with a note that read:

I am to ground this vessel at high water to-day, to command the approach to the castle and have little want of much of my stores. Send a boat for anything more that you need.
Jas Eagles,
Commander, 'St George'

The afternoon was thus occupied by boats from both vessels criss-crossing the harbour as the *Phoenix* was transformed into a man-of-war. In all this absorbing activity no one among her people sought to go ashore, or leave her. Whether or not it was the ingrained habit of obedience, which seemed on reflection to be unlikely among so hurriedly a scratched-together company, or some loyalty the men felt to the King, Faulkner was never able to decide. It never occurred to him that it might have been a sense of trust in their commander.

At high-water, towards three of the clock, Eagles summoned all the boats to the side of the *St George* and, with her pumps working, had his ship towed closer inshore. Carefully sounding his way in, he succeeded in swinging her shortly before she gently took the ground so that her starboard battery could be brought to bear on Arwenack House. The falling tide and the water rising inexorably in the *St George*'s bilge would do the rest, and Eagles could even lighten her, for he soon afterwards sent a request that Mainwaring should sanction the use of the ships' boats to carry ashore such of her larboard battery as could be safely removed, to be sent to augment the new defences being then dug round the lower glacis of the castle.

By the time the sun westered that spring evening, the first signs of the enemy disturbed their labours. The sharp crackle of dragoons' wheellocks could be heard from the woods north of the town on the road to Penrhyn, itself just obscured from the *Phoenix*'s anchorage by a bend in the creek. Then, through his glass, Faulkner could see the first of several laden farm-carts moving across that exposed ground and, swinging his glass south of west and laying it on the town itself, he could see a number of people milling with apparent aimlessness about the custom house. Before dark, the crack of small arms was interrupted by the heavy boom of a gun or two, and dense smoke was seen rising among the trees. More smoke appeared and the first stirrings of a westerly wind, accompanied by banks of cloud from the west that rolled up in the last of the daylight, bore the smell of it out to the anchored ships. In contrast to the fragrance of the morning it was, thought Faulkner, poor evidence of the work of man during the hours of daylight.

That evening, just after the dying of the light, Sir Henry Mainwaring came aboard.

'Tomorrow we shall be tested for our mettle,' he said, before going below, rolling himself in his cloak and falling asleep. Exhausted after his own sleepless night and day of labour, Faulkner followed him below and was, within minutes, oblivious to the world.

The breeze that had brought the smell of burning off to the ships the previous evening rose during the hours of darkness. It had begun to rain during the night and the morning began with a heavy downpour which sent sheets of water, driven by a freshening westerly wind, across the harbour and all but obscuring the visibility. A low scud tore across the sky and Falmouth lay a grey, indistinct feature, emerging from time to time in some detail, only to vanish again under the squall-driven sleet. The ships sheered somewhat in the gale and snubbed at their cables, so that it was necessary to slap canvas and grease in the hawse to prevent heavy chafe.

Faulkner stood the men down from their quarters, keeping only a few sentinels on deck with strict orders as to vigilance in case the enemy attempted to board under the cover of the weather in requisitioned boats. During the afternoon, however, the rain ceased, the sky cleared and the wind chopped round to the north-west. The clearing of the air was dramatic and it revealed a change of circumstances that, although anticipated, was no less disturbing. Arwenack House was in flames, burnt by the Royalist forces as they abandoned Falmouth and the little village of Pennycomequick, retiring into the fastness of the castle.

With the clearing of the air the men were stood to and both Faulkner and Mainwaring scanned the shoreline. 'Are the enemy in Pennycomequick?' Mainwaring asked, uncertainly. 'Eagles cannot command the village or Arwenack House from where he has taken the ground...'

'No, but I can see movement north of the town, where the road runs towards Penrhyn ... Yes, see there now: mounted troops, dragoons I suppose, and there! Pikemen!'

Mainwaring brought his own glass to bear where Faulkner indicated. 'And see there, a man on a white horse ... that is Black Tom himself...'

Faulkner swivelled and caught the image in the lens of the telescope: Fairfax, quite clear in black armour on his famous white steed, surrounded by his staff and standard bearer, rode south across the exposed ground towards Pennycomequick. But they were not the only people to spot the Parliamentary commander. Even as both men watched, a rumble from the *St George*, followed by the clouds of white smoke from her broadside, told its own tale. Mainwaring and Faulkner could see the sudden gobbets of earth thrown up by the shot as it ploughed at the end of its range through the sodden grass and mud. The horses of Fairfax's suite plunged wildly, rearing and kicking for a moment before their riders had them under control again and were heading off at a gallop, the standard streaming in gallantly as they made for the shelter of Penrhyn. A cheer from the *St George* was carried on the wind as the gunfire died away, echoing faintly into the distance. 'Not a single casualty,' Mainwaring remarked, lowering his telescope and turning towards Faulkner. 'That is hardly a victory.' He screwed up his eyes and seemed to be looking over Faulkner's shoulder. 'Hello, what have we here?'

Faulkner turned and followed Mainwaring's line of vision. A small sailing lugger was coming in from the sea, running inside the Black Rock and flying a large flag. Mainwaring raised

300

his glass with a sudden jerk and muttered an oath. Only a narrow sector of the distant horizon was visible from their anchorage but, to Faulkner's horror, it was no longer the sharp, empty edge of the world it had hitherto been. Now it was occupied by two, three and perhaps more, sails. Such a concentration of ships, arriving simultaneously, could mean only one thing; they were men-of-war and, with the navy in Parliamentary hands and those few ships raised for the King's service at Jersey or in the Isles of Scilly, that meant a Parliamentary squadron.

'We are cut off,' murmured Mainwaring. 'They have outwitted us and Pendennis is invested. That will be Batten, God rot him...'

'What, William Batten? Of Trinity House?' Faulkner's mouth was dry.

'Very likely. I knew him to be in command at Plymouth. Now, Kit, it is truly Brother against Brother.'

But Faulkner was thinking. He looked over the side and at the sky, then at the mast truck from which the flag of *St George* tugged bravely at its halliards. 'It is already late afternoon, Sir Henry. The tide is slackening and will shortly be on the ebb. With this wind they will not beat in tonight. We have a chance ... Ireland ... Jersey...'

'Scilly!' Mainwaring said decisively. 'Fetch me a boat!'

'At once!'

'And Kit?'

'Sir?'

'Make ready such preparations as you think

301

necessary.'

'Aye, Sir Henry.'

'Those for ladies, too.'

'Aye ... Mr White!'

White bustled up, his eyes flushed with the excitement of seeing Fairfax's party turn-tail. 'Captain Faulkner?'

'Have the men fed, tell off the watches and stand by in one hour to receive passengers. We shall weigh at nightfall, but I would have that last kept to yourself for the time being. Let us embark the passengers first.'

'Very well, Captain, May I ask—'

'No, you may not, but where this morning you woke the first lieutenant in a man-of-war, tomorrow you will be in the King's household – more-or-less.'

'The King's household, sir?' White frowned, puzzled. 'I thought the King in Oxford...'

'But his heir is in Pendennis yonder.'

White looked from Faulkner to the castle and gave a short laugh. 'Then he is much come down in the world, to be taking a trip in this tub, begging your pardon, Captain.'

'Well, White, make certain that you do not join him. I shall want the best out of you to-night.' Faulkner turned and indicated the approaching sails. 'They are likely to stop us if they get the chance. We are to see that they do not.'

It was after dark when the first of the boats came off from the shore, and Faulkner was in a sweat of anxiety to be gone before both the north-westerly wind and the ebb-tide had died. An hour before dark he had been out himself in a boat, to reconnoitre the approach of the enemy squadron and sound in the vicinity of the Black Rock, and ever since he had pounded the quarterdeck, bothering White with queries, eager to be off but beholden to the Prince, and Mainwaring, who had gone to summon him.

But the word came at last and Faulkner had prepared his ship as far as improvisation made possible. With a lantern at the rail and the men mustered in the waist, he and White waited by the entry, new neatly pointed and whipped man-ropes dangling over the side and a scrubbed ladder hanging down for the royal feet. They had found a red sash for White, which he wore with his sword and Faulkner wore his own sash over his blackened cuirass. Both men held their hats and bowed at the first sign of the Prince's head.

'Captain Faulkner.' Faulkner straightened up. He could see the features of the Prince by the fitful lantern-light. He was as tall as Faulkner himself, his eyes dark, his face well made but in the shadow of black hair, his own by the look of it. He smiled, his beard and moustache already darker and more substantial seeming than his father's, belying his fifteen summers. He held out his hand. 'I gather we are *in extremis*, Captain, and that our enemies are at the gate, or so Sir Henry informs me.' The voice was unusually deep for so young a man, but his tone was extraordinarily and surprisingly light-hearted, making his tardy arrival almost forgivable, Faulkner thought, as he briefly clasped the Prince's hand.

'I fear so, Your Highness. We shall endeavour to evade them, nevertheless, and will likely succeed with a little cunning.'

The Prince chuckled. 'I do hope so, sir. Sir Henry tells me you were with my father on the Spanish voyage.'

'That is so, Your Highness.'

'And this is...?'

'Mr White, sir, my lieutenant ... My *only* lieutenant, in fact, Your Highness.'

'You are short-handed.'

'Regrettably so, Your Highness. We had little time ... but may I make you welcome to the *Phoenix*.'

'I am obliged to you, sir. She is your ship, I understand?'

'She is yours to command, sir, and under charter to the King.'

'Very well.' The Prince looked about him in the darkness, catching sight of the assembled men whose pale faces showed curiosity. 'I am obliged to you all,' he said, raising his voice. 'Perhaps you can make a seaman of me on our voyage.'

A laugh went up among the men. 'May I show you to your quarters, Your Highness?' Faulkner said. 'I have, if you will forgive me, given no order for salutes.'

'Quite so, Captain.'

'This way, sir. And we must delay no longer if wind and tide are to serve.'

He heard the Prince chuckle beside him. 'Indeed, please proceed as you see fit. Sir Richard!' The Prince disappeared under the poop and a man Faulkner would later learn was Fanshawe, his military secretary, took over, followed immediately by Mainwaring who stopped alongside Faulkner only long enough to say in a low voice, 'I shall look to the ladies, Kit.'

'And I shall get the ship under-weigh.'

In the darkness he was aware of a stream of people, men and women to the number of perhaps twenty or two dozen passing across the deck. Where the devil was Mainwaring going to stow them all? And where the devil were he and Sir Henry – admiral and captain – going to sleep? And which among them was *she*?

The last of the baggage was coming over the side, some of it lifted in the boat as the yard and stay tackles drew tight, and the ship listed a little in response as the weight of the longboat came on them. Then it was settled in the waist and he sent the men to the capstan without a fiddler and orders only to tramp round in silence. On deck White tended the headsails and the topsails while Faulkner remained aft, by the helmsman. He recalled the night he and Brenton had slipped down the Thames and realized that he was much out of practice for this sort of caper. Caper? The Prince's insouciance was infectious and therefore dangerous! He was only a boy, for God's sake, while he, Faulkner, was a grown man with a wife and a family left behind...

He forced himself to concentrate as the word

came aft that the anchor was a-trip, and then aweigh. He ordered the helm over and the fore-topsail dropped. He heard the rasp of the canvas and a faint squeal from the blocks, and then Walker's voice calling the men to the braces. Striding aft, Faulkner stared over the rail. A faint light escaped through the shutters of the cabin and the murmur of voices came up to him, but he was looking for something else and at last he saw the ripples showing the ship had gathered sternway. He returned to the helm and called to White, 'Brace up!'

Round the ship came so that the backed fore-topsail fluttered, was braced round with the wind behind it and the *Phoenix* turned on her heel and gathered headway. 'Give her the sprit-sail and the main topsail, Mr White!'

'Aye aye, sir.'

'Leadsman in the chains. No calls over five fathoms.'

'No calls over five fathoms, sir.'

'Who is it?'

'Jackson, sir.'

'That's well, Jackson. You mind you take care to sound true.'

'Sound true, sir, aye aye.'

Faulkner moved alongside the helmsman, keeping his eyes averted from the dimly lit binnacle to preserve his night vision. 'How's her head?'

'East by south, sir.'

'Keep her so.' He stared out to starboard at the loom of the castle on its height, then crossed the deck and peered north to where the River Fal itself was slowly opening. Ahead the hump of St Mawes grew slowly larger in appearance as they closed the distance. He looked up at the set of the main topsail as White secured the braces. Above it flew the pale shape of the flag of St George.

'Keep the men handy, we shall brace her round again in a minute or two and strike that flag. We can't risk it catching the eye of anyone offshore.'

'Very good, sir.'

Faulkner sighed. It had been a long day and was going to be a long night.

'A tricky business, Captain.' The Prince's deep voice was unmistakable. 'I am sorry, I startled you.'

'Not at all, Your Highness.' He paused. Somewhat desperate he blurted out, 'You will forgive me, sir, but I must needs be active...'

'Of course. Take no notice of me. I merely wish to observe.'

'Thank you. We are about to turn south and make our way through the entrance. I am anxious that the tide does not set us down upon the Black Rock.'

There was no moon and the cloud that had gathered since sunset remained partial, so that the stars shone against the black heavens with a magnificent glitter. Casting a glance in the Prince's direction, Faulkner walked forward to stand above the starboard bumpkin, judging the moment to turn. The loom of St Anthony's Head

307

was close now; turning aft again he called White's men to the braces and ordered the helm put down, steadying the *Phoenix* on to a course of due south. Above his head as he again went forward, the yards swung and then men came forward to trim the sheets and braces of the little spritsail.

He stared into the darkness at the passage open before him, sensing as much as seeing the cast of the ship in relation to the shores on either side. If he had it right, and a theoretical line had been drawn across the narrows, their track should cut this at the three-quarter point, marked east from Pendennis Point. His eyes began to water from fatigue and strain. Somewhere ahead lay William Batten's ships, hove-to for the night and sure of descending and closing the trap on the morrow. Yet Batten was no fool; he knew as well as Faulkner himself that the tide was ebbing and the now dying north-westerly breeze was favourable for a ship leaving Falmouth Harbour. Would he not have at least one vessel on picquet-duty hard up under the land to seal off a would-be escapee?

Faulkner's mouth was dry again, and his heart thumped in his breast. Once outside he could seek darkness under the Lizard peninsula but even then the Manacles lay in his path. He had been dithering over this point since he first thought about their chances of escape, undecided and confronted by the greater problem of first slipping through the narrows. Now he was almost through, the *Phoenix* steadily

308

passing out under the impetus of wind and the last thrust of the ebb. Already the dark mass of Pendennis was abaft the beam to starboard and to larboard the land was tumbling away, falling to the sea. Suddenly he could see to the eastwards and, as the *Phoenix* began to rise and fall to the Channel swell, the starlight reflected off the vast expanse of the sea. He could see to the eastwards, the shape of a ship, some five miles off. He pulled out his glass and swept the horizon: there was another to the east of south, and yet another due south. No, two! He stared intently to the west of south, down towards where the land ended at the Lizard. There lay the ruins of Sir John Killigrew's abandoned lighthouse that had caused such argument at the Trinity House. He could see no ships and brought his glass steadily along the coast, catching the edge of the land where the Helford River lay: nothing! He waited a moment more, then, as sure of his observations as he could be, he made his way aft.

The binnacle light shone upon the crimson doublet of the Prince, illuminating from below his handsome face and in doing so, prefigured his appearance at an older age. White stood behind in the Prince's shadow with an air of frustration and deference.

'Well done, Captain Faulkner.'

'We have yet to run the gauntlet of the enemy, Your Highness. I have seen four of them. I hope that is all, but we cannot be too certain. Take a glass forward, Mr White.' He explained the approximate bearings of the enemy men-of-war that he had seen and White did as he was bid.

'He is not a naval officer, I think, Captain, not at least until now.'

'He is a good mercantile mate, Your Highness. You will find him competent enough and handy withal when an extra hand is required on the braces.'

'I meant no criticism, Captain. I am merely keen to know from whom I may learn, rather than importuning you all the while.'

If Faulkner wished to end this discussion and pass orders to make more sail, it was abruptly terminated for him by a shout from White forward and the sharp report of a gun almost under their bows. Faulkner caught the bright, near-simultaneous double-flash of small-arms, from match and muzzle.

'A guard-boat, God damn it!' exclaimed Faulkner, privately wondering why he had not thought of such an obvious precaution as he ran to the ship's side and peered into the darkness.

'Bastards!' a voice roared and he caught sight of a ship's longboat bobbing astern, and then another match-lock was discharged and a lantern was being held up and waved as a signal to the off-lying ships.

'Let fall the courses, Mr White! All hands make sail!'

The need for silence was over. From below came the squeals of startled women and this was followed by the boom of a culverin: one at least of the enemy ships was acknowledging the guard-boat's signal of alarm.

'We may expect a chase,' Faulkner remarked to the Prince as he took his station alongside the binnacle. 'I shall run to the southward of the Lizard as though for Jersey. We have some hours of darkness left and may yet throw them off the scent.'

'Is there anything I might do?'

Faulkner looked at the Prince. He thought of requesting he silenced the women, until he realized they were already quiet. Then a thought struck him. 'If you would care to take the helm with me, Your Highness, I can send these two men to help make sail.'

'Certainly...'

They relieved the men at the helm and Faulkner leaned on the heavy tiller, explaining the techniques of maintaining a compass course. 'The lubber's line marks the ship's head,' he said, 'and while the compass card moves within the bowl, it is the ship's head and not the compass that moves.'

'I understand.'

'That is one part of your task, sir. The other is to maintain our momentum. Unless you are with a very vigilant officer-of-the-deck, merchant mate, or man-of-war's man, you will likely be the first to detect a shift of wind. Keep your eyes moving from compass bowl to the sails, and remark any shivering that suggests a shift of wind and the need for a tug on the braces. If nothing else it will stop one from falling asleep.'

He stood alongside the Prince for half an hour

before asking whether he had had enough. 'No indeed, I am game for another ... what d'you call it?'

'A trick, sir.'

'Yes, I remember.'

'Would you care to try it on your own, Your Highness?'

'Why, yes, if I may.'

'Very well. You will better feel the ship without my corrections. Call for help if you require it.'

'I'm obliged to you, Captain Faulkner. This is vastly enjoyable, by God!'

'The ship off the Lizard, sir...' White said.

'Very well, stand by the braces. We'll put the wind on the larboard quarter and make him think we are for the eastwards...'

'Aye aye.'

'Your Highness,' Faulkner turned towards the Prince. 'We shall have to alter course and show that fellow on the starboard bow a clean pair of heels. It will put the ship on her best point of sailing and though we run the risk of drawing all of the enemy after us, we cannot double the Lizard now and have little choice.'

'Would we had yesterday's weather.'

'Yes, indeed. Now bring her slowly to larboard on to a heading of east-south-east, remembering always that the ship's and the lubber's line are the same thing.'

'Very well, Captain. It shall be done as you wish.'

The Prince stood another two hours at the

wheel until he declared he had done his fair share. It was now well into the small hours of the following morning and Faulkner sent White below to get some sleep. 'The chase will go on all night and probably most of tomorrow, if we have no luck tonight.'

'I'll go and pray for rain,' White said phlegmatically, touching his hat to the Prince, who lingered a while before going below himself. Towards dawn Mainwaring came on deck and insisted upon relieving Faulkner.

'The cabin is as crowded as a bed with fleas,' he said. 'And your lady is as well provided for as possible,' he added in a low voice. Faulkner rolled himself in a cloak and, tucking himself beside a gun-truck, slept on deck.

'By God he's a cool one,' Mainwaring heard one of the able-seamen remark as they coiled down the braces. 'Givin' 'is Royal bloody 'Ighness a sodding lesson on steering while we's a runnin' from the crop-head bastards.'

Mainwaring smiled to himself in the darkness and gave himself to thinking how they might outsail the crop-heads astern.

Ten

Escape

The chase ran on through the night with the *Phoenix* edging down to the southward as she ran east, in the opposite direction to her intended course and confirming in the enemy's mind the purpose of reaching France. This notion troubled Mainwaring not least because it ensured the persistence of the chase. 'It will be assumed,' he explained to Faulkner, who woke towards dawn, stiff and uncomfortable after his sleep on the deck, 'that we indeed have the Prince on board and are making for a French port to set him ashore to attend his mother.'

Faulkner shook his head clear of sleep and sent for a glass of beer with which to swill his mouth and set himself to rights.

'The wind is freshening,' he said, coming to his wits.

'Aye, and it has backed again. My guess is that we are in for another blow. We are not yet far from the equinox. One day is rarely the same as its predecessor at this season...'

'Stay,' Faulkner interrupted, holding out his hand in the dark. 'Is that rain, I feel, or only spray...'

'It's unlikely to be spray on this course ... No, by God, you are right. It *is* rain!'

Faulkner was fully awake now. 'Very well, let us haul her up on the starboard tack. We have an hour or two, and perhaps we may lose him. Call the watch! Stand to my lads! Fore and main braces there!' He waited until the men were at their stations. He could, perhaps should, have called all hands, but the men had laboured hard yesterday and there were just sufficient in the watch to handle the matter if he took a hand himself.

'What's about?' He saw the Prince loom up on deck and seized the moment.

'*Carpe Diem*, Your Highness. Be so good as to lend a hand here!' Faulkner led the way forward along the starboard side and, throwing a coil of rope off a belaying pin, unceremoniously grabbed the Prince's right hand and placed it on the pin. 'Sir, can you cast this off when I give the word? Do it smartly and stand clear of that coil.' He turned to a seaman who arrived to tend the sheet and tack. 'Watch your sheet runs clear and keep an eye upon His Highness's brace, d'you understand me?'

'Aye, sir,' said the seaman, his face cracking in a grin.

Faulkner raised his voice as he ran forward to the starboard forebrace. 'When you are ready, Sir Henry!'

Mainwaring gave the helm orders and shouted, 'Let go and haul all!'

The men posted along the starboard rail let run

the lee braces and sheets, allowing the majority on the larboard side to heave the yards round as the *Phoenix* came round on to the starboard tack. She heeled to the wind and her bow rose and then fell with a thump, sending a cascade of water up into the air from where the wind whipped it across the deck with a soft hiss. Faulkner leapt forward to help haul the foretack down to the bumpkin, before coming after to where Prince Charles and the seaman had been joined by others to haul the main-tack to the chess-tree.

Even in the darkness Faulkner could see the gleam of the Prince's wet doublet, and then the rain squall was upon them in earnest, cold and searching as it found its way under their clothes, setting them a-shivering and the ship bucking as the wind rose still further.

'Shorten sail!' Mainwaring roared. 'Clew up to'gallants!'

Faulkner resumed his station alongside Mainwaring. 'Damn it, she is over-pressed,' Mainwaring said. 'We must ease her or carry something away!'

'Aye, after the topgallants, we'll take in the mainsail.' Faulkner raised his voice again. 'Highness! Come here, sir!'

At the Prince's approach Faulkner grabbed the helm and indicated the Prince should do the same. 'Be off with you and lay aloft,' he shouted in the ears of the relieved helmsmen. 'Now, sir,' he said to the Prince, 'we are on the wind, you will find it best to steer by the wind and therefore watch the windward luff of the main topsail. Keep it just a-shiver – that's the wind just passing along its after surface. If you have it full, you are wasting effort and pressing the ship over. The sails must work now, harder than before. We require forward motion, not a heeling list. The trick is to get a flat belly across the bunts ... See, you can feel her responding...'

'I see ... This is a heavy job.'

'Aye, we're full-and-bye, and carrying a little lee helm, preventing the ship from paying off ... Once the men get the mainsail off her she'll stand her canvas easier and likely make more speed too. And with the topgallants off she might be the less easily espied,' he added hopefully.

Beside him the Prince digested this intelligence. Taking the occasional glance at his fellow helmsman, Faulkner thought that His Highness was indeed enjoying himself despite the cold and the wet. 'The men will be earning their breakfasts,' he said, at which the Prince nodded assent.

'And so are we, Captain Faulkner, and so are we, by God!'

They spotted the enemy ship only once more, a mere nick on the lightening horizon to the eastwards, actually in the act of cracking on sail having lost sight of their quarry ahead. It appeared that none aboard looked astern at where the sky was still dark, but the pale shapes of the *Phoenix*'s straining topsails might have been seen as she dodged out of one rain squall and into the next.

Three days later they lay at anchor off the island of St Mary's, the small settlement of Hugh-town under their lee and in company with five other small ships and vessels which had been gathered in the King's name. The small squadron, now all under Mainwaring's flag, lay anchored comfortably enough, for to the westward, out towards the Atlantic Ocean from whence came the strong westerly winds, lay a litter of rocks, islands, reefs and bird-inhabited skerries that were, so men said, all that remained of the flooded land of Avalon. Only when the *Phoenix* had brought up to her anchor did the ladies emerge, and only then did Faulkner catch his first glimpse of Katherine Villiers. She came on deck with Lady Fanshawe in bright sunshine and the promise of a smooth landing on the island, and she was followed by a black maid whose hand held that of a toddling child, a boy by the plainness of his dress. He was introduced by the Prince to Sir Richard and Lady Fanshawe, and then to Lady Katherine Villiers. She wore a plain travelling dress, as damp-stained as Lady Fanshawe's after the privations of their adventures and the passage in the *Phoenix*. Having apologized for the primitive and crowded nature of their quarters to the Fanshawes, he repeated himself to her, looking into a face that – he realized with a shock – was still stunningly beautiful, at least to his eyes. She was pale, drawn and tired, but the dark shadows under her eyes seemed to act like the *kohl* the *nautch*-girls

318

of the Indian coast were said to enhance their looks with, emphasizing depth and mystery.

'It was less comfortable than the *Prince Royal*, Captain Faulkner,' she said.

'It was all a long time ago,' he replied, but was afforded no further opportunity for conversation, for Lady Fanshawe interrupted to hasten her into the waiting boat. He followed them to the side where the men had canvas chairs ready to lower them into the boats, and for a brief moment they stood side by side.

'I hope you will have a moment to walk with me, Captain.'

'Tomorrow, ma'am. I shall walk ashore tomorrow, in the afternoon...' And then she was whisked aloft and lowered over the side.

The Prince of Wales and his entourage were destined to spend several miserable weeks in the Isles of Scilly, short of food and money, a burden on the islanders. For Faulkner, who was to spend a similarly depressing period at anchor offshore, nursing his ship through a series of gales, the walk with Katherine Villiers the following afternoon was to be a moment of pure delight.

She met him at the landing, having observed his boat put off from the ship from her lodgings. He walked up through the sand to where she stood, slim and elegant, despite her travel-wearied attire, a hat tip-tilted over her left ear and tethered by a ribbon as blue as that of the Garter.

'My Lady.' He bent over her gloved hand, his heart thumping like that of a youth.

'Captain Faulkner.' They stood for a moment, staring at each other, then she said, 'It is good to see a friendly face. They have been rare things of late.' There was an edge to her voice and he offered his arm. She took it and they began walking along the beach away from Hugh-town and over the low hill that rose to the north. 'I suspect nothing happens on this island without all knowing of it,' she said, referring to this very public demonstration of acquaintance.

'Nor will we be unobserved from the *Phoenix*,' he said drily, as they walked on in silence. After a few moments that dragged into an awkwardness that neither wanted, yet neither could break, he said, 'I have long wanted a moment like this and now it has come, I do not know what to say.'

'It is sometimes best to say what is uppermost in your mind,' she offered. 'I am wearied with palace intrigue, politics, self-perjury, deceit, insincerity, flattery, cajolery ... God knows there is enough of it!' She broke off, stopping and forcing him to confront her. 'You are married, are you not? And have children ... From what I know of you, you had no reason to join the King.'

'No. That is all true. Nor do I know really why I am here. I did not come to seek you, though I long dreamed of you, but I knew when I saw you at Court that, well, after the stupid hopes I had nurtured from the time of the voyage to Spain, I was a fool.'

'No, I was the fool.' She paused. 'It is true that

I had no intention of encouraging you at Court; it was simply inappropriate and I was a giddy girl, but I had not intended to hurt you, and hurt you I think I did.'

He shrugged. 'Perhaps.'

'Is that the truth? Perhaps?'

'I was mortified, but more by my own boorishness than your repudiation.'

'My dear Captain, you have no idea the boorishness I encountered at Court! But I did hurt you, and when I saw you no more I thought that you had forgotten me.'

They began walking again. 'I did my best. You are not an easy woman to forget...'

'But you married.'

'Yes, a man must, at some time or another, or else take a whore and I was not inclined to do that.'

'Not even an orange-seller?' she joshed.

'No. Never. Perhaps I would have done better to have done so and then I should not have left a wake of wreckage behind me.'

'Is that what you have done?'

'Materially, no, but emotionally, yes. My wife deserved better of me, as did my children, who are innocent.'

'Do you have sons, or daughters, or both?'

'I have two sons and a daughter.'

'How lovely,' she said. 'And your wife?'

'A lady of Puritan inclinations and headstrong views which I much admired ... I still do, but...'

'But? Love passes, is that it?'

'I had hoped not. To say I had not forgotten

you is not quite true. You ceased to trouble me. I heard nothing of you and assumed you had risen far above me in life, as was your birthright, and when I thought of you it was with that sadness that one recalls something long gone, beyond my practical grasp.'

'A sadness, like a dead friend?'

'Quite so; and the dead youth that I once was.' They walked on in silence and then he asked, 'Tell me, out of curiosity, what did you truly think of Lieutenant Christopher Faulkner of the *Prince Royal*?'

'I thought him kind, and handsome, and interested in me, a young and almost friendless chit of a girl who was not the person he thought her to be. Rutland scared me and though I recall I put a brave face upon it, I was sorely castigated for my insolence.'

'Insolence?'

'That is what I was told I had been. Why did you think that I failed to speak to you for the remainder of the passage?' He remained silent, recalling those distant days. 'You thought me haughty, did you? Did you?'

He nodded. 'Yes, and I felt humiliated.'

'Humiliated, why? You were a polished gentleman, a sea-officer of reputation, handsome in your crimson sash ... Why, Captain Faulkner,' she said with a trace of her old beguiling ways, 'I was enraptured, enamoured of you and flattered myself – before that fat oaf Rutland interfered – that you felt likewise about me.'

He gave a bitter laugh. 'If you knew ... if you

322

only knew...'

'Knew what? You were not married then, what was there to know? You were a King's lieutenant, for me that was a grand prospect. Whatever Cousin George aspired to, poor Katherine would have settled for a King's lieutenant if only to find bed and board.'

He stared at her puzzled. 'But the Duke, had he no plans for you?'

'Do you think I would have wanted to have been married off to some poxed goat that Cousin George wanted to favour. So, what was there to know about you, Christopher Faulkner?'

'I prefer Kit; my friends call me Kit...'

'Don't prevaricate, Kit. What is there that you are concealing from me?'

They had walked almost a mile from the town, and though some men were working in a field and they could see three fishing boats working among the rocks below, they were alone. He stopped and lowered his head. 'Katherine,' he said intimately and without thinking, 'Sir Henry Mainwaring, whom you recall as commanding the *Prince Royal* and who is presently with us...' He took a deep breath before ploughing on. 'Sir Henry found me a starving boy begging on the waterfront at Bristol, without mother or father, quite alone in the world. I am nothing. I have no land beyond a house in London...'

'You have ships,' she broke in almost angrily, 'you have men to command, you now carry the future King of England, if God grant success to his arms!'

'I come from nothing...'

'But we are alike...'

'How so? How so? You are a Villiers, your cousin was the most powerful man in England who influenced two Kings – not always well, I'll allow, but you cannot say for that, you are nothing. You were high-born, you inherited all that implies. Blood begot you and blood binds you, blood secures you land, a marriage...' He stopped, aware that he was breaking down, angry and stupid. He had never expressed such sentiments before, never given way to such self-pity or found himself so helplessly self-loathing. He pulled himself together. 'I am so sorry ... please forgive me, if you can.'

She smiled at him. 'There is nothing to forgive unless it be to chide you for sounding rather like a Parliament man. You are right in part, but not entirely so; my branch of the family was poor, George's less-so, though less well-to-do than you imagine. He rose ... well God knows how he rose. The stories about him are not pleasant and you have likely heard them. If you had not known of them before, I am sure you have heard of them since. Indeed, I thought perhaps they contributed to your repudiation of me, though heaven knows others are not so easily put off.'

'You have been married? Your child a father?'

'Oh yes, Kit, married, widowed by the plague, married again and then thrown over. Widowed a second time thanks to the King's folly at Edge-hill, then when with child, a kept woman and, after none acknowledged my child, I became, through the charity of others, a *companion*.' She spat the word derisively. 'Why, Captain Faulkner, were we to stand on the scales of approbation before any tribunal from here to Heaven you would outweigh me by your weight in gold!'

They stared at one another, then slowly began to laugh. 'There!' she said. 'Now you have an answer to your lack of proper manners and had better kiss me if you have a taste for such rotten meat.'

They stood stock still. The path had sunk a little and the low, wind-bitten hedgerow barely concealed them, but the sky overhead was full of the song of an ascending lark. He took her by the shoulders and gently bent to her mouth.

It was sunset before they had wandered back to the landing place. 'I do not like the look of that sky, Katherine. I think it may not be possible to see you tomorrow but you must know that, if you are willing and do not find the notion distasteful, until matters are settled in the country I am willing to take you under my protection.'

She put a finger on his lips, but he shook her off. 'I am quite prepared to speak to Lady Fanshawe...'

'I am sure you are, but leave matters to me, at least for the time being. You are to come to Jersey with us, are you not?'

'If that is what His Highness commands.'

'That is what His Highness is advised to do,' she replied. 'Sir Richard is his mentor. Anyway, we shall have time to talk further even if the weather turns against us tomorrow.'

'Let me see you to your lodging.'

She shook her head. 'No, your boat is coming in. They have been likely watching us from the deck with their telescopes.'

'Yes, they have. I shall dream of you tonight.'

'You are too old to play Romeo,' she said, laughing. 'But you have made me very happy, happier than I have been for a long, long time.' She turned and left him staring after her until he heard the crunch of the boat's stem on the sand. The oarsmen's silence as they pulled him back to the *Phoenix* was eloquent of interest and, as he reached the rail, he turned and tossed a florin back into the boat.

'If you get the opportunity, you may drink the health of the lady.' He was rewarded by complicit grins.

'Aye aye, Cap'n,' one of them responded.

Shortly after Faulkner had returned to the *Phoenix* another boat came off to the ship with an anxious Mainwaring. In the cabin he told Faulkner that earlier that afternoon seven ships had been seen approaching the islands, beating up from the eastwards, and that by the time he had decided to return on board, leaving the Prince and his people in the town or accommodated at Star Castle on the island's highest point, there were eleven in sight.

'It has to be Batten, Kit, with reinforcements. I fear more will be sent yet and that he will try and trap us here, and may well attempt an assault on us, here in the road.'

'If he leaves it until morning, he may prove to be too late,' Faulkner said. 'There'll be a full gale by the morning, unless I am very much mistaken.'

Mainwaring nodded. 'I am of the same opinion.'

And so it proved; the wind rose steadily during the night and by dawn the anchorage was streaked with white water and a low, troublesome swell was rolling into the anchorage, to which the ships curtsied in response, tugging at their cables and creating deep anxiety to those responsible. St Mary's Road is not renowned for its good holding ground and the added thrust of the gale created a strong possibility of dragging, so Faulkner ordered one of the guns slung over the bow and under the cable, sending it down on a messenger to back up the anchor. To further reduce the *Phoenix*'s windage, he had the topgallant yards and masts lowered, and dropped the lower yards a-portlast so that they lay across the ship's rail.

'God help us if we drag now,' he remarked to White, having thereby immobilized the ship. White nodded. It had been a hard six hours' work. 'Issue the men with an extra rum-ration, and tell them to stand easy.'

Fortunately the wind shifted a little north of west which, thanks to the rocks and shallows in that direction, eased the strain on the cables and, in the event and to the amazement of them all, not a single vessel dragged her anchor. How

Batten's squadron fared they had no idea but, once the gale abated after it had blown for three days and four nights, there was nothing to be seen of his ships.

For two further days nothing could be seen to the eastwards, so it was assumed that Batten had fallen back upon Falmouth, perhaps even as far as Plymouth, with his ships damaged by the foul weather. It was now that Sir Richard Fanshawe, aware that the islanders had barely enough for their own subsistence, advised Prince Charles that it might prove the decisive moment for his escape to Jersey. The Prince concurred and orders were given for the re-embarkation at a Council held in the castle in the Prince's presence.

'Sir Henry and I,' Fanshawe began, 'are of the opinion, Your Highness, that you should embark in the *Proud Black Eagle*. We are also of the opinion, confirmed we believe by Captain Baldwin Wake of that vessel, that she is exceptionally fast.' Faulkner looked across at Wake, a young man in extravagant dress who commanded one of the other vessels keeping them company in the anchorage. 'The enemy,' Fanshawe resumed, 'should we meet him, will assume that you remain in the *Phoenix* and we may let him continue to do so with the judicious deception of flags and so forth. Captain Faulkner will form the chief escort with the *Phoenix* and, should we encounter the enemy, act as a decoy. The other vessels will divide themselves accordingly as best suits the occasion, with at least one vessel in support of the *Phoenix,* but the remainder attending the *Proud Black Eagle.* I have no need to remind you gentlemen of what is expected of you if the enemy appears in overwhelming force. Any questions?'

'I am short of powder and shot,' said Faulkner. 'I obtained a little yesterday from the garrison commander but, now that we are departing, may I have a requisition order for more?'

'Of course, Captain. And I wish we had been able to increase our stores but all that the island can produce we have already taken.'

There were a few more details to settle but by noon Faulkner, having sent word to White to collect more powder and shot, walked down to speak with Katherine. Knocking at her lodgings, a small, mean stone fisherman's cottage almost on the foreshore, he was ushered in by the black maid. Katherine rose as he entered the room, as did Lady Fanshawe.

'Captain, how good of you to call. I regret there is nothing here to offer you by way of refreshment,' she said as he straightened from his bow.

'That is of no account, Lady Fanshawe,' he said smiling. 'I am grown accustomed to hard usage. I had it in mind to speak with Mistress Katherine since you shall shortly be embarking again.'

'So I hear. I must confess, I rather dread it. Yours is not the most comfortable of ships, Captain Faulkner.'

'Then perhaps it is as well that you will be

accommodated aboard the *Proud Black Eagle*.'

'The what?' Her ladyship's eyebrows shot up, 'What a preposterous name for a ship!'

He turned to Katherine. 'Shall you accompany her ladyship, Lady Katherine?' he asked. 'Sir Henry is to transfer his flag...'

'Of course she will, Captain,' put in Lady Fanshawe. 'We are inseparable, are we not, Kate?'

Katherine shot him a glance of resignation. 'Indeed, Madam, we are.' Faulkner felt the sharp pang of enforced separation.

'Then I shall have to master my disappointment,' he said, addressing himself to Katherine.

'So shall we all, I fear, if the *Proud Eagle* is that little ship which we passed in coming ashore.'

'That is the one, ma'am, but she is said to be fast. I shall take my leave of you. There is much to be done. I shall see you in Jersey, no doubt.'

'I devoutly hope so,' Katherine said, blowing a kiss from the tips of her fingers. He could hardly bear the look in her eyes and moved towards her.

For a moment they stood close; then he said hurriedly in a low voice, 'Perhaps it is as well that you travel with the Prince.'

She shook her head, tears welling in her eyes. 'No...'

He tore himself away. She had not attended the Council meeting and did not know the load laid upon his shoulders. Faulkner was in a black mood as he returned on board where Mainwaring soon afterwards joined him. 'I am sorry, Kit.

I know they have snatched the prize from you, but with luck you will be reunited in Jersey.'

'Let us hope so,' he said shortly, 'or the devil may take the consequence.'

The little squadron was off the Caskets when one of Batten's ships found them. The *Proud Black Eagle*, into which Mainwaring had transferred his flag, was in the van and made sail to the south-south-east and the refuge of loyal St Helier. In accordance with his orders, Faulkner hauled his wind and headed for Guernsey, as if making for the nearer island with his royal passenger and the enemy took the bait.

With the wind freshening again from the south-west, the two ships thrashed to windward, laying over, the spray flying. It was a dangerous game, for the spars and canvas strained and Faulkner worried about the extensive reefs that lay to the westward of Guernsey. The island lay like a slab into which the angry Atlantic had been slowly eating in its endless game of attrition; century by century the island had fallen back, leaving the bones of its skeleton to windward, hidden in a welter of white water which tore and broke as the waves dashed upon the rocks, while the sea itself ran under the impetus of the moon with fierce tides that could set a ship like a toy.

If the sturdy little *Phoenix* could not weather that muddle of rocks, and pass outside the Hanois reef, then she must turn and fight, and in these conditions, her crew worn with days of exertion and too small to man more than half her armament, she stood little chance of escape from a man-of-war of force, and the enemy was gaining upon them.

Faulkner stood by the helm. 'Keep your eyes on the compass,' he growled at the helmsmen, sensing their nervousness. It was scarcely surprising. The men on deck were casting frequently worried looks astern and many of them belonged to the watch below. 'Keep your eyes inboard, all of you!' he shouted above the noise of the wind. White came up and, touching his bare forehead, asked for orders.

'Seeing that we already have all hands on deck, you may load the guns but keep them inboard. Douse the galley fire and issue small arms.'

'Aye, sir.'

'But,' he said, restraining White from going about his business, 'I shall only fight if I have to.' White's face looked relieved, and for a moment Faulkner was puzzled until White revealed the source of his relief.

'You'll think of something, sir,' he said, before turning away to pass on Faulkner's orders.

He would think of something? Was that the burden of the men's faith in him which he carried? He felt a sudden fury; an outrage at being so put upon. It stemmed chiefly from the remark he had been about to confide in White, but which White's stupid remark had displaced. The only thing he could think about at the moment was the fact that he was bound in honour not to surrender; he had been about to tell this to White but to order him to save himself, the men and the ship, if he, Faulkner himself, were to fall.

Think of something! What was there to think about other than the overwhelming power of the enemy and the inevitability of the end of this encounter? He allowed himself a glance astern. It was always difficult in such circumstances to judge both the size of a pursuing vessel and her distance, the one being contingent upon the other, but she was as big as the Frenchman who had chased him off the Varne, all those years ago. Now, however, there was no friendly shoal under his lee over which he might hop to safety, sure in the knowledge that the enemy commander dared not follow. Nor was this a Frenchman; the fellow in command of the man-of-war astern was a determined Englishman hunting for the grandest prize, the heir to the English throne, possession of which would possibly end the war at a stroke and bring the King to Parliament's heel.

Faulkner tried to clear his head of such thoughts. Germane though they were to grand strategy, they were a hindrance to him in his present predicament. But they were difficult to shake off and he was conscious that below all his professional anxieties there lay another: that having found Katherine, he was about to lose her. The thought nearly overwhelmed him. He felt the unmanly prick of strong emotion, of the start of tears and a feeling of black rage. God was punishing him for his abandonment of Julia

333

and the children, or for his pride, or for his numberless sins.

A shower of spray rose from the *Phoenix*'s bluff and plunging bow. The wind caught it and whipped it to leeward so that it stung his face and had the helmsmen beside him spluttering and blowing the saltwater off his nose. It saved Faulkner from an onset of paralysing nerves and roused him from the torpor into which fatigue and anxiety threatened to thrust him.

'Mr White!'

'Sir?'

'Take the deck. Issue spirits to all hands. I am going to arm myself and will be but five minutes.' White acknowledged his instructions and Faulkner sensed the lightening of the helmsmen's mood at the announcement of a rum-issue. Did a tot of spirits really make such a difference when the enemy was at their tail? Faulkner certainly hoped so and he helped himself to a glass of wine the moment he reached his cabin. He stood a moment, glass in hand, braced against the pitch and roll of the *Phoenix*, and stared astern. The cabin windows perfectly framed the pursuing enemy vessel and he watched, almost mesmerized. Finishing his wine he pulled on his cuirass. Without a servant he had difficulty securing the clasps and straps, but the need to concentrate on so small but tricky a task steadied him. He picked up the crimson sash and wound it about his waist, buckled on his sword and looked about the cabin. He wondered if he would ever see it again. It had been his only home now for two months, during which his life had changed dramatically. Then his eyes were caught by the sight of the enemy, caught suddenly in a shifting patch of sunshine which threw her into highlights and shadows, the rise of her hull and the flat billow of her white sails. As he watched, her aspect changed slightly as her helm was put over and her head swung to larboard. He knew what was coming and saw the brief flowering of smoke with the bright flash of the discharge at its heart under her starboard bow. The smoke vanished in an instant, whipped away in the wind and lost, like the sound. The ranging shot plunged into the sea well astern of them, a hundred to a hundred and fifty yards away.

The shot had cost her time and distance, and the alteration of course had lost her some yards to leeward. She would recover, given time ... Odd that her commander had tried a ranging shot at such a distance ... The thought recalled him to his own duty with a start. He knew at once what had prompted that shot: the proximity of danger. Those reefs under their lee bow were troubling his opponent and ought, by God, to be troubling him. He made for the deck at a run and saw at once what had precipitated his enemy.

Almost under the larboard bow – or so it seemed from the lee side of the heeling and driven *Phoenix* – the seas broke on the outlying litter of dangers lying off the western coast of Guernsey. The spray from the breaking waves rose like smoke in the patches of intermittent sunshine and the white water over the shallows was broken here and there by the peaks of rocks and islets over which birds wheeled. Overhead the wind sang in the rigging, a near gale but steady. He looked up; the *Phoenix* was hard-pressed, but not overly so. He must hold his nerve and carry his canvas.

He reached the helm up the steeply angled deck. White looked at him expectantly. 'Shorten down, sir?' he prompted.

Faulkner shook his head. 'Not yet, Mr White, not yet awhile.' He caught the glance that passed between the two men at the helm. He thought better of interpreting it. It did not matter now what they thought; now the burden was his and his alone. He felt a pang of sorrow for them in their servitude and the thought, brief though it was, reminded him of Julia. The way of the world rendered such people helpless. He too was helpless, overborne by fate, or Providence, or the will of God. The difference, however, lay in the weight of his responsibility. That had been placed upon his shoulders by ... by what? By fate, or Providence, or God? Was he a smaller version of King Charles, claiming the right to decide the fate of others by divine right? But he had had a hand in it himself by way of his ambition and ability; Mainwaring, even the unknown apple-seller had helped too ... and Julia, the night she had repudiated his love-making. Where did it all end, this chain of cause and effect?

He stood for a moment, almost paralysed with

336

the import of this train of thought. To his men he seemed cool, the calculating fighting captain that they mostly assumed him to be. A man raised to command them and supremely fitted for such moments as they were just then embarking upon.

Faulkner recovered himself and raised his eyes to again study the chasing man-of-war. She had certainly lost ground to leeward and would run closer to the rocks than the *Phoenix* in consequence, but her commander was a man of nerve. Faulkner felt a sudden inexplicable lightening of spirit. He was filled with a sudden determination. He did not greatly care what happened. He had in fact little choice in the matter. He had found his love and would gamble all on that fact alone, let the Devil himself take it. A man had only a reputation to leave, and to die honourably was preferable to any other death. He would leave matters to God, or Providence, or whatever ruled the universe.

'I am going forward, Mr,' he said to White, his voice suddenly cold. 'Do you mind the men steer small.'

'What trick is that devil going to pull now?' one of the helmsmen asked of no one in particular.

'Hold your tongue!' snapped White, whose view of their situation was more realistic. He admired Captain Faulkner and knew him for a competent seaman and shrewd man of business, but doubted there was any trick he could pull right now. White expelled his breath. Well, perhaps it helped that the men thought their captain capable of such a thing but they were, for the most part, ignorant and superstitious fellows. He himself had a wife in London, and two fine pock-marked boys that he loved dearly, even though he beat them. Well, a man beat boys to make them men and the least he could do was make men of them if their mother was to be widowed in the next hour. White was not afraid of death; he had been at sea too long not to have seen its sudden, unexpected visitation far too often. Funny, but it so frequently carried off the best men, leaving the rotten to ruin the world. He watched, curious as Faulkner began to ascend the foremast ratlines on the windward side.

'Cap'n going aloft, Mr White,' the windward helmsman reported.

'I can see that, thank you, Matthews.'

'Reckon we'll sink or swim in the next hour, sir,' Matthews went on.

'I can see that too, Matthews, thank you.'

'Cap'n'll see us through...'

White held his peace. In his heart of hearts he certainly hoped so, but he knew he hoped against the odds.

'Cap'n's calling something, sir!'

White went forward and looked aloft. Faulkner was staring down at him. 'I'm going through the rocks!' he shouted. 'Send Matthews forward to station himself there, where you are, to pass my orders to you at the helm. I want you on the helm, White, and no one else!'

White waved his acknowledgement and hurried aft. 'Get yourself forrard, Matthews. The Captain wants you to stand where he can see you and I want you to shout what the Captain tells you with all your might. We're going through the rocks.'

'Jesus Christ!' Matthews' mouth dangled wide open.

'Can't imagine why the Captain chose you, Matthews, you look like a damned loon. Shut your gob and get yourself forrard.' On the far side of the tiller the second helmsman grinned. 'And you mind me, lad,' White chided him, 'this calls for real seamanship'.

In the foretop Faulkner had come to his decision quickly. It did not do to dwell on the risk. They might escape death if he brought the other ship to action, but they would not escape entirely unless he risked everything on a single throw of the dice. All, he had thought when ascending the foremast, decided upon the mere possibility of escape. If there looked like a passage through the rocks, then he must take it. Reaching the foretop he stared out over the scene of wild desolation. From this elevation the chaos of rock and sea that extended between the ship and the shore seemed intimidating but, if one took a cooler appraisal, there was deep water between many of the rocks, each of which – when it appeared from the seas breaking over it – was encircled by a garland of white. The white was composed, he knew, of the air left from the endless succession of broken waves and these trailed off to the south-westwards, drawn by the run of the tide. Many of the rocks were covered by the tide, and most which lay insufficiently under water for the *Phoenix* to pass over them were betrayed by the tumbling of waves and the white swirl caused by their submarine presence. Between such disturbances, dark, undisturbed water ran and several almost clear lines, most going in unhelpful directions, had already opened up and then closed again as the *Phoenix* drove past. Two circumstances had heartened Faulkner and kindled the bright flame of real hope in his heart, almost daring him to make his attempt at escape. The first was the tide, which by pressing against their lee bow would allow him to haul the ship a point further off the wind and thus increase their speed, and the other was the proximity with which they had already run past several rocks – such close acquaintance with these dangers meant that there was a good chance that most rose steep and sharp from the seabed. They were, he realized, what was left by the sea's attrition and likely to be the core of greater outcrops, and therefore chimney-like in their structure.

He seized upon these facts like a line thrown to a drowning man; he became convinced of their absolute veracity but he was aware that he must make up his mind upon an instant. The ship must be turned into the first and perhaps the only channel that led through the reefs to the south-east, cutting off the extreme corner of the great wedge of off-lying dangers that made of the west coast of the island a graveyard of ships and men.

He watched carefully, looking down occasionally to see Matthews patiently awaiting his orders. The minutes passed; perhaps there was no channel, perhaps ... And then he realized something else. Staring ahead he saw how the *Phoenix* could not weather the furthest extension of the reefs. There lay the Hanois Rocks, the final outwork of the island and, even if he gave up any notion of passing inside, he must tack and stand offshore, giving ground to the enemy that would, though he had to tack himself, nevertheless, finally catch them and bring the *Phoenix* to a fatal action. He craned under the foot of the straining main-topsail to see the enemy. She lay upon the *Phoenix*'s larboard quarter, still a little distance astern but she had already passed inside one, no two outlying rocks. The realization that he was up against a man of mettle, hardened Faulkner's resolution. He spun round and, as if God given, he could see a gap opening up. There was white water along it, to be sure, but...

'Matthews! Steer two points to larboard! Have the yards trimmed accordingly!'

'Two points to larboard! Trim the yards!'

Faulkner could feel the *Phoenix* turn as her helm went over. White could hear him at the helm. Thank God for White, for much would depend upon him holding his nerve in the coming hour.

'Hold on, sir!' someone called, and Faulkner felt the foremast tremble as above and below him the yards swung, the topsail parrel squeaking slightly as it did so. He stared ahead as the ship steadied and tried to judge the sideways set of the tide, but it was too soon. The *Phoenix*'s bowsprit was already pointing between white water with wet black rock showing intermittently. It was too late now for second thoughts; every fibre of his being must be stretched to his task. They sped past the first danger and then between a pair of submerged rocks. He thought he could see the tugging swirl of kelp on one, but had no time for such frivolous observations. Some way ahead and slightly to starboard, a large and prominent rock could be seen. It was almost a small islet, its summit permanently above the usual reach of the tide and stained with bird-lime. A number of seabirds could be seen on it and it served as a convenient mark of reference against which he could measure their progress and the set of the tide. After a few minutes he shouted down to Matthews to bring the helm up a touch, and to steer a course half a point to starboard, leaving the calculation of exactly which course to steer to White.

The close proximity of the dangers demonstrated the speed of the *Phoenix* as she rushed headlong in her attempt to reach the open water to the southward. The islet was steadily opening its angle on the bow with increasing rapidity as they drove past and suddenly it was abeam and then astern.

'Steer one and a half points to starboard!'

'One and half points to starboard, sir. Aye aye.'

Again the shift of the ship as she felt the swell under her and the tremble in the mast as the yards swung. Thank God, but he had a staunch and attentive crew. His eye caught sight of something ahead of them. It was a dark eddy on the surface of the water. The sea ran slick now, almost undisturbed by the wind-sea, though it rose and fell as the Atlantic swells rolled in. But here, with a foaming mass of white water now out to starboard absorbing the energy of the breaking waves, the sea state seemed subject only to the fierce thrust of the tide.

He had no time – the eddy was right ahead, the water running like oil over it. It was high on the up-tide side and swirled round an unseen obstruction which caused a cavity on the down-tide side. No white water could be seen on the surface, but how much water was over the rock below? He was too late to do anything about it; already the tip of the bowsprit was riding above it from where he watched. No one on deck will have noticed it but Faulkner bowed his head and briefly closed his eyes, his heart hammering in his chest, his expectation of falling in the wreckage of the tumbling foremast causing his hands to grip like vices.

He felt the first tremor then – nothing!

The ship swept on, the tremor caused by the disturbance in the water from the rock far below. He looked up again, the adrenalin of relief coursing through him. His relief was only momentary, however. White water lay in their path and he searched for their passage. For a split second he thought they had run into a dead-end and then he cried out, 'Starboard a point! No, two points!'

He heard Matthews relay the corrected order. This would be difficult, for the trend of the passage to starboard brought them back, closer to the wind and he could hear the boatswain calling the men to haul the yards sharp up, hard against the catharpings. Almost immediately he felt the windward edges of the topsail above and astern of him begin to flutter. He felt the heel ease and the ship slow. Then he could hear White's anxious, stentorian bellow, 'She's luffing, sir!'

He said nothing, there was nothing he could do except hope and allow the tide to carry them through. He heard the noises on deck, felt the foremast jerk as the boatswain and the men tried to get another foot on the lee forebrace, while another party hauled mightily on the tack so that the windward bumpkin bent like a longbow. Compared with her earlier dash, the *Phoenix* almost came to a standstill. The frustration and fear from below rose in almost palpable form, but Faulkner held his peace. He felt imbued by an almost religious serenity now, aware that the strong tide was carrying them sufficiently to windward as it drove through the deeper, unimpeded parts of the reefs. If they were taken aback, it would be a different story, but he did not think there was any danger of that, for they had not quite luffed and the sails still fluttered uncertainly, giving them just sufficient steerage way for the *Phoenix* to answer her helm when he called down, 'Up helm! Steer three points to larboard!' and was answered by a cheer.

Their ordeal had lasted no more than ninety seconds and ten minutes later they broke out into clear water to the southward. Faulkner descended to the deck and stared astern.

'She's hull-down, sir. Didn't have the nerve,' said White.

Faulkner found himself shaking with relief. 'That was very well done, Mr White. And well done, Matthews, you too. And you, Bosun, and all you men. Now pipe up spirits if you please...'

'You know, Mr White,' Faulkner said with a grin, 'going aloft in a cuirass, is a damned silly thing to do.'

Four hours later, they had skirted the south coast of Guernsey and laid a course to the southeast. It was long past noon but the wind held and the ship seemed skittish after her adventure, leaping, like the men's spirits, from one wave to another. Towards the end of the afternoon watch the horizon ahead was barred by the long, flat plateau that was the island of Jersey.

Faulkner levelled his glass, half hoping to catch sight of the squadron and the *Proud Black Eagle*. Lady Fanshawe had been right, it was a damned silly name for a vessel. But then, so was the *Lion's Whelp*, when one came to think of it. *Phoenix*, on the other hand, was a proper name for a ship. Notwithstanding the silliness of her name, he hoped the *Proud Black Eagle* had reached her destination safely.

'Shall we make it before dark, Captain Faulkner?'

He turned to find a yawning White beside him. The man was near haggard with fatigue.

'I devoutly hope so, Mr White. Our fortunes and futures depend upon it.'

Author's Note

Many of the characters in this story are based on real people. Apart from the obvious, King Charles I and his heir, Charles, Prince of Wales (afterwards Charles II), and figures such as George Villiers, Duke of Buckingham, Sir Thomas Fairfax and others, many of the less well known existed, including the Trinity House Brethren who commanded the expedition to the coast of Morocco in 1637 under their admiral, William Rainsborough. Chief among these, however, is Sir Henry Mainwaring whose life, obscure in detail, but rich in variety and incident, was real enough. It was in the contemplation of Mainwaring's life that the idea of this novel derived, for he was all the things claimed herein, from reformed pirate to reformer of the Royal Navy under James I and Charles I, by way of twice Master of Trinity House and admiral in the Royal Navy and the exiled Royalist forces. In one of those ironies inseparable from Mainwaring's life was the fact that his *Seaman's Dictionary* is thought to have been the chief book of instruction for the Commonwealth navy that was to found British naval sea-power.

Most of the major incidents in the storyline are

based on real incidents. I was attracted by the almost forgotten doings of the Royal Navy during the years of its neglect, under James I, and those of its mismanaged reform under Charles I. What we chiefly know is the imposition of Ship Money taxation, forgetting that this built the first proper three-decked line of battleship under the direction of Pett. As to Mainwaring's part, he commanded the *Prince Royal* on her voyage to extricate Charles and Buckingham from the mess of the proposed marriage of the former to a Spanish princess, led many of the improperly financed reforms that enabled the later Commonwealth navy to achieve so much and was party to the grounding of the *St George* off Falmouth for the purpose of annoying the Parliamentary attack on Pendennis under Fairfax. Moreover, her guns did indeed annoy 'Black Tom' whose habit was to ride a white charger.

And the man who would later become King Charles II had a lively interest in the sea and was, when King himself, a keen promoter of yachting and yacht-racing. It is known that he first learned to steer a vessel during his escape from the Isles of Scilly on his passage to Jersey in the *Proud Black Eagle*. I merely suggest he had done so first a few weeks earlier, when a hired 'frigate' called the *Phoenix* slipped out of Carrick Roads and conveyed the Prince from Pendennis to the island of St Mary's.

Faulkner is my own invention but there were those few who, raised by philanthropic individuals or private charities, found their feet and made their way in the world in this period of unprecedented change. For many the war itself was the vehicle for the encouragement of their talents and ambition, but who knows how many other men and women throughout England wished to remain occupied about their personal affairs, and avoid commitment during England's savage Civil Wars of the mid-seventeenth century? Not all were fervent Royalists, Parliamentary democrats, or religious zealots. And how many were cheated of this pacific desire, only to be swept up in events beyond their control, their lives broken, their families scattered, their fortunes squandered.

But the story does not finish with the escape of the Prince of Wales to Jersey. That is only the end of the first phase of a longer narrative. The year 1644 saw the King's forces defeated decisively at Naseby by the Parliamentary Army under Fairfax and with Cromwell as his lieutenant-general of horse. Bristol, too, fell to the Parliament while the King fell into his enemies' hands with the loss of Oxford the following year.

Sir Henry Mainwaring's pathetic end – along with Faulkner's fortunes – may yet be told in the sequel.